# Warrior's Vengeance

# Medieval Warrior's Legends Book 2

# By Gianna Simone

GIANNA SIMONE

# ωαꝛꝛιοꝛ'ꞅ ʋεɴɢεαɴϲε

Rosavin Publishing
Contact: rosavinpub@optonline.net

Warrior's Vengeance
Copyright © 2016 Gianna Simone

Cover Design: Gianna Simone

ISBN: 978-0692684931

This is a work of fiction. Names, characters, places and incidents either are products of the author's imagination or are used fictitiously. Any resemblance to actual events or locales or persons, living or dead, is entirely coincidental.

GIANNA SIMONE

# also by gianna simone

**The Norsemen Sagas**
Norseman's Revenge – Book 1
Norseman's Deception – Book 2

**The Bayou Magiste Chronicles**
Claimed by the Devil – Book 1
Claimed by the Mage – Book 2
Claimed by the Enchanter – Book 3
Claimed by the Zyndevine – Book 4

**Medieval Warrior's Series**
Warrior's Possession – Book 1
Warrior's Vengeance – Book 2
Warrior's Wrath – Book 3

Gianna Simone

# Praise for Gianna Simone:

**Warrior's Possession**
**BDSM Book Reviews:** Gillian is keeping secrets and Royce will use everything in his sexual arsenal to make her tell him all of them. A BDSM bodice ripper... if you enjoy spanking, bondage, subduing and sexual interrogation you'll have plenty to enjoy.
**The Romance Reviews:** As a period piece, I was impressed with the author's research into all aspects of the story (language, clothing, food, activities, etc.). And in typical period fashion, Lady Gillian is treated more as an object to be controlled than a partner. Something she wants nothing to do with. Well, mostly. For the Panther has a knack for turning his lady inside out. The sex scenes and the BDSM scenes are scintillating as it's easy to imagine your own skin warming under the Earl's capable hand.

**Warrior's Vengeance**
**The Romance Reviews:** The plot is so captivating that the reader feels compelled to know more. The story, the development and the end are, to put it mildly, peculiar and original. This is my first Gianna Simone novel and I must

say, she did a great job.
**Goodreads:** Impressive and totally hot bodice ripper!

**Warrior's Wrath**
**BDSM Book Reviews:** This story combines the richness of the 14th century history, meshed along with the stories of betrayal and the stories of love. There is a sweetness of Aeron as she is immersed in a sexual education she never knew existed.
**Goodreads: The menage scenes were H.O.T.!** Ms. Simone really does well with the heat and creativity of the triangle in action.

**Claimed by the Devil**
**BDSM Book Reviews:** The story leads you on an emotional rollercoaster, but it is well worth the ride. As Helene and Devlin get older their past is ever present, but Devlin works at gaining what he desires. Devlin fed into Helene's needs giving her what she wanted. Sex is here, often and hot, well written and intense.
**You Gotta Read Reviews:** This is one intense and hot story that grabbed my attention from the start and would not let go. While we are treated to the romance between Helene and Devlin we also get to find out about their lives outside of the bedroom, which include both friends and enemies. I loved watching the attraction between the two become so much more. Helene blooms

with the help of Devlin and his love.

**Claimed by the Mage**
**The Romance Reviews:** Gianna Simone does an excellent job with Aiden's seduction of Lily. He reads her well and understands, most of the time, when to push and when to give. He takes care not to overpower or frighten away his healer as he carefully reveals her submissive side to her. My favorite parts of the book are those moments when he uses everything at his disposal to make love to her, and magic can allow for some sinfully erotic maneuverings.

**Claimed by the Enchanter**
**BDSM Book Reviews:** The author did a wonderful job of contrasting Regine's need to control and be dominated. She also showed how much trust plays into a relationship. Once Cameron and Regine get together, the sparks fly. The chemistry between the two is intense and the scenes between the two, and later with David, are very hot.
**Coffee Time Romance:** Claimed by the Enchanter is published by a suitably named publisher, because it is a sizzler of a story. The struggle between self-perception and self-awareness is strong and the emotions it invokes mirrors the struggle between who a person thinks they are, and who they are afraid to be. The internal struggle was as strong as the struggle to solve the mystery. I absolutely fell right into the

story and lived as the characters lived with every emotion magnified. I am happy to say I am a new fan of Ms. Simone and look forward to reading more from this talented artist.


**Claimed by the Zyndevine**
**BDSM Book Reviews:** This is a fast moving magical story with many twists and turns. I enjoyed this book with its feisty characters, spells and hexes, evil forces and new lands. The romance was inevitable and the sex was hot. Even though BDSM was the main element to all romantic encounters, the prominent feel for me was one of true love conquers all. If you like magic, fantasy and happy endings this is the story for you.

GIANNA SIMONE

# Taken by her father's enemy, she soon craves her captor's ruthless passion

Near the Scottish border during the reign of Edward I, Marissa Langley, daughter of a powerful English earl is captured by a band of marauding Scotsmen. Completely at their mercy, she is desperate to escape. When the leader of the group saves her from certain rape, she believes she will be freed.

But Ian MacCallum is no savior. He takes her for his own, seduces her then makes her his slave. Her collar and chains are part of his vengeance on her father—the man Ian claims is responsible for the death of his beloved wife and son.

But her immediate death is not Ian's plan. He subjects her to daily suffering and punishments and goes so far as sharing her with another clansman. Yet, her spirit will not be broken. He finds himself drawn to that core of strength within her; finding it most exquisite as it cannot be violated.

When danger from within his clan threatens her,

Ian protects her, discovering at the same time that he does not want to lose her, ever.

Marissa makes her own discovery: she comes to crave Ian's torturous touch. When she learns the source of his hatred, she is certain he is wrong. Her father would not commit atrocities. She waits for the moment when she can escape and prove her father's innocence. But that would mean leaving Ian when she is no longer sure she wants to be free.

# featuring a kinky twist on history, including bondage, collars, spanking, multiple partners and more!

# chapter one

Marissa leaned low over the horse's neck, urging the animal to greater speed. The rain lashed her face with icy biting needles. She ignored the discomfort. The sound of the horses giving chase behind her incited crashing shards of fear. Panic shook her fingers and she gripped the horse's mane to steady her balance.

She choked back a sob, unable to shake from her thoughts the image of Leland's lifeless body sprawled on the field, an arrow protruding from his chest. Mere moments later, his attackers gave chase. Terror such as she had never known ripped the breath from her lungs. Had her companion truly been killed? If only she had her sword, she could hold her own against her pursuers.

"Hurry, Pride, just a little farther," she urged the steed, his powerful body taking the wet meadow in great strides. The shouts behind her sounded closer than before. She dared a glance back. Her heart seized. They gained on her! Ahead lay the small stand of trees, just beyond there, home and safety. She could evade the dirty Scots chasing her in the forest, and make a dash for the gates of Montchester.

She kicked the horse's flanks once again, her heart pounding wildly while she prayed for the time to elude her pursuers. There, she was almost to the trees now. Just a few more ...

She screamed when a rider drew up beside her, one hand reaching out to catch her hair which had blown free from its covering. The searing pain in her scalp seemed a minor annoyance when a meaty arm came around her waist and yanked her from the saddle. She fought her assailant, gouging her nails into his face. He let loose a yell of pain and released his hold. She fell to the ground and rolled in the muddy field, staring after her horse, which continued on toward the trees and the keep beyond.

Her attacker wheeled around, his mount blowing great plumes of steam in the cool wet air. More horses approached, and despite knowing the futility of her action, she leaped to her feet and ran in the direction of her fleeing horse. Laughter pounded her ears and she found herself surrounded by several mounted Scotsmen.

She raised herself to her full height and debated which way she might go to escape her captors. She suppressed a shudder as she looked at each one, all of them wild and unkempt. The one who'd grabbed her dismounted and stalked over to her. She would show this animal no fear and lifted her chin.

"Looks like we got ourselves a feisty lass, men," he said.

He reached out to touch her sodden hair and she slapped his hand away. The mocking laughter in his voice vanished.

"Now, lass, that ain't no way to treat your master." His fingers tightened in her hair and he yanked her close to him. She winced and tried to untangle his hand.

"Master? Filthy Scottish kidnappers. How dare you! When my horse returns alone, my father's men will soon give chase and arrest you."

"Dinna think so, lass, we'll be long gone afore anyone comes."

"You fool! Montchester is just beyond those trees. My horse has likely already reached it, and an alarm sent up!" She hoped beyond hope the half-truth and her vow proved right. The steed had a mind of his own, and could easily have taken refuge from the rain amidst the trees. Besides, Monchester was a bit further than she led them to believe. Why had she challenged Leland to that race? Marissa held back a moan of frustration. If only she hadn't worn out her horse then, she might have made it to safety. She'd been so close!

"We have plenty of time before your horse reaches Monchester's gates. We leave now. I willna risk losing a prize fair as you." His fast actions soon had her hands bound before her. She let loose a scream of outrage and jerked from his grasp. She barely got three steps before she came up against another. She stared in horror at the face of the man holding her still. A gap-toothed smile split his beard, and there was no mistaking the intent in his beady eyes. She jerked free of his hold, but found herself caught once more by her initial abductor. Damn it all to hell, how had she been so careless? Her mind replayed the events of the morning and not for the first time did she rue allowing Leland to talk her into the sneaking away for the unescorted ride, especially so close to sunset. She choked back a sob. Again, she wondered if he truly lay dead in the field. Had these filthy Scots succeeded in murdering him?

She had no chance to think further on it, finding herself tossed over the saddle of the Scots' leader a moment before he mounted up behind her. One beefy arm anchored around her waist. His low growl in her ear turned her stomach.

"Soon, lassie, we'll take shelter in one of the caves and we can share you properly then. Been a long time since I had me a fine English lassie."

She shuddered in revulsion at his meaning. Never. She would be free of him before she let that happen.

The rain eased when they headed toward the hills and the caves they concealed. She had to get free of these beasts before they reached the winding maze and got lost in them. She could die within days trapped alone in there. All knew the tales of travelers who sought refuge from the weather in the labyrinth of caves, only to be found months or even years later, dead. She tugged at the leather binding her wrists. She had to get free now.

But her captors picked up their pace, urging their mounts into a run, and she knew it was too late. She'd be gone before her father could get out of the gates with men to search for her.

What the hell would she do?

\* \* \*

Ian tended the fire. What took them so long? The scouting mission had gone well, and he had learned all he needed. Ian knew exactly how many warriors this siege would require, and he didn't want to waste more time than necessary heading back to the village to gather them. He'd spent the last two years preparing his vengeance, so readying the forces needed to launch his attack would take mere days. His eagerness to get this done had intensified over the last fortnight. He wanted his hunger for retribution satisfied. He could almost smell the Earl of Montchester's spilled blood. In a few short weeks, Ian would have his revenge. Montchester would return to find his home and family destroyed. Once the earl viewed the horror, he would pay with his life.

"From the looks of you, I'd say you're imagining what it'll be like when the Panther is no more."

At the sound of Monchester's nickname, Ian looked at his clansman, Jamie. He gave the younger man a smile and shifted to make room on the log beside him. Jamie settled beside him. "I've waited long years for this day. Sheila and Duncan will soon rest in peace."

He sighed at the thought of his beautiful wife and bright handsome son. They'd been gone nigh two years, Duncan only four years of age when his life was snuffed out by the Panther and his men. Ian had waited a long time for the day to face the man who'd brutally raped and murdered innocent villagers. His clan. They'd resided on their land quietly, farming and tending their sheep. Other than sometimes aiding The Bruce in defending against Longshanks, the MacCallums had mostly lived peacefully, though the occasional raid against neighboring clans sparked excitement. Until that bloody night when the Panther had raided, nearly destroying them all. Only by sheer determination had Ian and Jamie survived, along with a few other MacCallum clansmen. They'd sought refuge from the Crawfords, Ian's mother's clan, and had received it, for which Ian would always be grateful.

The Crawfords treated him as if they were his own now, yet, he yearned to reach his goal, so he could be free and rebuild his own clan. He would always miss Sheila and Duncan, but he needed to see his plans to the end so he could move on with his life, make the MacCallum name proud and strong once more, and become laird. He, Jamie, and Fiona were the only ones left. Old Man Henry had died last winter, the last of the handful who had survived the massacre besides Ian and his sister and clansmen.

"'Tis almost over. You'll have your vengeance."

Ian nodded and met Jamie's glance. "When it's done, we'll need to settle far away. Up in the Highlands where they'll never find us. There we'll rebuild the MacCallum clan."

Jamie smiled, his teeth white and even in his auburn beard. "Good. Sarah Crawford has been badgering me to ask for her hand. Glad I'll be to have that pressure gone when we leave!"

Ian chuckled. While several of the Crawford women had made their interest and availability clear, Ian wanted no part of the courting games they played. He'd taken comfort and relief from the loneliness when it became too much to bear, but nothing more. Jamie, however, loved the lasses' attention and had broken more than his fair share of hearts. But lately Ian had been restless and he knew 'twas because his heart was lonely. He longed once more for a loving relationship like he'd shared with his dear wife, the intimacy and companionship that filled his soul and brightened his days. When this was all over, when the Panther had lost his family as Ian had lost his, then and only then, would Ian be able to move ahead with his life.

He met Jamie's gaze. "The Panther has sent most of his men to join Edward in battle against The Bruce. Longshanks still seeks justice for Comyn's murder. The Panther remains behind for the moment, but he'll soon join his king. The keep will be lightly guarded. Another mistake Montchester will regret. The first was leaving survivors to bear witness to his attack."

"Aye. The attacks on the other clans left no one," Jamie agreed. "We were lucky."

Sometimes Ian wondered if that was really true. He hadn't felt lucky in the weeks and months following the murder of his family, the loss of his home, the entire village burned. He still didn't feel lucky to have survived, but grateful that God had given him this chance to avenge his people.

"Colin and the others should be back by now. Do you still plan to rest the night in the caves before returning to the Uplands to gather the men?" Jamie asked.

Ian nodded. "There willna be much time. If the Bruce tries to press the Crawfords into service, all of the warriors will be obligated to go and will leave none for this siege."

While he supported The Bruce's efforts against the English king, Ian had his own path to take. Just because The Bruce's actions aided Ian's plans did not mean he would stand with the newly crowned king in taking back Scotland. Nay, Ian only had his own piece of vengeance to strive for. One he now had in reach.

Hoof beats, still some distance away, echoed in the valley of the low mountains. That would be Colin and the others, returning finally. If all went well, they would be on their way to the Uplands at the first light of dawn.

He stood, dusting off his hands, and strode to the cave's entrance. The hazy moonlight gave him the ability to recognize the warriors of the Crawford clan who'd joined him in his quest. The clouds cleared long enough to reveal Colin in the lead, the other men trailing him. Finally, he brought his horse to a halt near the small stand of trees outside the entrance to the maze of caves. One of the others would take the animals to the hiding place deep in the woods while Colin and his men reported back to Ian.

"Lassie, dinna fight and 'twill go easier on you!"

Lassie? What the hell? Ian watched, realizing that sure

enough, Colin Crawford held a struggling woman in his grip. What did the fool think he was doing? Had he actually kidnapped a woman? Didn't he realize the folly and danger of such an act? Ian strode out of the cave and to the narrow path leading to the valley.

\*\*\*

Marissa jerked out of her captor's grip, but found herself trapped once more against another of his comrades.

"Filthy Scots! Release me at once and your lives may be spared!"

Her only response was laughter, as the leader, his name Colin she had learned, stalked over to her. Her bound arms gripped tightly by the man behind her, she could not evade him.

"Lassie, dinna think you can escape. We caught you and as is our right, we will take our turns enjoying you. And I'm first."

She held back her revulsion and fear, determined not to show any weakness before them. When he neared, she kicked out, catching him on the shin. He yelped with the sudden pain, his eyes narrowing dangerously.

"You wanna make it difficult, then? So be it." He reached out and yanked on her hair again, drawing her closer. Gathering what moisture she could from her panicked dry mouth, she spat fully into his face.

The roar of outrage echoed around her. Colin pulled harder, jerking her out of the other man's grip and toward him. Out of the corner of her eye, she saw the giant fist nearing her face. She closed her eyes, bracing herself for the blow.

Nothing happened. She slowly opened her eyes again, surprised to see another man holding Colin's arm.

"You fool!" he said. "What the hell have you done?"

"Found ourselves a lassie, Ian."

"Do you realize you've jeopardized the mission? No one was to know we were here. Now they will come search for us, before we can finalize our plans and return for siege!"

Siege? These Scots planned to attack Montchester? Why? Marissa stared silently at the two men while they argued, then realized the other men all watched just as intently as she. Here was her chance. She inched slowly toward the edge of the circle, taking care to draw no notice, the two men continuing to hold everyone's attention.

"You ruined everything!" Ian shouted. "They will come looking for her!" At that moment, he turned to where she'd been standing moments earlier. His gaze moved among the men and quickly landed on her.

"Oh, no, you don't!"

She turned and ran without considering the notion further. She'd barely managed a few strides when she found herself caught once again, a strong arm hauling her off her feet and against a solid muscled chest. She screamed her frustration, kicking against her captor. She twisted in his grip, her hands still bound before her and giving her little leverage. When his hand covered her mouth to silence her screams, she bit down hard on the nearest finger.

His furious oath blistered her ears, but somehow, she'd managed to gain her freedom. She ran, not caring which direction, but found herself quickly thrown to the ground, covered by a hard body.

"Dinna make me hurt you, lass."

"You'll pay for this!" she shrieked, trying to fight him as he turned her over. Her gaze locked on his, and she recognized a stony resignation in his expression.

"You've no choice but to remain as our prisoner now. We canna afford to free you, not yet anyway."

"You have no idea what you've done."

"Aye, lass, I expect you're more trouble than you're worth, but there isna choice now."

He stood and lifted her by the arms, and she detected something gentle in his actions, unlike the brutish treatment she'd endured at Colin's hands.

"You're a fool, Colin, for bringing this trouble upon us. I sent you to scout the surrounding areas and you do something foolish like kidnapping a lass. Did you learn anything useful at all?"

Colin sent Marissa a glare of pure hatred. She shuddered and shrank against Ian, choosing the lesser of two evils. She had no doubt Colin would have been the first of many to rape her, while she somehow sensed Ian would not be so brutal. She'd gone mad, surely, to think Ian, a Scot intent on attacking her family, could be a decent choice.

"Aye. After today, there be less than half the garrison present. The Panther is still in residence, but he will be leaving within a sennight to join his king." Colin spat on the ground. "There are several wooded stands that will give us cover as long as we make our approach at night. The Panther's family will not be able to defend against us when we attack."

Marissa stiffened at the sound of her father's nickname and barely managed to stifle her gasp. Ian's grip on her arms tightened. Before she could think on the meaning of the action, he'd spun her about.

"You're the Panther's daughter."

She shook her head. "Nay, I am not!"

A terrifying smile spread across Ian's face. She shivered against an icy chill, fear squeezing her heart.

"Mayhap this will be a better way to exact my revenge."

"Nay, you're wrong! I'm just a lowborn girl. Please, I'm not worth anything."

His dark eyes raked her body and she felt it as if he had touched her physically. He shook his head. "You wear the clothing of a lady. Methinks you will do nicely."

He turned and tugged her bound wrists. She stumbled as she resisted; he simply turned, bent and hoisted her over his shoulder. She kicked her legs.

"Bastard! Animal! Let me go!"

He laughed, tightening his arm across her legs and halting her movements. Seconds later, his large hand landed harshly on her bottom! How dare he strike her!

She shrieked, using every obscenity she'd ever heard her brothers use. She pounded at his back, but he ignored her as he strode toward the caves. Damn! She had to get free of him before they were lost in the maze and her father and his men would never find her!

\* \* \*

Ian didn't know how he held back his fury at Colin for kidnapping the girl. What had the fool been thinking? After he settled the hellcat on his shoulder, he would take the man to task. He'd come too close to allow a stupid action to ruin his plans. He needed to rethink everything up to this point.

At the same time, the likelihood of the squirming lass being the daughter of his enemy gave him an advantage as well. Her eyes gave her away. Whilst he'd never seen for himself, everyone knew The Panther had the eyes of the wild creature whose name he bore. This comely lass's eyes were the same tawny shade of gold. Who else could she be? He would ransom her, after he and his men destroyed the keep and brought the Panther to his knees. After that, who knew? He would have to think long and hard on this.

He strode deeper into the caves, until he reached the area he'd chosen for himself. Tucked away from the main path, the alcove gave him privacy, but remained near enough to the entrance to hear any who approached. He tossed the girl to his pallet. She rolled away from him and took up a crouching position, her bound hands held out before her. He smiled.

"You canna get away, lass, so you may as well get comfortable."

"Heathen! Filthy animal! How dare you kidnap me!"

Ian scratched his beard. "Actually, that would be my fool clansman who kidnapped you. Since you're here, and I'm the leader of this mission, you belong to me. I will decide what's to be done with you."

"I belong to no one." She slowly stood, her dark hair falling across her face. She tossed it away with a graceful wave of her chin.

She was a comely lass, he had to admit that truth. Her eyes, with their odd tawny shade, glistened in the firelight. Two bright pink spots adorned her high cheekbones. Her full lips twisted in an expression of rage. He had the sudden thought of those lips melting beneath his. He shook his head. He'd been too long without a woman that this scrap of a girl could give him thoughts of nonsense.

"Consider yourself my guest."

She sneered. He held back his chuckle. She would be fun to tame. As soon as the thought occurred, it took hold with a tenacious grip.

*The mission. Revenge. Don't lose sight of the goal.*

The more he thought about it, the more he realized this would be the ultimate revenge on the Panther. To destroy The Panther's daughter, as the other man and his soldiers had done to Ian's wife, would be true vengeance. He wouldn't take the lass before him in brutality. Nay, he would seduce her, make her crave his touch and what he could give her, and she'd be willing to do anything he asked, no, ordered. To tame her fire, to break her spirit, to turn her into his personal slave, that would be his revenge.

# Chapter Two

A sudden stab of fear ran through Marissa. The slow smile parting his dark beard revealed even, white teeth sent not only a frisson of alarm, but a shiver of excitement. She recognized a gleam in his eyes that hinted at his approval of what he saw. Perhaps this was something she could use to her advantage until she could get her hands on a sword or dagger. If she played along with the attraction, he might lower his defenses and she could find her way free. Pretending to feel an attraction should not be difficult. She found it easy to look at him as well. His dark eyes smoldered with heat as he stared, and a neatly trimmed beard covered his strong jaw. Long dark hair fell beyond his shoulders. Some of the chill of the cave left her.

She wasn't unfamiliar with the attentions of men. Many of her father's knights had openly admired her, some had even tried to woo her. While she'd enjoyed the flattering attentions, she'd dismissed most of the men. Leland had been the first she had agreed to meet. He didn't mock her skill or insist she tend to more feminine pursuits, such as needlework or running a household. She had no time for silly dalliances like her sisters. Instead, Marissa had trained with her brothers, handling a sword with ease and ability, until she'd become almost as skilled as they.

She longed for a sword now. Any blade would do. Damn Leland for convincing her to leave her weapon behind. She would use her beauty and feminine charms to get out of this situation. She should have paid more attention to her sisters' behavior around men. She truly had little idea of how to lure one to her bed, even if she planned to beat him senseless once she got him there. She concentrated, hiding her grimace and recalled how her sisters had simpered foolishly after some of the knights in her father's garrison. Could she do this? She had to; else she would never be free.

"'Twould be wise for you to release me now, before my father and his men come looking."

"Do you still deny you are the Panther's daughter?"

She shook her head. Better to let him think she had been subdued. "Aye, I am the daughter of the Panther. He will kill anyone who harms me."

"Who said anything about harming you?"

She held his gaze, sensing his suspicion ebb, while the interest in his dark gaze rose. She could do this. Her heart raced a little faster, oddly pleased to know he found her attractive. *Stop it, foolish girl, concentrate on freeing yourself.*

"You've kidnapped me, I assume for a ransom. That crime alone is harming me. I'm sure my father will see it the same way."

"I promise you, lass, you will find nothing but enjoyment in your stay with us. By the time the sun rises high in the sky, we'll be long gone from these caves."

A brief flare of panic threatened to erupt. Marissa tamped it down. "Certainly the caves are cover enough? Why leave?"

"I'll not tell you our plans. I suggest you settle in, 'twill be a long night if you insist on cowering in the corner."

"I am not cowering."

"Mayhap. But my order remains. You will obey me."

"I'm afraid I cannot."

"Why is that, lass?"

"This cave is simply unacceptable. I am used to being treated in a much better manner."

He laughed, and Marissa's temper fired hot once more. She held it inside, trembling with the force trying to burst through her calm exterior.

"You mock me?"

"Nay, lass, not entirely. You're lucky to have even these small comforts. Mayhap once we are back in my village, you'll find the accommodations more to your liking."

He stepped closer, and her senses came to full alert. Determined not to show the fear that now left her knees shaking, she held herself steady. All too soon, he stood before her, his massive height forcing her to tilt her head back to hold his gaze. One hand came up, and she winced, preparing for a blow. Instead, the backs of his fingers lightly brushed her cheek. The gentle and unexpected touch sent an unrecognizable sizzle along her spine.

"Dinna fear, lass. I willna hurt you."

"You already have, sir."

He nodded, his gaze turning thoughtful. "I suppose in your eyes, 'tis the right of it. Set your worries aside. You will be safe as long as I am here to see to it."

Deep inside, warmth continued to glow, and she found herself with the odd thought she believed she *would* be safe with him as her protector. He stared at her a few more moments, his fingers caressing her softly, sending more of those delightful tingles throughout her. She curled her fingers into fists, but refrained from lashing out. Now was not the time. Despite his assurances, she knew he didn't really believe her. She had to continue to play this game, until his guard lowered and she could make her escape.

Before she could give it another thought, he gripped her upper arms and hauled her closer, his mouth crashing down on hers. Her surprise was quickly lost on the yearning his lips inspired. His beard rubbed against her chin, creating an odd delight. All her careful thoughts faded when he tasted her, her body heating in response to the warmth rushing through her veins.

His tongue slipped along her lips and she didn't even think to resist, opening her mouth to allow him inside. The heat threatened to reduce her to cinders. She had never known such a thrill, and never wanted the kiss to end.

Abruptly, he released her and she stumbled backward. Without her hands to steady herself, she lost her balance and landed on her arse. The shock jolted her from the cloud of longing he'd stirred, her body suddenly chilled. Had she actually enjoyed his kiss?

"Forgive me, lass." He reached for her and helped her to stand. "Come, rest here for a while. I have tasks to tend to."

He led her to the sleeping pallet and eased her to sit. He planned to leave her alone?

He gave her a grin that told her he knew exactly what path her thoughts took. "Dinna get any ideas about escaping." He lifted a rope and quickly tied it to the leather strap binding her wrists. Once satisfied, he took the other end of the rope and fastened it to a rock protruding from the cave's wall. With dismay, she realized she could not reach it, even if he had given her sufficient slack to move about the area.

"I wouldna leave you a chance to flee. Not that you'd get far. You'd have to get through my men and that's as likely to happen as a sheep mating a donkey. I'll not have you wandering the caves alone. 'Tis too dangerous for a lass. You'll be safe while I decide what to do with you. I will return shortly."

With that, he turned and disappeared into the darkness of the caves. She stared after him, then turned to eye the odd branch-like stone the rope was bound to. Damn him! Yet, she knew, even if he hadn't secured her to his little alcove, he'd been right. She wouldn't have been able to get past his men or she would have wound up lost in the caves. She sighed and plopped down on the pallet. At least she had time to think and plan. Mayhap she could find something to cut the ropes. She crawled over to his pack, hesitating before lifting the flap and peering inside.

She gulped. Nestled in the bag lay many long lengths of rope. She also spotted a vicious looking whip, and many more leather strips like the one that bound her now. Alongside them lay a crudely drawn outline of Montchester, and the surrounding area. The two towers along the battlements had large X's over them. The earlier revelation that these Scots planned to siege Montchester came back to taunt her. Terror prickled along her spine.

Colin and his men had spoken of scouting the area. No siege could occur now; Ian did not have enough men. Marissa had a moment's relief at knowing her presence here in the caves could very well spare her mother and sisters from a horrific fate. She hoped her failure to return home would convince her father to remain at Montchester, instead of joining the king, so he could properly protect the keep.

Marissa would endure whatever lay ahead, if 'twould keep her family safe.

* * *

Ian headed toward the entrance of the maze. Colin and the other men who'd accompanied him on the scouting mission gathered around a freshly lit fire. Jamie sat among them. He glared at Colin with contempt, though the sot didn't appear to notice.

"The lassie has fire, I tell ya," Colin said. "I wanted to sample me the charms hidden under that fancy English dress." More than a hint of anger laced his tone.

"You never will, Colin, so put the idea out of your head." Ian strode over to stand beside his clansmen.

Colin leapt to his feet, eyes flashing with fury. "She was mine."

"And by taking her, you've risked the entire mission. As it is, the Panther and his remaining men are likely scouring the area for her. We risk being caught at any moment, and can only hope the cover of darkness and the rain will keep them away."

Ian glared in contempt at the younger man. All of his preparation had been tossed like used bathwater. The Panther would be on alert now. Any plans for siege, to occur under the cloak of a moonless sky, now lay in ruins and would have to be postponed.

"They wouldna find her, or us, in here. We covered our tracks, and the villagers claim the caves are haunted.

None will venture here."

"You better hope that's true. Dinna matter. Before dawn, we ride for home."

"I thought you planned to wait until daybreak," Jamie said.

"You and the others will leave before dawn. I will follow shortly after sunrise." He gave a stiff nod to the knowing glint in Jamie's eyes. He turned to face the other men gathered around the fire. "She is the daughter of our enemy, and she is mine to use against him."

"I demand you turn her over to me!" Colin shouted once more.

Ian held up his hand. "Enough. We'll not speak of this again."

Colin grumbled, but said nothing more.

Ian continued, "'Tis not safe to remain here with her. We'll continue with the plan, with a change or two. Perhaps a ransom request."

He caught Jamie's disbelieving stare. He couldn't blame his clansman, they were close to completing all they'd worked so long and hard for, but Colin's actions and the presence of the dark haired lass tied to his pallet had changed everything.

"I have decided to use the lass in our plan for revenge. 'Tis not wise to tarry so close to her home. We must set a faster pace on our return to the Uplands. When she is returned to her father, she will be broken. Then we strike."

Jamie's expression melted into an understanding smile. "Will you share her, Ian?"

The idea initially chilled Ian's blood. He shook his head, surprised at the hastily rising jealousy. Yet, as he pondered the notion, he realized it needed further consideration. Such acts would have to be planned carefully and were not to be taken lightly. 'Twould not be the first time he and Jamie had shared a woman. Doing so with the Panther's daughter could break her that much sooner.

"Nay, Jamie, not yet. I have plans for the lass. What I do know is, when I am done with her, the Panther will be on his knees begging."

"I found her," Colin insisted. "I demand you return her to me."

Revulsion knotted Ian's stomach. Would the man never cease? "She isna yours any longer, Colin. My uncle deemed me leader of Crawford warriors. *I* claim the lass. I canna change the fact she's here now. But 'twas your actions that imperiled *my* plan."

"Damn it, Ian, the lass was mine! She was to be our entertainment!"

"By acting no better than the Panther and his men, you would end up with your head on a pike. 'Tis not the way to handle this."

"And you know better? You havena proved your capabilities as a warrior to my mind."

Ian clenched his fists, and stepped closer to Colin. "You have no idea what I am capable of. Unlike you, however, I use my head for strategy. Not my cock. You made this mess. I'll fix it. If you argue, I'll have you hog-tied on the return to the village."

Colin's eyes flashed, and his mouth opened. Then, clearly deciding against making things worse, he shut his mouth and resumed his seat by the fire.

"Anyone else question my decision?" He glanced into each of the men's faces until he received an answer of nay from every one. "Good. Now spread the word. Seek your pallets so you'll be ready to depart ere the sun rises. By dawn, only I and Jamie will remain, and once we are sure the area is clear, we head for the border."

He ignored the murmurs that started when he walked away. He counted on Jamie to carry out his instructions. In the meantime, he had a lassie to tend to.

He found himself oddly eager to return to her, to once again taste the velvet of her lips. Her surprise when he'd kissed her had quickly turned to an eager response, and his cock hardened at the thought of her innocence. For 'twas no doubt, she was pure.

Yet, the idea of the vengeance he needed to take from her innocent body turned his stomach. He had no wish to subject her to the same fate his Sheila had suffered. The irony in the act was justified, but he would not behave like an animal. Despite her father's barbaric deeds, the girl was merely an innocent lass. A tool to be used, one he would wield carefully.

His earlier idea came into clearer focus and he found himself seeking a way to ease the level of degradation she would suffer, though, in order to adhere to his plan, he could not spare her. He pondered it further and knew he could follow through with the plan, yet not brutalize her entirely. He would seduce her, give her pleasure. Sometimes. Surrendering to her captor would be the best way to break her.

*You don't want to break her.*

He forced that taunting thought from his head.

He realized with a start, he didn't even know her name. His lips curled in a grim smile 'Twould change soon enough. Tonight, he'd give her a taste of the pleasure a woman could experience and by morning, she'd be eager for more. She'd offer herself, and he would be a fool to refuse. She would be willing. Therein lay the key to his success. Knowing she gave herself willingly would be the worst humiliation she could face. Breaking the girl would break the father.

Ian stared at the lass lying on his pallet. Drained from her ordeal, she'd fallen asleep. A twinge of pity tore at him, but he hardened his resolve. She might bring unexpected disaster to his original plans, but with this new strategy, he didn't want to waste a moment. He wanted to taste her again, to bare her skin and feel the creamy flesh tremble under his touch. He looked forward to the enjoyment to be gained from the game about to commence.

He took a deep breath to clear his thoughts and studied

her closely. Her dark hair fanned out behind her, her bound hands clutched tightly against her chest. He frowned. Her skin looked red and raw. He bent, retrieving his dagger from its sheath and slicing through the leather. He took her wrists in his hands and gently rubbed the sore area. She moaned in her sleep, a sound of discomfort, intensifying the conflicting emotions tearing at him like a brutal coastal storm.

He sat beside her, wondering again at her name. He would have it from her ere the night was through. He eased himself to the pallet and drew her close. The sense she fit perfectly around him drew a startled shudder. He glanced down and found her staring at him, her tawny eyes clouded with both sleep and confusion. He grasped her chin and forced her to lean back, a moment before covering her mouth with his.

Her entire body shivered against him and his cock hardened as it hadn't in over two years. He drove into her brutally with his tongue, finding each dark secret buried inside her heat, and savoring the surprised and panicked gasps he drew. He ravished her mouth for several more moments until her frantic attempts to evade him sank through his lust dazed mind.

He drew away and she jerked back. He tightened his grip on her waist, catching one of her hands at the moment it came up to strike at him. He chuckled, loving the defiant fire lighting her face.

"Careful, lass, or I'll bind you again, tighter than before. Then you'll be powerless to stop me from doing as I wish."

She stilled, fear creeping into her gaze. A split second later, she turned into a hellcat, kicking and screaming. She jerked her hand from his and pelted him about the shoulders before he caught her flailing arms and jerked them behind her. Gripping her hands in one of his, he rolled her onto her stomach and reached for another leather thong from the supply in his pack, the ones he'd been preparing since he had regained consciousness. He'd imagined binding the Panther's family before killing them, tying the servants and other members of Montchester with the carefully crafted ties.

Before he had recovered enough to resume his battle training, he had prepared these bindings, the task keeping his focus on his plans. Hours and days and weeks, he had trimmed the leather, adding each newly cut strip to the store. He had eagerly anticipated using them on the family of the Panther, as the man's soldiers had done to Sheila, leaving her unable to fight their attack. The task had given him purpose when he could do little else. Now, he carried them in his pack as a reminder of what Sheila had suffered and how he would ultimately avenge her. Forcing the recollections from his thoughts, he quickly secured the strap around his captive's wrists, knotting it tightly then flipping her onto her back.

"Filthy bastard! I should have known you'd rape me. Fine, then, do your worst. I assure you, when I am free of you, I will see you dead."

The venom in her voice sparked his frenzy further. "I'd like to see you try, lass."

He studied her. Despite her rage and the way she defied him, he saw fear in her golden eyes. He hated what he was about to do. She would hate him more. He held her gaze, and knew he could never take her in brutality and anger, not after he'd watched the agony his wife had endured. Yet, he would not spare the lass.

His perfect revenge had been handed to him, but he knew he could never attack this trembling girl with hate. The conclusion solidified his earlier idea. Seduction must be his path to take, and his ultimate victory would be that much sweeter.

\* \* \*

Marissa stared up at her captor, hating him for what he was about to do. While she may not have played the court maids like her sisters, she had always hoped to gain a husband who cherished her and would make her his with love and kindness - not hatred and brutality. Yet, she was helpless now, the man looming over her free to do whatever he chose. The strange tingle of anticipation alarmed her. How could she possibly anticipate this? Her fear, mingled with a strange anticipation, mocked her, taunted her. She clenched her jaw.

For several moments, he simply stared at her. She wondered what thoughts lurked behind that dark gaze. He lifted a dagger and her eyes widened. He didn't plan to kill her, did he?

She panicked and tried to jerk away, but one hand landed firmly on her hip, preventing her flight. He lowered the blade to her bodice and she gulped in a deep breath when he sliced through the fabric, then set the dagger to the side. His hands returned to the cut material of her dress, ripping it away, baring her breasts.

"Heathen beast! You will pay for this!" She screamed the words, gaining some leverage with her feet to push herself up along the pallet. Her arms ached, her shoulders straining with the movement, but she continued to wriggle, until she came up against the stone wall of the cave.

Ian's grin turned positively menacing. "You're well caught now, lassie. Why dinna you stop fighting? 'Twill make it easier."

The seductive burr in his voice added to the turmoil. A shiver passed over her, not an unpleasant one. She tried to ignore it, with little success. "I will not willingly submit to you, you bastard."

He threw his head back and laughed, and her fury exploded within her. Yet at the same time, she found his genuine amusement transformed his rugged features, his eyes sparkling, the wide full smile open and warm, and her heart changed rhythm. What was wrong with her that she could find anything attractive about her rapist?

He leveled his stare on her once again. She shivered, tugging against her bindings. He inched closer and she cringed against the wall.

"Lass, when we're finished, you will be willing to serve me in any way I choose."

His meaning sunk through her frantic and chaotic thoughts. "You sick animal! I will never serve you!"

"Once I show you the pleasure I can give you, you will. I own you, lass. I'm about to prove it."

His voice deepened, making his words seem an actual caress. Her body trembled in a maddening response that left her more bewildered, and strangely eager to experience the next moment. His gaze lowered, reminding her of her exposed state, and she bowed her head, trying again to shrink into the wall.

She sensed him beside her and squeezed her eyes shut. All that happened was a gentle finger stroking her jaw. She opened her eyes and stared at him. His thumb slid along her lower lip, and despite her resolve, another shot of heat spread through her and she fought with all her strength of mind not to give into the need to press against him, to seek more of his gentle caress.

He leaned in close and she felt his breath on her mouth moments before his lips slid over hers, soft and languid - not at all what she'd expected. She tugged once more against her bonds, fighting them as much as the need to give into this delight.

She moaned, her lips trembling beneath his when he teased her with lazy kisses. His hand cupped the side of her head, holding her still while he deepened the kiss. A fog engulfed her. She could no longer think, and responded, returning his attentions with fervor.

A need, sharp and sudden, sliced through her. His tongue lined the seam of her lips; instinctively, she opened, fear and anger fading under the tender assault. Her tongue tangled with his, jolts of hunger startling her and making her want more.

When he drew away, drawing a steady breath grew difficult. She took some satisfaction in knowing he appeared as unsettled as she, even as she hated the flare of disappointment that he'd stopped. How could she want more? She couldn't answer that question, could only acknowledge the desire simmering within. To consider anything else now would surely drive her to madness.

His finger continued to slide along her jaw, now trailing down her neck. His stormy gaze held her captive as surely as the leather binding her wrists. Still, he continued the tender exploring touches, igniting sparks that traveled her body, settling with a shocking pulse deep inside her. Between her legs, her sex clenched and she knew what that meant. Innocent though she may be, she'd heard enough talk from her brothers to know what happened when a woman was aroused. Ian had certainly aroused her.

Heat burned her cheeks, yet, he continued the soothing caresses, and her moment of panic faded. His touch felt too good to deny, and she was tired of fighting. Her intentions were to play along with him, until her moment for freedom presented itself. If he continued to make her feel this good, she might as well enjoy it.

"See, lass? It can be enjoyable, if you dinna fight. Surely you see the futility of resisting."

"I should not give in so freely." Her voice cracked. "'Tis a sign of weakness."

"Nay. 'Tis a sign of strength to recognize the pleasure and enjoy it for what it is."

She gave a little shake of her head. Yet, reason sounded clear and strong. He will take what he wants, regardless of your choice. If she succumbed to his seduction, would it hurt less?

"I'm afraid." She didn't know why she admitted it, but satisfaction burst free at the concern softening his features. Perhaps she'd found another way to deceive him. Play to his pity, and mayhap she could even escape before he harmed her further.

"Have no fear, lass, I will show you pleasure. First,

you must tell me your name."

She hesitated. He knew who she was, but she had never confirmed her name. The idea of doing so now troubled her, as if telling him would give him additional power over her.

"Marie," she said. "My name is Marie."

# Chapter Three

Ian sensed she lied, but didn't press the matter. While she appeared to respond to his kisses and caresses, he knew she calculated the first chance she would have for escape. She was smart, but he was smarter. He would have her, and she needed a clear demonstration of his intentions.

"Well, Marie, mayhap you'd prefer to get more comfortable. That stone wall must be cold. Come closer, and I'll warm you, lass."

She hesitated, a brief shiver passing over her. Finally, she nodded, and he helped her back so she lay on the pallet.

"Won't you untie my hands, please?"

He shook his head. "Sorry, Marie, but I canna trust you. You will remain bound."

She sighed. "This hurts."

He frowned. He wanted to pleasure her, well, to a point, and surely her arms were terribly sore by now. He sighed, gently rolling her to her side, straddling her legs to prevent her from kicking. He removed the leather around her wrists and eased her to her back, refastening the thong so her hands now lay bound before her. With quick movements, he hauled her arms up over her head, securing them to yet another protrusion of rock.

"There, lassie. Better?"

"I'd rather be free."

He grinned. "Nay, Marie. I'll not have you escaping before I've had a chance to ... finish this."

She concealed it well, but he'd caught her brief expression of anger, before her face melted back to mild acceptance. Ian congratulated himself on reading her so well. He contained his amusement and stretched out beside her. Her tawny eyes focused on his face, and he could see her wondering what he planned next. He leaned over and kissed her, gently, until the tension eased from her taut muscles, and she responded to his kiss. He had to taste her, driving his tongue deep inside to savor her heat. A soft whimper escaped her when he resumed his caresses along her neck, trailing slightly lower with each stroke. Her warm flesh seared his fingers as he slid them between her breasts. Immediately, she stiffened.

"Hush, lass." He ran his hand lightly over one breast, then the other, her nipples peaking beneath his palms. A tremor passed over her and he repeated the motion, leaning back to watch her face while his hand moved over her.

"Oh, that's..."

"Feels nice, doesna, lass?"

She nodded and he firmed his caresses, gently massaging the creamy trembling mounds, this time avoiding the rosy tips until she arched up against him. Triumph resounded through him, but he held it back, trying to maintain his focus on tormenting the lass quivering beneath him.

"I can't... no more," she moaned.

At that moment, he took both nipples between thumbs and forefinger, and gently squeezed. She cried out, a violent spasm taking her over. He tugged at the swelling buds, his cock throbbing as he watched her moan and writhe.

He released her and she fell back, panting. "'Twould seem you liked that, lass."

She licked her lips, her golden eyes now hazy with desire, and gave a small nod. He leaned over and kissed her again, not lingering this time, trailing trailed along her jaw and neck, his mouth following the earlier path of his hands. All the while, he continued his gentle caresses on her breasts, squeezing and patting, every now and then, lightly pinching her nipples. Each time, she gave an intense groan, her body rippling under his touch.

Lust clouded his senses as he trailed his tongue along the side of her breast. Marie gave a little shriek, her body now moving frantically beneath him. If she thought this was good, wait until he truly started his torment.

\* \* \*

Marissa moaned, the heat of Ian's mouth on her breast shocking and exhilarating at the same time. He continued to toy with her nipples, and they grew ever more sensitive with each pinch. When he stopped, her breasts throbbed, heavy with pleasure and the need for more.

She stared at him, wondering what he would do next. Never had she imagined something could feel this good. When he leaned over her, his hot mouth sucking one peak inside, she cried out. This was so much better than before. His tongue laved the hardened peak, sensation exploding throughout her, settling with even more ferocity between her legs. A heavy wetness coated her sex, and she shifted her hips, trying to gain some friction to ease the intense hunger.

Ian chuckled, the vibration against her heated flesh too much to bear. She arched against him, cursing her bound hands that kept her from holding on. She needed to steady herself against the tumult, yet at the same time, she wanted him to continue bringing her such delight.

A sharp tearing broke through the haze, but she didn't even care that he ripped the rest of her dress open, leaving her naked except for the undertunic he had destroyed when he'd cut her bodice. His hands made short work of the thin fabric, and she lay bare before him. A cool breeze fluttered over her burning skin, and her nipples tightened further. A smile split his beard, his gaze moving over her and sparking with approval. Why did the sight thrill her? He leaned back, settling between her legs and using his knees to keep her spread open. Heat scorched her face and she closed her eyes, embarrassed he would see her disgrace.

"Dinna worry, lass. 'Tis no need to be shamed in finding pleasure. Though you will likely hate me after I'm done."

The reminder of what he intended raised alarm, yet not enough to chase away this need still pulsing through her. She tried in vain to close her legs, but Ian didn't budge. He laid one hand on her belly, and she trembled, the spark from his touch sliding through her veins. He did nothing more than caress her belly and breasts, stirring her once more to the feverish pitch he'd held her at earlier. She tossed her head, her fingers clenching as she tugged once more on her bonds. The urge to touch him became almost as powerful as the riot of need taking over the last of her senses. The hunger burned in her mouth, and she whined, not knowing why the sensations continued to grow.

Slowly, the large hand on her belly moved lower, creeping through the dark curls that hid her sex. She found her hips straining upward, seeking the contact she knew was coming. The moments seemed to last an eternity before his hand finally cupped her, pressing lightly against the throbbing flesh that desperately sought his touch.

A sobbing moan escaped her and she bucked her hips, trying to silently convey her want. His fingers slid along her cleft, slick and hot, and moved up to circle the hardened bud where all sensation seemed to gather. He teased her, making her moan and pant.

"What is it, lass? What do you want?"

"I... I... I don't know. Just... more."

He continued to torment her, his touch light and slow while he explored her most private area, returning again and again to the spot where she wanted it most. She watched him through eyelids growing heavy. A sharp gasp escaped when he abruptly lowered his head. The heat of his tongue sliding in her folds became too intense and she screamed against the searing pleasure. He found her sensitive bud and suckled it between his lips. Marissa strained against the ever surging desire intensifying with each second. She had the sense of reaching for something, a pinnacle that eluded her. Ian pulled his mouth from her core and she moaned in disappointment.

"No, don't stop," she sighed.

"I think that's enough for now, lass."

Her eyes snapped open, her mind not comprehending his words. "But you... I thought... why?"

"You should rest. You have a long day ahead of you."

She blinked, still caught in desire's tenacious grip. Her body burned, ached, and she felt so close to something she quickly realized she craved.

"B-but, isn't there... Aren't you going to...?"

"Nay, not now. Tomorrow's ride will be long and difficult. I must rest."

He couldn't leave her like this! She bit back her scream of frustration. "But I thought you wanted... that you would..."

"I find I dinna have the strength right now. Settle down and sleep, lass."

He slid up beside her, turning her so he spooned against her back. He wasn't serious!

"Please, you can't leave me like this!"

"Like what, lass?"

"I... I don't know. I... I ache. I need... something." The plea slipped from her lips before she could think to stop it. She didn't care. He had stirred this fire within her, and she wanted him to quench it!

"I'm sure you do. But you don't get that pleasure unless I decide to give it to you. Right now, I need to sleep. You should too."

Sleep? Now? Like this? Her body remained on fire, she couldn't stop trembling, and her core felt like it might explode. He couldn't be that cruel. She turned to look at him and found his expression a mask of cold indifference. She held back a frustrated moan and turned away. Her anger flared yet again, anger at herself for falling under his wicked spell and giving in so easily.

The heat from his body taunted her further. At least she could press her thighs together, that seemed to give her some soothing. As soon as she had found a rhythm, Ian pried her legs apart with his own, thwarting her attempt at relief.

"Nay, lass, the only pleasure you'll receive is at my hand. Now go to sleep."

She fumed in the darkness, fighting the urge to cry over the unfulfilled pleasure. She had no idea what she wanted, but she knew she had to have it. Somehow. The thought of begging crossed her mind, but she refused to give the idea further consideration. How was she supposed to sleep like this?

* * *

Ian held the girl in his arms while she fidgeted and tried to get comfortable. With her arms still above her head, she had very little leeway, with the way he embraced her. He suppressed his chuckle at her squirming, trying to close the legs he ruthlessly held open, preventing her from achieving any sort of relief from the need he knew coursed through her. His own desire remained painfully hard, but he forced it from his mind. By the morn, she would be ready to beg him to take her innocence. He could hold out a few more hours.

After several minutes, she finally settled, but an occasional tremor still passed over her from time to time. When he felt her breathing turn slow and deep, he put the next part of his plan in motion. One hand slid to her cleft, still drenched and throbbing with desire. She moaned in her sleep, her hips thrusting toward his touch. He skimmed his fingers along her folds, sliding up to teasingly circle the hardened nub that held her passion. He flicked it lightly, and she quivered and sighed, her body responding without her being aware of it. He wanted to keep touching her, but soon her legs strained, a sign she sought greater contact with his fingers. He drew away and savored her moan of disappointment. Had she wakened? He peered down at her.

Nay, she still slept. The fire in her body still raged and he would ensure the flames burned all night long.

He dozed in brief spurts; each time he awakened, he once again slid his hands to Marie's sex and teased her, making her writhe and plead. Twice she awoke, her sleep roughened voice begging for more as powerful an aphrodisiac as any of her body's responses. He denied her each time, leaving her near sobbing by the time he fell into a deeper sleep.

When he awoke, the fire had almost died. Noises from the cave's path drew his attention. Jamie peered around the wall shielding Ian and Marie from view.

"'Tis dawn. Are you ready to leave?" he asked.

"Nay, gather the men and go, I will catch up to you soon enough." He caught a glimpse of Jamie's grin before his clansman disappeared from sight once more. He raised himself up and studied the girl on his pallet. Her tawny eyes were wide open and focused intently at him. In their depths, he read the need still seething within her. He held back a smile.

"Are you ready to leave, lass?" he asked.

Her eyes widened. "Leave? But nay, you can't just take me ... "

"I can, lass, and I will. One way or another, you are coming with me."

She tugged on the rope holding her arms above her, wincing. He loosened the rope and she cried out as she lowered her bound wrists, the discomfort of being in the position too long obviously great. A tear fell free of her eyes and he fought the urge to wipe it away. Still, her gaze held more than a shadow of desire, and he knew his torment of her throughout the night had taken a different sort of toll.

His still hard cock reminded him he needed relief too, and 'twas time he got it. He stretched out above her, savoring the way her eyes widened in realization.

"Aye, lass, 'tis time for me to take my pleasure. I fear

the ride will be difficult enough."

"You bastard! How can you do this to me?" Her voice cracked and she tried to lift her arms to strike him, but the limbs remained weak from the enforced bondage. Ian lifted his kilt and settled between her spread thighs.

"Nay! Don't do this, please!" Her plaintive wail tugged at him, but he strengthened his determination, using a hand to tease and caress her soaked pussy. Despite her protest, she quickly responded, her hips bucking against his when he circled her clit, using her own cream to slide gently around the hardened nub. She moaned, her protests melting into soft pleas for more. He obliged her, increasing his attentions until she finally gave a shriek, her body convulsing wildly beneath him. She even cried his name, passion evident in her voice. Before the tremors had subsided, he rose up and drove his hard cock into her heat.

Her cries changed, filled with pain at the sudden intrusion. Her bound fists pummeled his chest until he caught them and held them above her. Damn, she was gloriously tight, hot and wet, and his head swam trying to hold on, wanting to make it last. As she bucked against him, driving him deeper, the thread of his control frayed further.

He eased his length from her, noting the blood that adorned his cock, along with her glistening juices. With a groan, he sheathed himself inside her once again, noting with surprise the way her moan was no longer pained, instead he clearly heard her pleasure in the sound. He stroked harder into her, pleased when her legs wrapped around his waist, urging him still deeper. He was caught up in the tempest, as surely as she, and he released her hands to steady himself as he pounded into her now welcoming body. A shriek pierced the silence of the cave moments before her pussy convulsed wildly on his cock, her body writhing with such force, he thought she might buck him off. Instead, he drove faster into her, the release overtaking him in a blinding rush, and he poured his seed deep. Breathing heavily, he collapsed atop her, her body still twitching around his.

Several minutes passed before he regained his senses, and he raised himself up and stared into Marie's tear-streaked face. A wave of regret surged through him, but he forced it back. He had a mission to complete, and she was merely part of that. Caring for her comfort would jeopardize what he had to do. Her disruption to his careful plans had cost him too much already. From this point on, he had to ensure her presence only helped his goals. Feeling any emotion for her other than contempt would get him killed. He had to remind her of what she was to him.

"Get up, lass, 'tis time to go."

Her eyes cleared and she resisted when he tugged her bound wrists, urging her to stand. She swayed unsteadily, the remnants of her gown hanging off her shoulders. He frowned. Perhaps he'd been too hasty to destroy her dress. He couldn't drag her to the Uplands half-clothed like this. He reached into his pack for another tartan and turned.

"Come, lass, let me remove those rags."

She shook her head and backed up a step. "Nay, 'tis bad enough you ruined my clothes, I will not let you strip me naked."

He rolled his eyes. "You can't travel like that. Let me wrap you in something to keep you warm."

She backed away again, but he rushed toward her, catching her easily and pulling the tattered remains of her dress free until she stood before him, bare-arsed as the day she'd been born. He took a moment to admire her feminine curves, the flare of her hips and the swell of her breasts, before wrapping the plaid around her as best he could. At least she was covered, even if her arms remained bare. He eyed the leather holding her wrists together. 'Twould have to stay now, he didn't dare risk her taking any chance to flee. He pointed to the floor. "Sit."

Pleased she obeyed; he quickly gathered his belongings, pulling some dried meat from his pack. Biting off a piece, he handed it to Marie. She shook her head.

"Eat it lass, you'll need your strength."

She hesitated a moment more, then nodded, taking the meat and biting off a mouthful, While she chewed, he lifted his skin and drank some ale before passing it to her. She took a healthy swallow and returned it. He packed it away and turned back.

Her cheeks flamed, and he held back his laugh. He knew what she wanted. "Aye, lass, when we are free of the caves. Now come."

"No."

"Still stubborn, eh? You would do best to obey, since to disobey will earn you a punishment. Which would you prefer?"

"I'd prefer to be freed."

"Sorry, lass, willna happen. You belong to me now, and you can make it easy or hard. Your choice."

She debated for a moment, then fixing a fierce glare on him, she stepped toward him.

"You're smarter than I thought. No dallying, we have a lot of ground to cover before we reach my village."

He led her through the maze, looking for the marks that none but he and his men would recognize as directional signs. After a bit, the end of the maze came into view, as light from the outside brightened the cave's entrance on the other side of the mountain. He slowed his step, and Marie stumbled into him. He turned and steadied her, then crept closer to the mouth of the cave. He peered around the edge and seeing no one, led her out into the morning sunshine. Sure enough, his horse was tethered a few feet away, saddled and ready for him. He silently thanked Jamie and threw his pack atop the animal. He turned to Marie, scowling when she backed away.

"You said I could ... relieve myself."

"Soon enough, we must make haste to put some

distance between us and England."

# CHAPTER FOUR

Marissa stared at him. If he forced her to go, there'd be no way her father could find her now. She glanced around the clearing near the cave's mouth. Could she make a run for it? Before she could decide, Ian's arm came around her waist, hauling her off her feet and carrying her to the horse. She struggled briefly, but he tightened his grip, forcing the air out of her lungs. Lightheaded, she went limp just before he tossed her into the saddle and climbed up behind her.

"Once we're safely away, I'll let you tend to your needs." With a noise to the horse, they were off, a slow trot at first, then a faster gait until the mountain and caves were no longer in view. She knew because she peered over his shoulder and realized her chance at freedom was, for now, gone.

"Dinna fash yourself, lass. I think you'll find being my slave will not be a totally terrible experience."

She stiffened. Slave? "You can't be serious!"

"But I am. I own you now, or have you forgotten?"

"I'm not a slave; I will not be treated like one! Release me, or I'll -"

"You'll what, lass? Look at you, bound and helpless now, what can you do? Besides, last night and this morning proved how much you will enjoy being my slave."

With those words, he reached up and fondled her breast. She gave a shriek of outrage and used her bound hands to push him away, but he merely returned, squeezing her flesh harder. Despite her anger at how she'd been tricked, again, his rough touch ignited more of that alarming sensation in her core. How could she like this? He treated her like a whore, and her body responded to his ill-treatment. She choked back a sob, knowing now that he'd taken her innocence, any chances of a powerful marriage alliance were gone. She was damaged, used by a heathen Scot. Despair and fury mingled, still entwined with a healthy dose of desire as he continued to manipulate her breast, first one, then the other. She held back the bitter tears burning her eyes, hating how her body responded to his touch.

Abruptly, the horse stopped and she found herself tossed to the ground. She managed to hold her stance, and gave a brief moment's thought to flee when Ian's hand clamped once again on her bound hands. She wiggled her fingers, now growing numb and gave a moan of relief when he sliced through the leather binding her. She rubbed her reddened and raw wrists, wincing when the feeling returned to her weakened hands.

"Dinna think you'll be making a run for it here. You'd get lost and starve to death before anyone could find you."

Knowing he was right, she glared, but refused to speak. Her gaze caught sight of a stream nearby and the urge to relieve herself once again overtook her. She headed for the bushes beside the water, halted by his grip on her upper arm.

"I'll be watching, you, lass. No stupid moves. If I have to chase you down, I'll punish you for it."

She gave him a curt nod and turned away when he released his grip. After tending her personal needs, she strode to the water, cleaning herself off. How she longed for a bath, to remove the grime of her ordeal, and the still-lingering scent of her captor. She debated whether to enter the creek when he appeared beside her.

"If you'd like to bathe, feel free. I'll be right here." He settled down on the banks of the stream. She resisted the urge to protest. He truly intended to treat her as no better than his slave. Fine. He found her comely; the heat in his eyes had given that away. Her appearance became a tool she could wield against him. She wouldn't cower, she would stand straight and proud. If he wanted to watch, so be it. It might help in her plan to trick him into lowering his guard so she could escape. With careful and deliberate motions, she slowly unwound the plaid he'd wrapped around her. She marveled at how the one piece of fabric covered her so completely, even as she hated the reason she had to wear it. Would her father search the caves and find her tattered gown? She hoped such a discovery wouldn't lead him to abandon his search, thinking her dead.

Finally naked, she dared a glance toward her captor. He sat with arms folded, the hunger in his gaze revealing his interest in her nudity. She took care to move with grace, hoping the sight of her tormented him, even as the knowledge he watched her filled her with that now familiar heat. Her nipples hardened painfully and she forced herself to the water's edge to try to ignore the sensation. She daintily dipped her toe into the creek, then quickly drew back. The water was cold, though she should have expected that in late spring. Nevertheless, gritting her teeth, she waded into the stream and slowly lowered herself into the water. She had no soap, but used the weeds growing along the banks as a cloth to scrub some of the grimy dirt from her body.

Aware Ian still watched, she avoided his gaze until she had nearly completed her ablutions, as best she could. Too late, she realized she had no cloth to dry herself with. She turned to him, eyes widening to see his hand slide under his kilt. His sly grin told her he knew of her awareness. She stood, shivering in the afternoon breeze, and crossed her arms before her. He stood before she even had time to blink, pulling her hands away and baring her breasts. She shivered, partly from cold, partly from the flames dancing in his eyes.

"Dinna cover yourself, lass. I'm enjoying the view."

Heat flamed her face and she looked at the ground. He tilted her chin back, forcing her to meet his probing gaze. He said nothing, merely covered her mouth in a hungry kiss that left her panting against him when he drew away. Before she had the thought to question him, he had urged her to the ground, covering her with his body. His hands stroked everywhere along her naked flesh, stoking her desire yet again.

She reached for him, tangling her fingers in his long hair, holding him close and kissing him back. His fingers found her sex again, stroking and teasing and making her forget, just for a moment, where she was. His skillful caresses had her writhing in need, aching to feel that wondrous pleasure he'd given her earlier. He thrust his hips against hers, and his hardness ground briefly against her sex. She moaned, undulating against him, lost in the sensations overpowering her. Somewhere in the riot of her thoughts, reason battled to be heard, but she disregarded it, trembling against his seeking fingers, wanting more.

He abruptly released her and rose. "Put on your tartan. We have no time to waste."

His gruff, clipped words sent an uneasy chill along her spine that had nothing to do with her wet body in the morning breeze. Oddly pained by his suddenly icy demeanor, she gathered up the plaid fabric and wrapped it around herself. No matter how she tried, she couldn't make the material cover her as Ian had earlier. She struggled to arrange the cloth, when his hands suddenly pushed her aside. Did he growl while he tugged and twisted the fabric so it once again covered her bare form?

"Thank you," she said, catching his stare.

Something flickered in his gaze, chasing her chill. The brief moment vanished when he turned and practically dragged her along behind him to his horse. Once more she found herself settled in his saddle before him, but now her hands were free. As if her thoughts had somehow reminded him, he drew another leather strap from his pack and wrapped it around her wrists before securing them to the saddle. Uneasiness consumed her thoughts. How many of those blasted things did he have? Why?

"There's no need for this," she said, tugging at her arms.

"I canna trust you." With that, he kicked the horse into a lope and they sailed across the fields.

Marissa marveled at how long the horse maintained the rapid pace, her own horse would have quit a long time ago. The rocking motion of the animal's gait, combined with the heat of Ian's body at her back made her drowsy and her lids drooped. She jerked herself to awareness. She had to keep a close watch on the journey, so when the chance arose, she could find her way back. She'd need a horse. She'd have to steal Ian's when her opportunity came.

For now, though, she had no choice but to hold on. Finally, after what seemed like hours, Ian slowed the animal to a walk and Marissa heaved a sigh of relief. Her spine ached, but she fought the ever-growing longing to lean back against Ian. She continued to hold herself as far from him as she could, not really far at all, since the saddle left no space to maneuver.

Ian's arm around her waist tightened, drawing her fully against him. She fought against his hold for a moment before his rough voice near her ear sent a frisson of excitement through her.

"Relax, lass, you'll be unable to walk once we stop if you don't."

Knowing she needed to keep her wits sharp, she acquiesced. She wouldn't escape him if she couldn't move without pain. Just when she became comfortable, his hand slipped up to idly cup her breast. She sucked in a breath and tried to dislodge him, but his grip was relentless, caressing her until heat licked at her body. With her hands bound to the saddle, she had no way to stop his assault, yet she found her attempts to evade him weakened further with every touch. His lips slid lightly along her neck, and she trembled with delight, biting back the threatening moan.

He moved to her other breast, and teased her flesh with the gentle caresses, finally taking her nipple between his fingers and squeezing gently. She gasped, arching against his hand. His chuckle vibrated against her shoulder, magnifying the desire taking over her senses.

He moved lower, sliding his hand under the plaid between her legs. His sure fingers found her sex, sliding along her damp heat. Her head fell back against his shoulder, and his mouth latched onto her neck, suckling in time with his stroking hand. He circled her hardened nub, the sensation maddening and delightful, and her hips shifted, seeking deeper contact.

As if to oblige her silent plea, he slipped a finger up inside her and she cried out, her fists clenching. Still his mouth tormented the sensitized skin of her throat, his hands working her to a fiery peak she ached to reach. Her body seemed about to burst into flame, her yearning so great, it nearly consumed her.

Then he stopped, withdrawing his hands and mouth, leaving her hanging on the precipice of bliss.

"No," she moaned in frustration. Her body trembled with unfulfilled desire, and she bit her lip to hold back the plea for him to continue.

"Sorry, lass, I choose not to reward you just yet." Suppressed laughter tinged the cruel bastard's words.

"You are no gentleman, sir." Her voice wavered, betraying the need holding her in its persistent grasp. The urge to weep with the intense desire tearing at her nearly overwhelmed her, but she resolutely forced it back. She would not show such weakness.

"Nay, and I never claimed to be. Remember, slave, you're mine and I decide if you deserve pleasure."

If she could have, she would have scratched his eyes from his head. Instead, she took a ragged breath, trying to ignore the riot still pulsing through her body. Damn him, his game was sadistic, and yet all she could think about was finding a way to get him to give her the pleasure she now craved.

For the next hour, she squirmed uncomfortably, trying to find some relief from the fiery excitement gnawing at her, to no avail. Every now and again, Ian resumed his torment, determined to keep her on the edge of this hunger, until she practically sobbed and begged him to continue when he stopped. Somehow she managed not to break down, even as she could no longer think clearly through the haze. All she could think of was the urgency throbbing in her sex, one that would need soothing soon, or she would go mad.

\* \* \*

Ian smiled at the girl squirming in his arms. Her breath came in ragged spurts, and her heart raced against his arm. He knew exactly how desperate for release she was, he damn near was in the same position. He wouldn't give in. Yet. He wanted her to crave his touch so thoroughly she would do anything he asked. He had a long list of things he wanted to make her do. Watching the Panther's daughter humiliated and broken when he showed her off to his clan would be a sweet delight. Then he would display her before her father; show him what he had done. His final act would be to destroy the demon who had destroyed his life.

Yet, even as he savored the sweetness of the revenge, his conscience warned him he played a dangerous game. As much as he wove his spell around her, he could easily get caught in his own web. He must take care not to let the lass worm her way into his good graces. She was a means for vengeance, nothing more. He found himself anxious to bury his cock deep inside her again, to watch her come apart with release, to hold her against him while she slept. To catch a glimpse of her smile, something he had yet to see.

'Twas a shame he could make out the dust of his clansmen's horses. Despite the brief dalliance near the stream, he had managed to catch up to his men quickly. No time now to indulge any further private moments. As soon as they reached the village, he planned to take her as soon as possible.

She finally slumped against him, sleep overtaking her. Good. He'd rather she not hear what he planned to discuss with his clansmen. He urged the horse into a gentle trot, closing the vast space between him and his men.

Jamie wheeled back to meet him when Ian was within a mile. His clansman grinned at the girl sleeping in Ian's arms. "How was she?"

"Sweeter than I could have imagined," Ian admitted. "Breaking her will be an enjoyable task."

"I envy you, Ian."

"There may be a way for you to help me when we reach the village. 'Twould be a perfect way to hasten the process."

Jamie's eyes glittered with eagerness. "Aye, I'll bet Colin would be willing to help as well."

Ian's anger quickly rose to the fore. "Nay, that brute willna touch her. The way to break her is through kindness. Give her hope then take it away. Colin doesna know how to touch a woman except in violence."

"He's been talking about making you give her to him."

"Willna happen. She belongs to me. As leader of this mission, I claim all bounty, and share as I see fit. I willna share her with Colin."

"He's threatening to take it to your uncle."

"My uncle gave me authority to do as I need with the Crawford men. He willna gainsay me."

Jamie nodded. "Let me know when you need my help. I canna wait to sample her charms."

Ian grinned. "She'll serve us both well before we show her father what we've done to his daughter."

"Will you free her then?"

"I havena decided. Mayhap when the Panther is destroyed, I'll sell her. Her position and beauty give her a value that would aid us in rebuilding the MacCallums."

"Or you could keep her."

"Aye. Havena thought past her usefulness to our goal yet. There's time enough to decide. Come on."

Ian kicked his horse to a faster pace. He and Jamie quickly caught up to the other men, and Ian took his place at the head of the group. Aware of Colin sending icy looks his way, he fell back to ride beside the other man.

"We'll settle this at the village, Colin. I willna give her up, so decide what you want in payment."

He didn't wait for a response, simply resumed his place at the fore of the group. They rode in silence for several hours. The sun had crossed much of the sky when Marissa finally awakened.

\* \* \*

Marissa stirred, the soothing rocking motion making it difficult to relinquish the peaceful haven of slumber. Wakefulness remained relentless, forcing her out of sleep, until she recalled exactly where she was. Remembering too late her wrists still tied to the saddle, she stiffened and jerked upright. Pain lanced up her arms and she cried out before she could stifle it.

Almost immediately, a blade sliced through the leather, and painful feeling returned to her wrists. She held back the urge to break down in tears, refusing to show weakness.

"So the lass awakes. Ian, what are you planning for her?" one of the men called out.

She hadn't realized they'd joined the others. She lifted her head, looking around. An ominous stare from Colin made her shrink back against the seeming safety of Ian's embrace.

"Nothing I'll share with the likes of you," Ian bantered, laughter infusing his words.

"But you will with Jamie?" Still another, clearly disgruntled.

Ian threw his head back and gave a full throated laugh. Marissa continued to rub her sore wrists, the sharp discomfort fading. He would share her? Which one was Jamie? She glanced at the man who'd drawn alongside them. The knowing glint in his stare provided her answer. She shivered at the heat in his gaze, alarmed at the way her body recognized his intent - responded to it. It must be because Ian had so thoroughly aroused her body, she *would* react in such a way to another man. Another Scot.

"Aye, he will," the man said, continuing to hold her stare, and she gulped. He was near as handsome as Ian, his shoulders as broad. She had a brief flash of being held in Jamie's embrace, and the imagining set her heart to a panicked racing.

He gave her a grin and continued, "Already promised me time with the lass. Apparently he needs help in training her to be his slave."

"See, I knew you favored Jamie," came the reply.

Marissa stiffened, heat searing her face. How dare they talk about her as if she were nothing more inconsequential than an animal to be bought or sold! Anger at her foolish musings spurred her fury as she realized just how they intended to humiliate her. At another laugh from Ian, she twisted in his arms, rage now controlling her and not caring what she risked. She swung her arm toward Ian's head, catching him in the temple. His head snapped to the side and she moved to strike again, but he caught her wrist in his iron grip. She froze under the fury in his eyes. Yet, she refused to cower and met his stare evenly.

"You heathens! How dare you treat me like this! I am the daughter of an earl!"

Ian's eyes narrowed, just as a nervous laugh from the side broke through the sudden silence. Jamie watched her with that same hungry intensity as his clansman. But 'twas the Scot holding her, and glaring so menacingly who demanded her full focus.

"You are nothing more than my slave. I will share you with any and all I choose. The sooner you accept your fate, the better 'twill go for you, lass. Make no mistake, I willna tolerate disrespect or disobedience. Both will earn you a harsh punishment." His voice, low and dark, held a threat she couldn't discount. She lifted her chin.

"You will hang for this, I promise you."

His tight expression eased and he gave a simple shrug. The indifferent gesture irritated her further. To her shock, he reached up and grabbed her breast, squeezing tightly in warning. A bolt of discomfort shot through her chest, yet her nipple hardened, the familiar heat stirring yet again. She silently cursed the hunger for him to capture the peak in his mouth, as he had last night, hating the way his touch, any touch unraveled her senses so quickly.

When he released her, she held back a sigh of relief. If he'd continue, it wouldn't take him long to reduce her to a writhing mass of yearning, willing to do anything to feel the pleasure he stoked so easily in her body. Likely he would then deny her the very pleasure he had promised with his torment. She couldn't bear any more, her body had come alive just from that one touch, and it hadn't even been the connivingly gentle caresses of earlier. His rough handling of her body had brought her lust to a fiery peak almost instantly. What could be wrong with her to enjoy his brutal siege on her body?

She had to resist, had to fight the desire even now pulsing between her legs, making her wet and achy. Her legs spread so wide across the saddle didn't ease the discomfort of her desire. She discovered, though, if she positioned herself just so, the horse's gait created a rhythmic pattern against her sensitive flesh. If she could ride this way long enough, surely she could find her own relief from the tenacious hold of passion.

Suddenly, his hands slid under her legs, lifting her and spreading her even wider across his lap. The bulge pressing against her arse clearly proved he was as affected as she. Why did he persist in this? She realized her new position kept her sex away from the saddle, hovering above it. Her balance precarious, she found herself oddly thankful for the arm around her waist, anchoring her in place.

"Dinna think to take your pleasure now, lass. Slaves don't get to choose."

His low chuckle against her ear added to her mounting frustration. When his hand slid to cup her damp sex, she tried to squirm free. He would do this in front of the others? Heat scalded her cheeks and she caught Colin watching greedily. She bit her lip, hard, to keep the cry from escaping when Ian teasingly ran his fingers along her folds and around the hard nub of her clit. Oh, she wanted that pleasure he'd given her this morning, and despite her best intentions, her hips quivered, and she sought closer contact.

Just like before, he pulled his hand away, leaving her panting and hungry for more. Shame as she'd never known engulfed her. How had he, in the matter of a few hours, turned her into a harlot? She'd heard her brothers talk about the camp followers who would do anything before anyone, for the attention and coin tossed their way. Sex was all that mattered to them. Now she was no better, allowing him to fondle her in front of his men, allowing herself to respond, to practically beg him for more. Her hands were free, she could have fought him.

She hadn't wanted to. She'd wanted *his* hands on *her*, had found the idea of the other men watching exciting somehow. A great tearing sob ripped from her lungs, despite her best efforts to contain it. How could she have fallen so low? Her father would not want her back, once he knew what she had become.

She was being shifted again, this time, lifted and

cuddled close to Ian. She let the tears flow, her disgust with herself growing. She allowed Ian to settle her against his chest, his hand stroking her hair, oddly soothing her while she poured out her despair.

When she had nothing left but heavy gasps for air, he tilted her head back. A gentle finger wiped the tears off her cheeks. She almost fell to weeping again.

"Hush, lass. 'Twill be some time before we set up camp for the night. Think hard on how you want your life to be."

He continued to hold her for the remainder of the day, and when they did pull up just inside a large forest, he waited until Jamie stood beside him before passing her down and dismounting. He and Jamie helped her stand when she swayed unsteadily. She had never gone this long in the saddle, and her legs protested, even if she had spent most of the afternoon cradled in Ian's arms. Despite all that had happened, she felt oddly disappointed she didn't still remain there.

All too soon, the gentle way they handled her became more insistent, and Ian roughly dragged her to a tree. She tugged against his tenacious grip, but couldn't break free, and all too soon, she found herself with her back against the tree, her arms pulled behind it and bound securely once again. She cursed him, spitting before his feet when he stepped back.

"I've tasks to see to and I dinna trust you not to run while my back is turned. When I'm finished, I'll release you. You'll have work to do."

He turned and strode away, leaving her tied to the tree. She screamed after him to release her, calling him every obscene name that came to mind. He ignored her and gathered his men, speaking in low tones she couldn't make out.

Her throat raw from yelling, she fell silent, taking note of her surroundings. If only she hadn't fallen asleep, she might have some idea where they now were. A day's ride had given Ian and his men a big advantage over her father, if he even searched for her. A moment of despair overtook her, longing for her family and home where she was safe. It was not to be, not yet anyway. Besides, she wasn't the girl who'd been stolen from her home. So much had changed in just a single day, she wondered if she'd be welcomed at Montchester anymore. Once everyone knew she'd been in the possession of these filthy Scots, her life would be ruined. There was nothing left for her but the convent.

An idea sprouted in her thoughts. Mayhap when she freed herself, she could petition her father to allow her to fight as a soldier in his garrison. She was as capable as any of her brothers, had proven herself in training many times. But she was a woman. The tiny hope she might convince her father to agree withered and died.

That left her with very few other choices. She could build a new life, maybe even in London, where she could lose herself in the anonymity of the city. No one knew her there, not really. What could she do? She possessed few skills, other than her ability with weapons. No one would take her seriously as a warrior for hire, even if she could prove her skill. She hadn't learned needlework; she had no trade to practice. A brief image of being reduced to a tavern wench or beggar left her struggling to breathe. There was nothing for her, nothing but a life as Ian's slave. She could never accept that.

For now, her best chance at survival would be to play along, until the opportunity for freedom came her way. Once she returned home, safe, then she would worry about the future. She tugged at the bonds securing her to the tree. They didn't give, but she hadn't expected they would. The men busied themselves setting up their camp, ignoring her. For a long time, she used the distraction of watching them to keep more troubling thoughts from assailing her. The men's movements did little to divert her thoughts from her plight. She noticed them huddled together, their voices too low to hear their words. More plans about the siege of Montchester. Her thoughts raced now and she focused on a new goal - that of preventing an attack on her home. How? She hung her head, exhaustion making her sag.

"Now here's a sight for me tired eyes. All alone, he's left you, has he?"

She stiffened at the cruel voice a few feet away. She turned but didn't see who spoke, even though she knew who stood nearby. An icy stab of fear cut through her and she shivered, tugging at her bonds once again. Her heart raced unevenly.

Colin stepped into her line of vision, the malevolent, hungry look in his gaze alarming her further. He grinned as he neared.

"All alone and helpless. Looks like I'll finally get to sample your charms."

She opened her mouth to scream, exhaustion slowing her reflexes, but he clamped a meaty hand across her lips. The other hand tangled in her hair and jerked her head back painfully. She winced, and drew a breath when he pulled his hand away from her face, his mouth slamming down on hers stirring her fury. She screamed against his slobbering that muffled any sound, and lifted her knee. He anticipated the move, pressing against her and blocking her attempt to drive him away. At the same time, his hand captured her breast, squeezing it painfully, pinching the nipple hard. Fear, panic controlled her and she tugged against her bonds, desperate to escape, even though the rope held tight. No chance to escape existed.

He suddenly vanished, and she gulped in deep breaths of air, her vision clearing. Ian had his arm around Colin's neck, hoisting the large man off his feet and choking him in the tight hold.

"You dare to touch her? You'll pay for this, Colin, clansman or no!" Ian's shout echoed in the quiet forest, setting birds to flight.

He hurled Colin to the ground and set on him, landing

blow after blow to the cowering man's head and body. A part of Marissa was delighted with Ian's protection of her, but when he finally stepped away from the now moaning and limp man huddling on the forest floor, the look in Ian's eyes triggered alarm. He sneered at her.

"You cause trouble again and again."

He stepped behind her and untied her hands. With a tight grip on her arm, he pulled her toward the fire Jamie had started. Ian shoved her to the ground before the flames.

"Prepare these." He tossed a couple of rabbits at her. She stared at him, then the animals in confusion.

"Get to work, slave. I expect you to prepare our meal."

How dare he? She started to protest, then remembered the necessity to go along with him. She nodded, forcing her expression into one of mild acceptance. Her exhaustion had faded, replaced with restlessness and a pounding heart. She held his stare, and knew he awaited her defiance. She wouldn't give him that satisfaction.

"Yes, sir."

His eyes narrowed, but he gave a curt nod before turning away. Jamie appeared beside her and handed her a small dagger.

"Dinna think of using it against one of us, complete your task and you may be permitted to eat with us."

Marissa didn't respond, but her heart jumped unsteadily at the intense stare he focused on her. He reached over and rubbed his fingers against her cheek, and the soft touch stirred myriad emotions, each one more disturbing than the last. Her breath hitched, her skin heating beneath his lingering hand before he finally drew away. Several more moments passed, his gaze steady and penetrating. Heat flooded her veins and she pulled her eyes away and studied the dead animals in her lap. Forcing herself to concentrate, she set to work skinning and spitting the rabbits with the branches Jamie provided. While she appreciated his help, his continued study of her left her with trembling hands and a strange fluttery feeling low in her belly.

Before long, the scent of the rabbits roasting over the fire reminded her she'd had little but some dried meat and water since awakening this morning. Her stomach rumbled again, now from hunger. A handful of root vegetables were shoved into her hands. Someone had laid a pot with water from a nearby stream on the fire. She peeled and chopped the legumes, dropping them into the water.

It wasn't long before the aroma of the food drew the other men back to the fire. Some of them murmured thanks while they scooped vegetables onto old bread and tore hunks of meat from the roasted rabbits. In minutes, all of the food had been cleared from the fire and the men ate noisily.

Tears burned her eyes. Weren't they going to allow her to eat as well? Her stomach rumbled again, louder than before. Her hunger spiked almost painfully. Rotten Scots, they'd let her starve. She moved away from the fire, seeking some privacy. From the corner of her eye, she spied Ian leaning back to watch her, fully aware they both knew she would go nowhere this night. She found herself near the tree she'd been bound to earlier. She curled around the trunk, trying not to savor the smell of the food and resisting her burning eyes.

A hand on her shoulder drew her attention and she rose. Through blurred vision, she found Ian standing over her, his bread laden with the meat and vegetables a taunt. She scowled and turned away.

"I apologize for my men's rudeness. Come; eat something before you become ill."

She sniffed, hating to reveal any sort of weakness. Ian hunkered down before her, holding out a piece of meat.

"Eat, lass. You need to keep up your strength."

The gentleness of his tone brought fresh tears to her eyes. Somehow, she fought them and accepted the offer of food. The meat burst with juices on her tongue, the gamy texture sweeter than any pie her father's cook had prepared.

Ian handed her another and another, and she accepted each one, one hunger finally soothed.

When she refused the last piece of bread, Ian set it down and pulled her into his embrace. Her full belly and the stress of the last hours overcame her and she curled into him, seeking the comfort he offered. She was too tired to fight anymore.

# chapter five

Unable to look away, Ian stared at the girl in his arms. A healthy surge of regret speared him. She'd endured so much in the last day. When he'd noticed she hadn't taken any of the food for herself, that his men had left her nothing, guilt stung nastier than an entire hive of bees. She'd been so brave through her entire ordeal, and though he knew he would ultimately achieve his goal, he admired her courage and strength. Even when she'd given in to tears, he hadn't thought her weak, though he somehow knew she viewed herself that way. Why did he have the mad urge to build her up, instead of break her down, as he intended?

He would not change his plans, but mayhap 'twas time to show her more kindness. She had done nothing to deserve being kidnapped and mistreated. Despite his reminder that neither had Sheila deserved her fate, the idea he could be as ruthless as the Panther and his men unsettled him. He wanted revenge, aye, and he would have it, but he didn't need to abuse a woman to gain it.

Yet, no matter how much kindness he showed her, his plans for her *were* cruel and abusive. He hardened his resolve. No reason he needed to coddle her. He cared nothing for the chit, and he would use her as he planned. 'Twas time for another lesson in what he expected of her.

He stood, lifting her easily. Her arms came around him and hugged him. Another twinge of guilt speared him. He scowled, knowing he had to follow through with his plans, new and un-thought out as they were. Yet, the odd longing for her to always seek comfort from him intensified. He shook his head. He must remain focused on his goal - destroying Marie's father. She was the tool to his success.

He moved to where he'd laid his pallet, a short distance away from the others, yet still close enough for them all to hear what would happen. Ere the night was over, he would have her begging for him to please her, the humiliation of knowing the men had overheard her downfall bringing him one step closer to his goal.

He gently laid her out and she lifted her gaze to his. The bleakness in her eyes stirred another stab of remorse, but he pushed it aside. 'Twas time to continue his path of turning her into his slave.

He stretched out beside her, pulling her flush against him. She quivered, her hands curling into his tunic. He stroked his hands along her back, in an attempt to soothe her agitation. Her quivering soon eased and she snuggled into his chest. Her warm body nestling close stirred him fiercely, and he knew 'twould take a monstrous amount of control to keep a clear head.

He lifted her chin, and the sight of her eyes softened with fatigue and desire made his cock throb. He gave in to his urge and took her mouth in a hungry kiss, driving his tongue deep into her warmth to taste her every nuance. She moaned, meeting each stroke with a ferocity that left him addled and ready to forego his plan.

Her hands had somehow found their way to his hair, tugging with insistence and clearing the haze of lust consuming him. He eased back and gave her a knowing smile, before untwisting the tartan covering her secrets. Her sharp gasp and wide-eyed expression made him pause momentarily, but he continued, soon removing the fabric and baring her luscious breasts to his gaze. The creamy mounds beckoned and he cupped one, flicking his thumb across the hardening nipple. She panted and arched against him and he held back a satisfied smile.

He continued to flick at the tip of her breast, finally lowering his head and sucking the red and swollen nipple into his mouth. She went wild, her fingers scraping through his hair, her soft cries escalating. He tugged the flesh between his teeth, savoring her ragged wail and the ensuing ripples that consumed her.

He drew away again, relishing the way she tried to draw him back. He reached around and smacked her ass. She stiffened, a growl of outrage escaping her lips, now twisted in a scowl.

"You dinna make any demands, lass. The sooner you learn that, the sooner you'll make it easier on yourself. Now, dinna move, unless you wish to be punished."

Her eyes flashed, but she held her tongue. Her mouth twitched, her jaw clenching, and he almost laughed aloud at her struggle to contain her anger.

"Good, you're learning." He lowered his head once more, sucking the tip of her breast deep into his mouth. He sensed the struggle she fought to remain still. Her fingers, still holding his head, tightened again in his hair. He slowly continued unwrapping her from his tartan, until she finally lay bare before him. Taking her hands in his, he laid them beside her.

"Hold still or I'll bind you again."

He thought she might protest, but she remained silent. He smiled, and the tight lines in her neck eased. He sat back, deciding how to begin.

A crack of a twig alerted him to someone nearby watching. Jamie? He hoped so, he'd asked his clansman to join in tonight, and between the two of them, they would soon know what Marie could endure. Jamie's observation could determine what methods worked best on Marie, what reduced her need to the most basic cravings where they could command her to perform any task, no matter how humiliating, Yet, even as he thought it, Ian realized he didn't want to do that, much as he knew he had to break her spirit in many ways. He wanted to make her willing to do as he asked, to serve him in whatever way he chose because it pleased her to do so. The distaste at the thought of her behaving like a terrified animal rose swift and sharp. She was a beautiful young woman, and he wanted her to revel in her beauty, to share it with him willingly. He wanted her obedience so he could reward her. Watching her give in to sexual satisfaction was as enjoyable as burying himself into her body.

What was wrong with him? How could he feel such tender emotions toward his enemy's daughter, the weapon that would wield his ultimate revenge? He studied the trembling girl lying before him. She was merely a vessel to be used. With slow movements, he caressed her legs, her sides, sliding up to cup her breasts fully. Her back arched, a low hiss escaping her clenched teeth and he flicked her hardened nipples. Her moan carried on the evening air, and he sensed movement beside him.

Marie stiffened beneath him, her hands coming up, but not to push him away. Before he could rebuke her, Jamie had taken her wrists and drawn her arms up above her head. Panic cleared the desire in her gaze and she squirmed to free herself. Ian smacked her ass again.

"Dinna fight us, lass. You canna stop it, and 'twill only make it harder for you."

"No, damn you!" she cried.

"She's too loud," Jamie complained.

"Aye." Ian tore a strip from his kilt and leaned over her. She must have realized his intent, shaking her head violently to stop him, but he soon fastened the strip of fabric across her mouth, sliding it deep between her teeth and garbling any sounds she might make. Her protests, now muffled, still betrayed her fury.

"Tie her down, Jamie. 'Tis time the lass learned exactly what a MacCallum does with his slave."

As Jamie obliged, Ian held her still as his clansman bound Marie's arms, and using strong branches buried into the ground for stakes, secured her in place. Ian set to work on her ankles. Before long, she lay spread-eagled and staked to the forest floor, her cries muted by the fabric gagging her. Jamie came to stand beside him.

"A beautiful sight," he said.

"Aye," Ian agreed. "I wonder if she can handle us both."

"She's got fire, I'm sure she's up to whatever we decide to do."

Despite the fear, Ian also read a hint of excitement in Marie's gaze. Her feminine perfume surrounded him, betraying her desire. He smiled and knelt between her legs.

"'Tis a good thing you're gagged. When we're done with you, your screams could summon any other souls who may be about this night. Dinna want anyone who might be searching to find us."

\* \* \*

Marissa fell silent at his words. She stared in shock as Ian knelt between her legs. She tugged against the leather keeping her secured and open, but couldn't free herself. She glanced at Jamie and the hunger in his gaze ignited more heat, her sex dripping. How could she want this? Her heart raced, from excitement, or fear? Mayhap a little of both. Her gaze landed on Jamie's hands, resting on his knees. Large, powerful, with long, strong fingers, she had a vision of those hands tormenting her breasts, or sliding deep into her sex. She inhaled sharply and tore her gaze away.

Ian's touch on her legs chased any remaining rational thoughts, leaving her moaning behind the fabric garbling her half-hearted protests. His fingers teased as they crept higher, his movements torturously slow, until she moved her hips frantically, urging him closer to where she wanted him to touch her. The desire he'd stoked all day fast reached a terrifying intensity, and all that mattered was somehow making him continue.

He finally reached her throbbing sex and gently pulled her open. A sense of embarrassment mingled with her need, but was quickly forgotten as he tickled along her sensitive flesh. She quivered and tossed her head.

Movement beside her distracted her from the

sensation of Ian's fingers exploring her folds, using her own moisture to tease and tantalize her. Her gaze once more landed on Jamie as he knelt beside her head. He reached out to cup one breast, lightly, as Ian had done earlier. His touch burned nearly as much as Ian's, and he drew lazy circles around her nipples, and the flesh hardened almost painfully. He made no move to touch her aching nubs. She wished she could beg him, but a sharp pinch on her clit reminded her of Ian. She looked between the two of them, their large hands moving insistently over her body, driving her to a mindless state.

Her gaze focused squarely on Ian, and her lids fluttered when he lowered his head. The heat of his tongue in her pussy drew a squeal as she thrust herself up against his mouth. At that moment, Jamie leaned over, taking the tip of her breast in his mouth, catching her nipple in his teeth.

Fire seared through her, her core clenching in delight. Ian's tongue circling her clit, Jamie's circling her nipple had her in a frenzy, and she writhed as much as her bonds permitted. She rose higher and higher, the pleasure escalating, and she fought to reach the glorious peak she sensed just out of her reach. Another swirl of Ian's tongue had her ready to explode when both men drew away, studying her while she writhed.

She shrieked into her gag, frustration creating bitter tears. She closed her eyes, hating that they watched her still quivering, her hips moving, her sex desperate for more attention. She was shameless, but she didn't care. The last day and night had driven her to this mindless point of craving, and everything else fell away in the tempest.

After several long minutes, her heart steadied, her breathing slowed. They began again, each man using his mouth and hands to bring her right back up to the edge of release before easing away, feather-light caresses keeping her hanging on the precipice. She fought against tears, need tightening her body and driving her slowly mad.

Again, they resumed, forceful contact that stole her breath; again they paused, her entire body quivering, unfulfilled. By the time they repeated their torment for a fourth and fifth time, Marissa openly sobbed at the denial. If she could have, she would have begged them to continue.

"It's time," said Ian. "Jamie, take her."

She should fight, somehow, but all she could think of was having Jamie's hard cock inside her. He stripped off his kilt, taking Ian's place between her legs. She caught sight of his erection, long and thick, and standing ramrod straight. A brief moment of panic made her struggle, but Ian's hand on her cheek soothed her.

"Relax, lass, and enjoy it. Jamie knows how to pleasure a woman."

His fingers at the back of her head loosened the knot of her gag, and she sighed with relief, wiggling her tongue.

"But we still need to keep you quiet. Open up, lass, and suck me."

She stared up at him. He couldn't be serious! The determined look in his eyes convinced her he was. She shook her head, clamping her mouth shut. She wouldn't do it!

He grinned, as if expecting her response. "Go ahead, Jamie."

She sealed her lips against a cry when Jamie thrust his entire length into her with one shove.

The sensation of fullness gave her desire still more force. Stroking into her, he played with her clit, and the urge to cry out grew stronger, delight consuming her.

Ian rubbed the head of his cock along her sealed lips. "Lass, open your mouth."

She noted the warning in his tone, but refused to comply. He gave a shake of his head, then pinched her nose shut.

Panic overcame her and she struggled, but was

quickly distracted by Jamie's continued thrusting, his fingers sliding harshly over her clit. She had to breathe, she arched against Ian's hand, but he didn't release her. Lungs burning, her lips parted to take in air. Ian slid a finger into her mouth, dragging it open. Before she could shake him off, he had slipped the tip of his cock between her lips.

"Dinna bite me, lass, or I'll whip that hungry little pussy til it's raw."

She held perfectly still, the feel of his hard flesh in her mouth both alarming and exciting at the same time. He thrust deeper, slowly, a low groan escaping.

"Use your tongue, lass, and lick me. Suck me."

She didn't know what he meant, but when he reached behind himself to pinch her nipple hard, she tentatively ran her tongue along the ridged flesh. He shuddered above her, and drove a little deeper into her, startling her. She squealed around him and he groaned again.

"Suck, lass, suck on my dick."

She should find disgust, yet his words fueled her need, driven by Jamie's incessant stroking in and out of her. Her head swam, she couldn't think, and she obeyed Ian's order, sucking hard on the throbbing cock. Her fearful shock faded as she grew accustomed to the hard flesh filling her mouth, her tongue fluttering along his length. He groaned, a harsh sound roaring in the clearing. The sight of his face, pleasure melting over him, eyes closed, drew a startling realization.

He enjoyed this. Oddly, knowing that she pleased him deepened her own hunger, and her sex clenched on Jamie's thick cock. He gave a hoarse moan, and her head seemed to float, knowing she pleased these two men as much as they did her. A sense of power strengthened her lust and she sucked hard on Ian's cock, her tongue catching a spot near the base that made him jerk above her.

"That's it, lass, just like that." His voice, roughened with passion, tingled along her spine as if he'd touched her. He cupped her head, holding her still as he surged even deeper, hitting the back of her throat. She gagged briefly, but that action seemed to make him swell in her mouth. The urgency to bring him satisfaction inflamed her further and she regained her rhythm, drawing another growl of gratification from the man straddling her chest. The sound sent a shot of heat along her spine.

Though out of her line of vision, every moment of Jamie's continued tender assault started a riot in her core, her pussy clenching hard around him each time he flicked her clit. Being taken like this stoked the fire, until she thought her entire body would go up in flames. Then she couldn't think at all, could only feel as she suckled Ian's cock, accepted Jamie's into her body and let the pleasure consume her.

The building pressure continued, and when Jamie gently fondled her breasts, she couldn't contain the blaze scorching through her, the blinding bliss overtaking every sense. Her soul seemed to erupt into great waves of ecstasy, her body trembling violently under the onslaught. Unable to see, to hear, to do anything other than feel the two cocks spearing her and driving her climax so high and so long, her remaining vision faded.

When awareness returned, Ian cradled her head in his lap while Jamie gently cleaned her tender sex. She moaned.

"Hush, lass. You fainted."

The realization of what they'd done, how she had enjoyed it, hit her as if she'd been slapped. A moan of regret was all she managed, even though Jamie's gentle touch between her legs stirred her again.

What was wrong with her? She'd been forced to do what she'd previously considered despicable things, yet she had enjoyed them. Wanted more. Had loved the feeling of being helpless between two men who knew how to pleasure a woman, knew how to make her yearn for release. Another sob, then another and she found her bonds released and she was hauled into Ian's lap. Jamie sat beside them, watching her closely.

"I could tell you liked that, lass. That pleases me," Ian said.

Her response was a strangled groan. She didn't know what to say, too stunned by the warm glow suffusing her at his words. Why should she care if he was pleased? But she did, and a strange contentment stole over her to know she had given him satisfaction. She dared a glance at Jamie. He grinned.

"You are a delight, lass," Jamie said. "All the clansmen will be clamoring over Ian, hoping for a chance to taste you."

Her eyes widened. They wouldn't! She held little doubt they would. They were cruel and sadistic, even if they had given her ecstasy she'd never dreamed possible. How could she have found pleasure in the acts they'd forced on her? They'd bound her and taken her, used her. Yet, much as she wanted to, she couldn't deny she *had* enjoyed everything that had just passed between them. Still, the idea of being shared among the entire clan terrified her.

"You can't! Please, haven't you humiliated me enough?" she managed to croak out. What if he gave her to Colin? Terror sprouted at the thought.

"Nay, lass, only Jamie will get to taste your charms again. You'll serve us both, and the others will learn to accept their envy." Ian held her gaze and her frantically racing heart slowly calmed.

Both men fell silent. Ian gathered her close against him, cradling her in his lap. Jamie took a seat beside him, and gently stroked her hair. She couldn't fight them, feeling strangely safe, embraced as she was. The sensation added to the riotous conflict.

\* \* \*

Ian cradled the trembling girl, an odd sense of

completion engulfing him. An image of Sheila swam in his thoughts, and the shame he felt overpowered his brief moment of contentment. His dear departed wife seemed to be scolding him; he recognized the look on her face. He shook his head to clear it, but Sheila taunted him, he could almost hear her taking him to task for his treatment of Marie.

He resolutely forced her from his thoughts. 'Twas clear her soul wouldn't rest until he accomplished his vengeance. The girl clinging to him now was merely a means to that goal. But he couldn't push her away. If his plan was to work, she had to need him in many ways. Pleasure was one, but she also needed to feel safe with him. He could never truly break her if she didn't trust him. He would earn that trust, and annihilate it along with her father. Only then could his wife and son truly rest. Only then could Ian move on with his life.

He met his clansman's knowing gaze. He glanced down at Marie. She had fallen into slumber, and he eased her out along his pallet.

"She's an innocent lass, Ian."

He remained silent, tucking a blanket around her and turning to Jamie. "She is the way to destroy the Panther. A siege on his keep wouldna send the message this will. Losing his daughter as I lost Sheila, lost my son, is all that I want."

"She responded to us both. She wanted to fight, and she did, but she is drawn to you. You canna destroy her without destroying your manhood. Take her, keep her, what could be better revenge?"

In a strange way, Jamie's words made sense. The Panther would lose his daughter, ultimately, one way or another. The idea of keeping Marie with him, to serve him always, excited him. More than he liked.

"Jamie, 'tis a long ride ahead of us on the morrow. Find your bed and we will discuss this further when we reach the village."

Jamie gave a curt nod and with a lingering caress of Marie's cheek, rose. He disappeared into the night, back to the camp where the other men slept.

For a long time afterward, Ian leaned over Marie, watching her sleep, his thoughts filled with the ways this minx could occupy his nights. And his days.

# CHAPTER SIX

When Marissa awoke, the sun had already risen. Ian lay behind her, his arm around her waist. Her mind jerked to awareness with memories of the night before. Both Ian and his clansman had taken her, had used her body. She had loved everything they'd done. A heavy weight settled into her chest. She was a harlot, a whore, to enjoy such depravity. She couldn't lie to herself. She *had* enjoyed everything that had passed between her and the two clansmen.

Even now, she recalled the feel of Ian's hard cock in her mouth, the sensation of Jamie's shaft stroking in and out of her. God help her, she wanted to feel those sensations again, wanted them to pin her down and take her, show her again the blinding pleasure that had taken over every part of her. Spurred by the recollection, her sex throbbed with hunger, wanting to be filled and stroked and sucked until she came with a mind shattering release.

What had happened to her? Two days ago, she was a proud girl of noble birth, a strong woman who had trained with her brothers and was capable as any warrior. Now, she was reduced to little more than a mindless creature wanting the pleasure these two heathens had given her. She couldn't go home, even if her father rescued her. She was not the daughter he knew, would never be again.

Even though despair threatened to overtake her, Ian's hand moved along her body, his touch stirring heat and need. She stiffened. His mouth at her ear brought another rush of hot wetness between her legs.

"Easy, lass. Don't fight the pleasure you're meant for."

She moaned in protest, unable to form any words. She couldn't want this, but when Ian's fingers toyed with her breasts, plucking at her nipples, she found her ability to think clearly once more taken. Along with everything else.

Soon, his mouth moved along her neck, nipping, licking, and sucking. She bucked toward his seeking hands, wanting him to continue to move lower, to touch her hungry sex. Nothing mattered but the fire he stoked, his hard cock pressing against her arse.

"I want you, lass." She found herself suddenly beneath him, and the brief thought to resist evaporated as he stroked her pussy, finding her wet and using the moisture to tease her further. His fingers were magical as they moved over her, stirring her. When he squeezed the hard nub of her pleasure, she cried out.

"Please," she moaned, unable to stop the plea.

"Aye, lass, feel it. Your body is made for this pleasure, and only I will give it to you."

She sensed a commitment, a vow, in his words, and knew without any doubt, no one would ever touch her this way, even after her ordeal had ended. When she gained her freedom, and she would, no one would ever make her feel this way again. How she knew that, she wasn't exactly sure, but the knowledge settled deep into her consciousness, a low hum in the background of the tempest as Ian continued to touch her, sliding his fingers deep inside her sex, her hips thrusting against his hand. Her head tossed. She shouldn't want this, but God help her soul, she did.

His low chuckle surrounded her, the sound of his enjoyment heightening her awareness of him. He trailed his mouth along her neck, the scratch of his beard another delightful torment, adding to the sensations tossing her about like a fierce wind. The heat of his tongue licking at her skin drew a strangled plea, her hands finding a hold on his shoulders, digging in, needing to hold on, lest she get lost in the fury of passion.

"You taste of fine sugar. I dinna think I'll ever tire of you."

His mumbled words sent a jolt of joy through her and

she held him tightly, his hand buried in her pussy driving her on. His sure strokes, the way he circled her clit with insistence sent the pleasure soaring higher, stealing her wits as it crashed over her, her body afire with heat and bliss and breath-stealing intensity. Ian crooned soft words, she couldn't make them out, but they soothed her as she shuddered in release. When she could finally take a breath again, the sensation of being held tenderly in his embrace furthered the oddly familiar feeling of safety. If he hadn't been her captor, she might almost imagine a future by his side, living her days being the center of affection of such a passionate man.

'Twasn't to be. She stiffened as Ian rose above her, his eyes dark with hunger as he contemplated her. Suddenly, she knew he'd felt that same sense of rightness in their coupling, despite the terrible reality of the situation. The knowledge calmed the rising panic and she pulled him closer, wordlessly giving her submission when she placed a soft kiss on his lips, then drew away to await his response.

One dark eyebrow arched while he considered her, then he took her mouth hungrily, spreading her legs. Holding her wide, he thrust into her and her head arched at the way his hard flesh filled her

still quivering sex. A long groan escaped him and he remained still for several moments. She wrapped her legs around his waist, and he drew back, giving her an affectionate smile. He stroked her cheek, brushing aside her hair. Burning tears threatened at the tender gesture.

He moved then, drawing out until just the tip of his cock rested inside her. Two breaths and he drove back into her, and she cried out at the delight. His rhythm, steady yet forceful, had her writhing beneath him, her hands scraping along his shoulders and back while he took her. The white heat intensified, she held on tightly as they moved together, the world ceasing to exist.

He sealed his mouth to hers again and she responded

with ferocity, the fiery lust driving her higher again. A long loud groan came from Ian and he stiffened above her. His cock swelled in her pussy, pulsing as he released his seed. He pulled free, panting, drawing out of her arms.

Marissa blinked, still hanging on the edge of release. Her now empty pussy pulsed and throbbed with need. Not again! The bastard would kill her at this rate.

"Up you go, lassie. We've a long ride ahead."

"Where are you taking me?"

He didn't answer at first, simply stared at her. "My home. Another day's ride at least."

"Where are we now?" She needed to know, needed to think about something other than the yearning still relentlessly twisting her insides.

"Dinna think to trick me, lass. All I'll tell you is we're in Scotland."

She suspected that, Montchester wasn't far from the border, but the question was, where in Scotland? They'd kept a rapid pace the day before, and if she hadn't slept, she'd have some idea of how far they'd come. Ian wouldn't tell her if she asked, of that she had no doubt. She accepted his offered hand, and let him lead her to the nearby stream. Unlike yesterday morn, he turned his back as she tended her needs. She didn't understand the way he treated her, sometimes as if he treasured and respected her, other times as if she were no more consequential than a dog. Her head spun trying to keep up with his changes in mood.

When she finished her ablutions, he once again took her hand and led her to where his men had broken camp. Jamie stood near his horse, the others mounted already. Ian gave a wave of his hand and they rode off, leaving her alone with the two men.

The slowly cooling desire flared back to life at the way Jamie looked at her, hungry and intense. Like his clansman, but different. Almost as exciting. She hesitated, aware of Ian turning to give her a curious glance.

"We havena time for play now, lass," he said.

Her eyes widened. He thought she wanted... She held back a hysterical chuckle.

"You don't mean to... again?"

Ian grinned at her, and she glanced at Jamie. He wore the same amused expression.

"Nay, lass, not now. Tonight, though, when we are safe in Castle Crawford, Jamie and I will further instruct you on your... position."

Outrage flared, but she managed to keep it from showing. She lowered her head to conceal her anger, following when Ian tugged her toward his horse. Jamie reached over and took her wrists, wrapping a leather strap around them before she could pull away. She wondered if they had an endless supply in their packs.

"Nay, you don't have to do this." Her efforts to evade him failed and she found herself once again bound.

Ian's amusement faded to a grim coldness. "Aye, lass, we do. Jamie, take her."

He turned and walked to his horse, mounting without another glance at her. She gulped, aware of Jamie guiding her to his horse.

"Nay, please ...."

"Dinna fret, lass, I willna hurt you. Up you go." Hurried movements had her mounted, Jamie quickly taking position behind her. He took the end of her ties and fastened them to the saddle, securing her. He slipped the arm holding the reins around her waist, anchoring her against him. 'Twas the other hand that brought alarm. And anticipation.

He rested his hand on her thigh, his fingers slowly moving over her in gentle, soothing circles. Mayhap not soothing. Her body still caught in passion thanks to Ian's leaving her unfulfilled, it didn't take long before Jamie's touch stirred her needs to a higher level.

She squirmed, trying to dislodge him, but he squeezed her leg harder.

"Dinna fight, lass."

She should resist this abuse of her body. Was it abuse if she liked it? Finding pleasure so easily with both men couldn't be right. The realization of what that meant burned the back of her throat like bile.

She stared off at the cloud of dust raised by Ian's horse ahead. The barbarian! How could he?

\* \* \*

Ian drove his animal hard, desperate to put some distance between him and Marie. The lass affected him like no other had. Not even Sheila. When Marie had looked at him with such adoration, the guilt had nearly driven him to leave her then. His cock had ruled him, needing to find pleasure in her welcoming body. She had welcomed him. No doubt existed any longer that she wanted the physical delight he could give her.

Even now, his cock stirred at the thought of driving into her wet heat. He couldna afford to let himself get consumed in the lass, he had to remember what she was. The hurt in her eyes when he'd handed her to Jamie had confirmed that he had chosen the right way to achieve his goal. She cared for him, even if only a wee bit. 'Twas what he wanted, so he could use it against her. Even in his head, his arguments sounded empty. He stiffened his spine. She was a weapon to be wielded against his enemy, nothing more. He must not lose sight of that. Giving her to Jamie had reminded her of her place, as Ian had intended. Still, the betrayal shining in her gaze stung.

He scratched his beard, silently cursing the rambling thoughts. Marie was no more than a means to revenge, a slave to be used and broken, then abandoned. The idea which had come to him rose again, and he knew that act would make his intentions clear. As soon as they arrived at Castle Crawford, he would see to it. She would hate him for it, but her hatred would make it easier for him to keep to his plan. If nothing else, mayhap it would keep the sadness from her eyes. Or give him respite from the remorse that grew stronger with each loping stride of his horse. When she was broken, a shell of herself, he would deliver her to her father, and then take his final vengeance. His family's souls would rest, and mayhap he would finally find peace as well.

He wondered how she fared with Jamie. Hopefully, his clansman would use some of the time to wear her down further. Ian had no illusions that his captive also found Jamie attractive. Oddly, the idea did not bother him. It stirred him, and he imagined watching Jamie take Marie in various ways.

Jamie's words came back to haunt him. If only he *could* keep Marie. Ian harbored no false hope she would want to, not after he took his final revenge. She would never willingly stay with him. Why did the thought inspire a despair that rivaled his loss of Sheila and Duncan? God's bones, Marie would not affect him that way! He wouldn't allow her to become dear to him, for madness lay on that path. Yet, he already cherished her, in some small way. He couldn't deny it, and reluctantly accepted it. After all, she pleased him physically. Of course, he would care for her, even if only a little like he would for his horse, or any other pet.

He set his jaw, refusing to acknowledge he lied to himself.

\* \* \*

Marissa shifted, her awareness of Jamie's hand on her leg her main focus. He had rested it there since they set off, not moving, just sitting motionless on her upper thigh. The struggle to keep from squirming, to urge his hand closer to her core, grew more and more difficult to resist. Desperate to keep from shaming herself further, she forced herself to think about why she had been stolen away.

"Why have you done this?" Her voice cracked, her effort to control the hovering lust taking much of her concentration.

"Because Ian asked me to. I suspect he needs the time to think further on his plans."

Damn him, that told her nothing! "What plans? Kidnapping me is not enough? Why would he need to be alone?"

"You're a distraction, lass. And I certainly understand that. You are a comely lass with enough fire to always excite a man. I suspect Ian still hasn't determined what to do with you."

Somewhere in his words, she believed a compliment lurked, but she refused to think on it. Her focus needed to be on her freedom. "Then let me go and I'll distract him no more! Free me now, and I will do everything in my power to see you are not caught and punished for this! My father is a close confidant of King Edward."

"Aye, he is. But I willna trust the Panther, or his daughter."

"If my father requests it, the king will send a party to find me."

"I have no worries there, lass. The Bruce is giving Longshanks enough trouble to keep his focus on the Scottish king."

"This will be one more on the list of crimes Scotland has committed against England."

Marissa had heard more than she'd wanted about the aggressions William Wallace and Robert the Bruce had perpetrated against the English. While Wallace had been executed two years earlier, Marissa knew her father and the king were still vexed about The Bruce's continued attacks, and their lack of success in capturing the renegade Scot. The day word had come that Bruce had been crowned king of Scotland had sent her father into a rage. Marissa suspected 'twas because of his failure, rather than any sort of success by The Bruce.

"The Bruce is no king. He will be stopped, just as Wallace was."

Jamie gave a disgusted snort. "Wallace lost sight of his own way. He paid dearly for his mistakes. The rest of us have learned from his failures, and from the evils your king inflicts on us."

Marissa realized from Jamie's perspective, her father, King Edward, all of the English lords and soldiers would seem to be in the wrong. Didn't they know 'twas only because Edward sought to unite all the countries, just as he had done previously with Wales?

"Why do you despise Edward?"

"Do you not know what the devil has done to our country? The taxes and fealty he requires are taken, whether we wish it or not. 'Tis forced from us, on punishment of death."

"Nay, Edward seeks to make England stronger, by uniting all the lands." Surely Jamie was wise enough to see that.

Another laugh, one tinged with anger. "You are a fool, lass, if you truly believe that. Longshanks has installed his men on our lands, he takes the finest this land offers for his lords and leaves us with almost nothing. Our children starve, our men are forbidden to hunt to provide for their clans. If we refuse, they slaughter us."

She shook her head. This could not be. Her father had always told her Edward's cause was righteous. Yet, she also recalled her father's frustration with some of Edward's brutal methods. Perhaps there was some truth to Jamie's words. Perhaps she could prevent any further bloodshed, at least with Ian's clan.

"If you free me now, mayhap I can -"

Behind her, she felt him shake his head. "Nay, lass. I see your ploy, but willna work with me."

"Don't you understand? My father will come for me. When he does, you will all pay with your lives."

"Your father already failed once before."

"What are you talking about?"

"Your father made a fatal mistake when he attacked

our clan. He left us alive, to seek vengeance."

Marissa was more confused than ever. "I don't understand. My father attacked you?"

She twisted around to see her captor. The fury on Jamie's face, the rage burning in his eyes, terrified her.

"He and his men came in like cowards, under the cover of night, determined to slay us all as he did to several clans before us."

Nay, this could not be the truth! "You are wrong. My father would not do something like that." Her father was an honorable man, did not ambush helpless villages as Jamie suggested.

"He does. The MacCallums were not the first. He and his men killed all in the MacLiam, MacBray and Geiren clans. But the MacCallums are strong and some of us survived."

She shook her head. This couldn't be real. She grabbed tight to the one fact she'd almost overlooked. "You say it was at night. How can you be sure my father was responsible?"

"'Twas his pennant the fires revealed. Our village was burned to the ground, and the flames lit up the night. The Panther's banner was clearly visible."

Marissa refused to accept his words. This could not be. Her father was not a ruthless murderer.

"You must be mistaken."

"Nay, lass. I saw the pennant myself."

She remained silent, her mind racing with what she had learned. "Jamie, what happened to Ian?"

Several moments of silence passed before Jamie answered. "His wife was raped, right before his eyes. He watched as man after man brutally used her. Their son was forced to watch. When it was done, they made Sheila watch as Duncan's throat was cut. Her screams were silenced by the sword of your father and his men."

Marissa's stomach rolled. Nay! Her father would not have committed such crimes! Even under order from the king, he would not. She knew, for she had heard her father complain to her mother about Edward's deceit many times. Her mother had feared the king would turn on them, for her father's numerous refusals to blindly obey Edward's orders.

"You are wrong. I don't know how, but I know in my heart my father would not have done that. I will prove it." She had to learn more about these attacks, for there had to be clues they had missed. The words of the Scotsmen on her first night of captivity taunted her. They had spoken of a siege at Monchester. Understanding dawned, and with it, an urgency to uncover the truth.

Jamie chuckled. "Your loyalty is to be expected. There is naught you can do but accept your fate. You would do well to seek what pleasure you can."

He moved, sliding his hand on her belly. Outrage stiffened Marissa's spine. After relating such horrors, he would dare to assault her? The fingers creeping toward her sex threatened to undermine her determination to resist. She couldn't stop the images flashing in her thoughts.

"You beast! I will see you dead, if not by my own hand, then my father's!"

He laughed and the sound spurred her fury. She slammed her head back, catching him hard in the chin. Though the pain resounding through her skull grew fierce, she took satisfaction at his bellow of pain.

"You will pay for that!" His low, menacing voice was more terrifying than any war cry.

He moved suddenly, one hand squeezing her breast, the other grabbing her sex. She cried out, the rough touch spurring a fire that became a blaze in moments. She managed to resist the rising need for several moments, trying to hold onto all she had learned and what it all meant. Two fingers shoved deep into her sex scattered her concentration. She jerked back again, but Jamie was ready for her this time and evaded her movement. His fingers clamped hard on her nipple, squeezing and twisting until she cried out. To her horror, heat and wetness slicked her legs and she bit her lip hard, trying to keep from responding. She behaved no better than a tavern wench, his harsh mauling actually spurring desire.

"You bastard! Let me go!" she cried. Her entire body trembled with heat, making her voice hoarse and uneven, betraying the traitorous desire he so ruthlessly stirred.

"Nay, lass. You belong to Ian. He has given you to my care and I will do what I need to keep you still."

He wiggled his fingers inside of her and the blaze singed along her spine. No matter how hard she tried to withstand it, the lust overcame her, and she moved her hips, responding to his rough touch. He caught her clit with his thumb, and she threw her head back with a scream as the pleasure crashed over her. Her body shuddered and trembled in his hold. The force of the release blurred her vision and robbed her of any rational thought. When the last tremor passed, she slumped against Jamie and choked back a sob.

These ruffians had turned her into a wanton! When Jamie pulled his hand free, another ripple of passion slithered in her core. She moaned, a desperate, keening sound that echoed around them.

Jamie did not attempt to touch her again for a few minutes and she felt a moment of gratitude for the opportunity to gather her wits. Her head spun, both with all she had discovered today and the force and aftermath of the intense sexual pleasure she had just experienced. Nothing made sense, and she wondered if it ever would again.

How had she fallen so low? Two days ago, she would have taken up a sword against any who dared what these Scots had. Now, she found herself unable to resist their cruel treatment. Even worse, she actually wanted more of their masterful touch.

As her thoughts became clearer, her rage returned. If she could get her hands on a sword, she would be free of these barbarians. She tugged her hands, wishing she could get loose. An idea sprouted.

"My hands hurt, my wrists are nearly bleeding. Please untie me."

She worked hard to maintain an image of weakness. Several moments passed before Jamie finally nodded and slid a dagger free.

"Verra well, I see no harm in it, but try to escape, and I will rebind you, tighter than before. Ian willna be pleased."

"What more could he do to me?"

"He would punish you."

A frisson of alarm skittered along her spine. Punish her? How? Ian had threatened her with punishment before, but she had no idea what that meant. Would he whip her? Or worse? She didn't want to think about the possibilities.

The sharp and burning prickle arced through her arms as the leather was cut. A pained cry escaped before she could stop it. Jamie's large hand came down on her wrists, rubbing her bruised and raw skin. The soothing motion eased the discomfort. She clenched and unclenched her fingers, until she finally felt she had control of her hands once more.

Soon. She would make a move soon. She leaned back against Jamie, and tried to ignore the pulsing desire that ran through her veins when he nuzzled his face into her hair.

The ride continued in silence, and Marissa waited for a chance to make her move. All her focus needed to be on escaping Jamie. Once she'd accomplished that, making her way to freedom would be a simple task. Realization of what she would need to do roiled her stomach. Jamie would have to be rendered threat-free, and she would have to steal his horse. No doubt Ian would eventually realize something was wrong and come in search of his clansman. He would find Jamie, but she would be on her way back to England. She prayed for enough time to put plenty of distance between them so he would not recapture her before she reached Montchester.

An image of Jamie lying unconscious on the ground warred with her last recollection of Leland, left for dead. Still, the idea of leaving Jamie for dead brought a despair she had never known before. Why? She should want him, and Ian, dead for what they'd done. Yet her body wouldn't let her forget the pleasure they'd given her.

She wanted to scream with frustration. She didn't know what to do. She wanted to avenge her honor, defend her family and free herself. But she didn't want to harm Jamie, or Ian. In spite of what they'd done, a certain affection had grown. Had the pleasure they were capable of giving changed her so much?

She wondered what her mother was doing right now. Probably urging her father to search for her. If anyone could make The Panther do her bidding, 'twas Gillian Langley. All of England knew how much the Panther adored his wife. Marissa had always envied the love her parents shared, had hoped to be as lucky as they in her marriage. Now she had no chance of marriage. None would have her now that she had been ruined. Would her family even want her back, once they learned what she'd endured? The convent was not a choice she would consider, but what else was left for her?

Once again, the idea of being a warrior crossed her mind. Mayhap if she disguised herself as a man, she could succeed. 'Twould be tricky, but she could do it. First, she had to get free.

As if sensing her thoughts, Jamie's arm tightened around her waist. She could wait. She had no choice, but she possessed patience and a strong will. When her opportunity came, she would be ready to act upon it.

After another hour or so, Jamie finally pulled the horse to a halt. Without a word, he helped her down and pointed to a low gathering of shrubs. She nodded, keeping her head lowered, hoping she appeared truly broken. Better to take him by surprise. She quickly tended her needs and returned to his side. He peered along the horizon. He seemed at ease, one hand shielding his eyes against the afternoon sun, the other resting casually on his hip. Marissa took her chance.

With a sudden lunge, she closed her fingers around the hilt of the dagger in his belt, as she reached around him for his sword. Before he could react, she had pulled the dagger free, but didn't have enough leverage to pull the sword from its scabbard. She released her grip on the sword, and held the smaller, but just as deadly, blade before her. She only needed to get close enough to land one blow.

"Dinna be foolish, lass. Ian willna be pleased when I tell him of this."

"You'll tell him nothing. By the time he finds you, I will be long gone, and you will hopefully be dead." Oddly, she almost choked on the words. Still, she waved the blade before her. Damn it, why wouldn't he come closer?

"Nay, lass. 'Tis a foolish mistake you're making." He unsheathed his sword, and despite knowing his blade gave him a much greater advantage, she refused to retreat.

"The only mistake I will make is leaving you alive."

He aimed his sword at her heart, and it skipped in her chest. She lifted her chin, willing to die with what little dignity she still possessed.

"Kill me then. I would rather be dead than let you shame me further."

Jamie grinned and her fury exploded. All sense of logic fled and she lunged. He blocked her blow with his sword, and grabbed her wrist. She curled her fist and landed a hearty punch to his jaw. Startled, he released her and she slashed the blade at him, nicking his sleeve, even though he evaded the strike. He swung his sword and she raised the dagger at the last moment, preventing the steel from slicing into her. But the smaller blade easily gave way under his sword, and she was unable to push him away. Once more, he clamped onto her wrist, his grip painful, but she clenched her jaw and tightened her hold on the dagger. His vice-like hold quickly grew excruciating and she cried out, releasing the dagger. Without letting go, Jamie bent and scooped up the blade, re-sheathing his sword at the same time. Both hands now free, he hauled her against him.

"You will be punished for this, lass. When Ian learns what you've done, he will see you beaten. And you'll need to mend me shirt."

She choked back a sob at her failure. She barely even flinched when Jamie retied her wrists. The pain seemed minimal compared to the agony of her disastrous attempt to flee. She let him lead her to the horse and didn't protest when he tossed her up and quickly took his seat behind her. A harsh hand on her breast didn't stir her from her stupor. She wanted to weep, but somehow kept the weakness from showing. She would never know where the determination came from.

# chapter seven

An hour later, Marissa nearly choked from controlling her sobs. After the ruthless pleasure he had inflicted on her earlier, Jamie kept her on the edge of release for hours, denying her the rapture she so desperately craved. At this rate, she was willing to do just about anything if he would only continue. How did these men know just when to stop to make the denial so much more painful? Their debauched ways proved all she'd heard about the Scots - uncivilized and barbaric. Yet, she found herself unable to resist their depravity.

Sweat trickled down her cheeks and she longed to wipe away the irritating itch. Her sanity hovered near the breaking point and she wanted to scream her frustration.

"Is this your way of punishing me?" She hated the way her voice cracked, revealing her desperation.

"Easy, lass, this isna how you'll be punished. This is merely to teach you your place."

"You are as vile as your clansman."

To her increased annoyance, he merely laughed, his fingers once again sliding around her folds, maddening her with the teasing touch.

"Do you think so? Dinna let Ian hear you say that. Could make your penalty far worse."

"Where do you get such depraved ideas to torture a woman this way?" She panted heavily, his thick fingers penetrating her, his thumb crushing her clit. The brief sensation of discomfort quickly gave way to a powerful hunger, against which she had no resistance. She bit her lip hard to keep the plea from escaping. Enjoying his harsh attentions horrified her, yet she was unable to summon the strength to stop him.

"You think this torture? Be glad you arena man. If

you were, you'd be whipped and set to hard labor. Or worse."

"Like this is any better?"

"Well, there's one thing in common. You'll be whipped, except after, you'll be fucked."

She gasped. "Wh-whipped? You would whip me?"

"For what you dared? Aye. You'll feel the kiss of leather. Dinna fash yourself. As a woman, I'm sure Ian will go easy on you. Besides, he and I both know how to whip a woman so she finds pleasure in it. Course, I've never whipped a slave before, I imagine 'twouldna be as pleasurable, since punishing slaves with no rights is quite a different matter."

The idea of being whipped pleasurable? These Scots were not only barbaric, they were mad!

"Aye, lass, a good flogging can be pleasurable."

God's teeth, she'd said that aloud? Heat scalded her face. "I ... I don't understand. How can that be?"

Despite the fear a whip might actually be used on her, Marissa also recognized a disturbing fascination in feeling the leather strike her skin. She shuddered. From fear or excitement, she couldn't truly say. Mayhap a little of both. That frightened her more than the thought of the whip.

"The strike can be pleasant, not hard enough to break your skin or the like, but enough to bite into sweet, creamy flesh. After the sting, pleasure follows."

"Nay, I don't believe you." She stifled a moan when his fingers now tickled her sex, her hips moving, seeking more contact. Instead he pulled away at the critical moment, and she let out a wail. He laughed.

"Lass, when Ian lays that whip into your arse, you'll love it."

She shook her head, trying to steady her uneven senses. 'Twas only his insistent touch that made her consider the idea of being whipped intriguing. She tugged at her wrists, and not even the ensuing shard of pain was enough to cool the yearning searing her body. She lowered her head, her eyes burning. The tears were not of sorrow, or fear, or anger. Nay, these tears were born of frustration and weariness, and a desperate need for release. Not freedom. Release.

\* \* \*

Ian waited impatiently for Jamie to reach him. The turmoil eating at his gut turned to alarm to see Marie unconscious in Jamie's arms. Or was she asleep?

He dismounted and took Marie from Jamie's arms before his clansman had a chance to explain. Ian stared at the pale girl in his arms. Her limp body revealed that she wasna asleep, but truly unconscious. Damn!

"What the hell happened?"

"She went for me dagger, tried to escape."

Ian clenched his fists. Why did this news feel like a knife to his gut? "She didna succeed."

Jamie shook his head. "She also tried for me sword, but failed. She's fierce, Ian. And she looks to have some skill with a blade."

"How could you tell?"

"She wielded the dagger like 'twas a sword. She knew moves any seasoned warrior would know. And look at my shirt! Another hair over and she'd have sliced me arm! You best watch your back."

Ian nodded. He glanced at his clansman. The way Jamie purposely avoided his gaze raised the hairs on the back of his neck. "What else happened, Jamie?"

Jamie sighed and looked out over the landscape. He seemed to be searching for the right words. Ian didn't need to hear them. He knew.

"You told her." He couldn't keep the anger from his voice.

Jamie turned and met his gaze steadily. "Aye. She wanted to know why."

"God's bones, Jamie, 'twasna your place to tell her."

Jamie nodded. "She needed to know. Besides, I couldna help it. The lass argued for her father's innocence, of course, but she didna deny Longshanks tyranny."

"What do you mean?"

"She swore she'd prove her father didna attack us, or the others. Though I hate to admit it, Ian, her questions ... before we siege Montchester, mayhap we should look closer at the attack."

"What is wrong with you, that you could let the lies of one English lass raise any doubt as to what we need to do?" Ian's rage blurred his vision red, yet some minute part of him realized Jamie was not being unreasonable.

"Ian, think on it. The attack came at night. You took a blow to the head. What if we are wrong? I say we use the coming days to search deeper for the truth. Now, I think I will catch up with the others. We canna be far, judging from his step, my mount smells home."

Ian said nothing as Jamie turned away. Aye, they were close to Crawford Keep now, true, but that wasn't what troubled him.

He wasn't ready for his captive to know what he'd endured, what drove him. Not yet.

Barely aware of his clansman kicking his horse into a gallop, Ian strode to a nearby stand of trees and carefully laid Marie out on the soft grass. He sat back to study her and the ferocious desire he'd worked all day to put behind him flared back to life. What was it about this lass that the sight of her could put him in the state of an untrained lad being led to his first whore?

When she stirred, he eased her up into his arms, watching when her tawny eyes opened. Her gaze cleared, settling on him. So many things flashed in the depths of her eyes, fear, concern, understanding. He held back his curse, his annoyance with Jamie giving way to the realization her knowledge of his past could actually work to his advantage. Yet, the thought of using her gentler emotions against her boiled his innards with guilt.

She said nothing, simply stared. Words eluded him; instead, he pulled her closer, covering her mouth with his, giving in to the need escalating within. She whimpered, the sound driving him to taste deeper of her. Her still-bound hands clutched at him, but he didn't even take the time to free her before he rolled her to the grass, covering her with his body. He lifted the fabric of her tartan, sliding his hand along her pussy, finding her swollen and wet. A flare of jealousy that he hadn't brought her to this state was forced aside when he drove a finger into her. Her muscles spasmed around him, her hips rising to seek deeper contact. With a low oath, he shoved his kilt out of the way, baring his hungry cock. One sure stroke and he sheathed himself to the hilt within her. Why did the sensation feel like coming home?

He focused on taking her, driving fast and hard into her body. She cried out with each thrust, arching against him and meeting his strokes with eagerness. Her eyes, locked on his face, widened, and she gave a keening wail, a second before her body rocked, her pussy clenching furiously around him, her release taking over. She bucked and shuddered wildly for what seemed forever, finally dragging him over the edge with her. The delight blinded him and silenced every sound except the blood rushing furiously through his veins and pounding in his ears.

He held himself still above her until his heartbeat steadied and his vision cleared again. The sight of her, her face softened with satisfaction, tugged at a place inside him he'd thought long dead.

With a muffled oath, he withdrew from her warmth, ignoring her husky protest. He stood, straightening his kilt.

"Get up, we've a journey to finish." He tried to ignore the confusion in her golden eyes, the brief flash of hurt she quickly concealed. 'Twas harder to ignore his guilt at causing that hurt. With a firm grip on her bound wrists, he pulled her to his horse, tossing her into the saddle before mounting behind her. He urged his horse into a trot.

"Ian?"

His heart thawed at the soft sound of his name. "Aye,

lass?"

"I'm sorry for what happened to your family."

"Jamie shouldna told you anything."

"Well, he did. While I don't doubt what he told me was the truth, I don't believe my father is guilty of those crimes. He's not that kind of a man."

"Dinna speak of things you know nothing about."

"I know my father would not have allowed what happened to your family."

"He is a man of Edward, is he not?"

"Aye, but -"

"Leave it alone, lass, or you'll find you won't like the consequences."

Thankfully she fell silent, but he sensed her anger and her need to defend her father. 'Twas likely she had no idea what the Panther was capable of. But Ian knew, all too well. He would see the Panther paid for his deeds.

Why did he worry how Marie would feel when he achieved his goal?

\* \* \*

Marissa remained silent, wishing for a way to convince Ian of her father's innocence in the attacks. Yes, the earl was a warrior, she knew that. She knew of the cruelty King Edward was capable of. She also knew her father was often the one who advised Edward against such brutality. Marissa had heard him speak of such things with her mother, confiding in his wife how he tired of holding Edward back, but thankful he had done so. Was it possible Ian and Jamie had made some sort of mistake, that her father hadn't committed those acts, but someone else had, and Ian merely thought 'twas her father? It had to be. Who would have done such a thing? Who possessed a pennant similar to her father's, someone as ruthless as the raiders?

Somehow, she would find out. So much time had passed since the attack on Ian's village, the trail of the real murderers had surely grown cold by now. But someone, somewhere, knew the truth. Other clans had been attacked.

There must be others who knew of those incidents. Finding those people would be a monumental task, one she had no choice but to undertake. She would prove to Ian her father was innocent of the crimes for which he stood accused.

In the meantime, however, she still remained in Ian's possession, and doubted he would allow her to seek the real story behind the sacking of his village, or help her in any way. Unless she could convince him her father would not rescue her; that his plans were for naught. He wouldn't believe her. Not yet, anyway. The task looming ahead of her suddenly seemed insurmountable.

Skepticism that Ian would believe anything she told him weighed heavily, but if she remained vigilant, she had to have faith eventually she would make him listen. Mayhap, he would help her find the real killers. Ian would have no choice but to release her then.

Why did the thought of returning home, to family and safety, unleash a well of sorrow? How could she have changed so much in a few short days? She'd been kidnapped, assaulted. But she hadn't been raped. While she had not asked for Ian to take her innocence, she had enjoyed it, and wanted more of the physical joy they shared, even when it became wicked and raw. Despite her initial resistance, after a few kisses, she had given of herself freely. She wanted to continue. Even when he'd shared her with Jamie last night, she hadn't refused, not entirely. Not that she had a choice, silenced the way she'd been. The desire flared, hotter than before, and she knew, if Ian were to bring Jamie again, she would not rebuff either of them.

She lowered her head, wishing for a way free of condemnation of her behavior. If she'd been a man, 'twould be expected that she seek her pleasure wherever she could. But she wasn't, and although she had trained with her brothers, she was still a woman. Her skills hadn't earned her any admiration as a warrior, not amongst the men in her father's garrison anyway. She'd heard the whispers. As a woman, none would think her capable of possessing a warrior's state of mind or behavior, even though she was as strong and fierce as her brothers and many of her father's men. While she sought to find a way to ease her situation, as any man would do, she would most likely be shunned for doing so. 'Twas not fair!

The few opportunities otherwise available had disappeared the moment Ian had taken her captive. She had two choices now. A convent or a brothel. Neither one appealed, but again the thought of starting a new life, on her own terms, difficult as that would be, poked through her sorrow.

She needed to keep her wits, and not get lost in the sensual pleasure that intensified with each encounter. There were plans to make, many things to think on, and she couldn't afford to lose sight of that. Her future, bleak as it now seemed, lay before her. Acceptance of her lot was not an option she would consider.

Even as she thought about what choices she had to make, another realization settled over her. She would need coin, and supplies. How she would get it, she didn't know. She found herself with a surprising reserve of patience. Good. She needed it.

\* \* \*

The sun had nearly set when Ian guided his horse through the gates of Crawford Castle. Marie had fallen asleep in his arms hours ago and he had savored her warmth curled against him. The time to end that distracting pleasure had come and he wished he could delay it a wee bit longer. He glanced at her, hating what he was about to do. She would hate him more.

"Come, lass, time to wake. We're here."

The oak doors opened and several people spilled out of the keep, Jamie in the lead. Marie stirred, glancing around in confusion and trying to stretch, the movement halted by her bound wrists. Ian freed her from the saddle, but left her tied, and handed her down to Jamie, aware of the murmurs growing louder as the Crawfords neared. Despite the way they'd taken him and his fellow survivors in, and though they were his mother's family, he still thought of them as separate from the MacCallums. They had become his clan when he needed them, but he'd never really belonged here. Soon he would leave, and rebuild his own clan, somewhere far away, perhaps up in the wild Highlands.

"Ian, glad to see you've returned safe. Jamie's told us a little about how the scouting trip went, but I'm eager to learn the rest." Donal Crawford pulled Ian into an embrace when he dismounted, slapping his back with affectionate force.

"Aye, I have to speak with the smith first. I will share the entire tale when I return. Jamie will see to the lass until I get back."

He ignored the frightened confusion in her gaze in the brief glance he spared her. He headed toward the smithy. His business shouldn't take long. After completing his objective, he strode back to the keep, his pace slower, hesitant. The others had all gone inside already. He paused by the door and stared at the sack in his hand. When Marie saw this ... He lifted his head and stepped inside. This task, while necessary, churned his stomach.

The voices in the room fell silent when he entered, immediately the focus of everyone's attention. He caught Jamie's gaze, his clansman standing near the hearth, holding Marie against him. She curled into him, seeking protection, her fear-filled gaze darting about the hall. Ian sighed.

He strode to the hearth and took up a position beside his clansman. Jamie released Marie and pushed her toward Ian. She stared at him and he could almost read the questions in her thoughts.

He cleared his throat and turned to the others awaiting his words. "My plans for revenge on the Panther have changed, 'tis true, but 'twill be a much sweeter vengeance. While I hadna intended to do this, the daughter of the Panther found her way to my possession."

Murmurs and gasps filled the room. Many of the clan turned their attention to Marie. She inched closer to him, gripping his arm with her bound hands. He shrugged her off, ignoring her sharp gasp.

"I will use his daughter to destroy him, as he destroyed my family and the Clan MacCallum. As such, with you all as witnesses, I claim Marie as my slave."

He removed the iron collar from the sack. Marie stared at him wide-eyed and backed away.

"Nay! Nay, you will not do this!" she screamed. She turned and tried to run but Jamie caught her, halting her flight. Despite her bound hands, she fought fiercely, swinging her arms wildly and kicking. Jamie barely managed to hold the struggling girl. Ian nodded to two others, who stepped forward. One, after much careful maneuvering, knelt beside Jamie and restrained her kicking legs, while the other took a strong hold on her swinging arms. Between Jamie and the two men, his captive was now completely at his mercy.

Ian strode over, and she flinched away when he reached for her, squirming violently against the restraining hands. "She's a hellcat; do you need another to assist?"

"Nay, just hurry up and do it, Ian," Jamie said.

Marie struggled in Jamie's hold, but Ian swept her hair aside and opened the collar. While not the final collar he would place on her - he'd asked the smith to forge one especially for her; he'd had this on hand, used when the Crawfords had held prisoners of war. The collar was too heavy for Marie's slender neck, but in another day or so, one more befitting her gender would adorn her throat.

He slipped the two pieces of iron together and quickly padlocked the collar. Marie's scream of outrage echoed through the keep, an eerie wail of anger and despair. Jamie released her and she made another attempt to flee, but Ian tugged on the chain attached to the collar. She came up short, horror widening her eyes.

"You are my slave now, Marie. In front of these witnesses, I've claimed you and collared you. If you try to escape, everyone here will stop you, and you will be punished. Publicly."

She shook her head, her mouth open, her lips moving, but no sound came out. She turned to Jamie; he gave a regretful smile before stepping back. Her head swung from side to side as she sought assistance from someone, anyone. None came. Finally, those tawny eyes settled on him again. She shook her head, her face ashen.

"Nay." The word came out a low moan and before Ian realized it, she had fainted. He barely caught her before she hit the floor.

\* \* \*

Royce Langley, Earl of Montchester, dismounted and handed his reins to the stableboy. He removed his helm and stood silently for several moments, staring up at the battlements of Monchester. He dreaded the coming moments.

He barely had a chance to consider what he might say when the heavy wooden door to the keep opened and his wife, Gillian, appeared at the top of the steps. He recognized her anxious expression even from this distance. Slowly, he headed toward the steps as she came down.

"Have you found her?" The fear and desperation in his wife's voice cut through the inner bailey as if silence hovered over the manor.

He waited until she had reached his side, but knew from her crumbling expression she already had her answer. He shook his head, his heart squeezing when a sob escaped her. He slid his arm around her shoulders and turned toward the steps.

"Fear not, Wildcat, we will find her." He began to doubt his words. The Scots who had carried Marissa off had vanished, not a trace could be found. Surely they had to have left some sign of their presence. Why would they venture here? If his men had been able to find Leland, Royce might have more answers. For now, he had no idea which clan had trekked this far into England without being seen by Edward's forces. The king had soldiers heading north to face The Bruce, surely a group of half a dozen Scotsmen wouldn't be hard to spot.

"Royce, she could be dead or..." Gillian's voice trailed off, but Royce knew his wife feared what he did as well. That their first-born daughter, with the heart and skill of a warrior, had been raped and broken. He didn't want to admit to Gillian that after this last sennight, he began to doubt he would ever see his daughter again.

"She is not dead." He hoped his wife would not notice the lack of conviction in his voice, but her own sorrow saved him from having to explain himself. No one else in the world knew better when Royce withheld the truth, but her worries and dread kept her from recognizing his bleak thoughts.

"Send word to the king. You cannot be expected to join him now, not until we've found Marissa and brought her home."

"I have already sent a messenger, but 'tis doubtful Edward will care. He needs my men, he needs me, by his side for this battle."

"He already has your men. He doesn't need you."

"He needs my aid in strategy." Royce led his wife into the great hall and toward the hearth. He eased her into her chair.

"He does not listen to your advice anyway, has not in many years. Warwick is there, he doesn't need you too! Please, Royce, if he refuses, you must insist. If we don't find her soon, those heathens will destroy her!"

The sharp note of his wife's voice tore another shred through his heart. He hated hearing and seeing, feeling, her pain. 'Twas as if it were his own. He could not refuse such a desperate plea.

"I will do everything I can to find her, Gillian. You know that."

She nodded, her beautiful violet eyes filling with tears. He stifled a groan. The sound of her weeping always felt like a knife slicing his innards, and each time he heard it, he almost wanted to cry himself.

"Come, I am hungry after the last days of searching. I need to be alone with you."

He held his hand out to Gillian, who took it and allowed him to lead her to the stair. She hesitated for a moment, summoning a maid and asking for a meal to be brought to their chamber. When she turned back to him, the despair in her gaze nearly sliced him in two. He pulled her close, and her head rested on his chest. The sight of her dark hair against his tunic always made him feel as if he had been granted every boon in the realm. This night, the sight reinforced the fact he could not ease his wife's pain. Not this time. Only one thing would soothe her sorrow, and he feared he might never be able to provide her with what she so deeply longed for.

He wanted nothing more than to forget the horror of the last several days, but knew 'twould be impossible. Mayhap, he could make his wife forget, even if just for a little while. Pleasing her would help ease his own battered heart.

# chapter eight

Marissa's awareness slowly returned, a haze of hushed voices greeted her.

"Poor lass."

"Fetch some ale."

"She's awakening."

Strong arms cradled her against a solid chest, warmth chasing the chill from her shivering body. She opened her eyes, her vision still blurry. She tried to move, but the arms tightened around her.

"Easy, lass. Let's make sure you didna break anything when you fell."

She'd fallen? How? She tilted her head back, a heaviness around her neck bringing swift recollection. Fury swelled in her chest, and she came fully awake. She pushed at Ian, curling her lips in a sneer.

"You vile bastard! You'll pay for this." She touched the metal on her throat, holding his stare with her own hostile glare.

He said nothing and she shoved at him again, surprised when he released her. Unprepared for his action, she fell off his lap and landed hard on the floor. She winced and immediately moved to stand. Before she could rise, Ian tugged on the chain, and she halted on her knees.

"I see you've recovered, slave."

"I won't recover until I'm free of you and this place! My father will kill you for this! If I don't kill you first!"

Ian reached for a mug and took a long swig from it, seemingly unconcerned by her threat. He looked down at her from his chair, his face free of all emotion. His eyes were hard and unyielding, and a tremor of apprehension shivered along her spine.

Once again, she tried to rise, and once again, Ian's tug on the chain attached to the collar halted her.

"You'll remain there, at my feet, where you belong."

No words formed in the force of her rage. He would dare! She curled her fingers into claws, tugging at the bonds keeping her hands together. Her gaze darted to his sword. Could she move fast enough to reach it? She had to try. She lunged.

Her fingers barely brushed the hilt before he caught her arm and wrenched her away. A sharp pain in her shoulder caused her to cry out. He stared at her, and for the briefest instant, she thought she saw a glimmer of regret in his gaze. Then his eyes hardened, into angry burning coals.

"You're either foolish or brave, I dinna know which." His growled words drew a shiver of fright. He shoved her back to the floor.

"Ian, give the lass some consideration," a voice called from the end of the long table. Marissa couldn't see, but 'twas a woman.

"Fiona, mind yourself, this doesna concern you." He turned back to Marissa and pointed at the floor beside his chair. "Kneel here."

She lifted her chin defiantly. Her courage wavered at his feral grin, moments before he leaned over and grabbed her arms, dragging her to the spot he wanted her. She tried to fight him, but he was simply too strong.

"If you move from there, I will punish you."

She glared at him. Her fingers clenched. She should have gone for his face, ripped his eyes out. He gave a low chuckle then turned back to the table.

The conversation resumed, and Marissa could make out snippets, but her rage thundered through her, her concentration scattered. The bastard had collared her as a slave before his entire clan. How dare he! One day soon, her father would see her honor avenged. She would savor the day that happened.

The aroma of roasted meat and vegetables teased her nose, and her stomach rumbled. Once again, she had gone most of the day without food, and the pungent scents reminded her. Her mouth watered. She noted Ian had a trencher before him, eating heartily while he discussed the change in his plans.

At least the threat Montchester faced had been stayed. For now. Her kidnapping had delayed his original plot, and while that thought did bring some relief, it also reinforced her own situation. She'd hoped to use her time to uncover clues about the truth of the attack, but collared and chained as she now was, greatly reduced her chances of solving the mystery. Even so, the more time she spent in this God-forsaken place, the longer her family remained safe from harm.

She held back a whimper of despair. No doubt her parents knew she was missing. If Leland had survived, had he told them of the Scots? Did her father even now search for her?

She dared a glance at Ian. He ignored her, still eating, just as the others did. Nobody paid her any notice. Angry tears stung her eyes. Damn him, wasn't he going to allow her to eat? She sat here like an animal, no better than a dog, while he glutted himself on food and ale.

"Ian, you've near starved the girl," came the woman's voice again. Fiona?

"Sister, you have no say in how I treat my slave. She'll be fed when I'm ready."

He caught Marissa's gaze. In response, she narrowed her eyes. He scowled and proceeded to ignore her once again. Several minutes passed before a small piece of bread was tossed to the floor before her. How she managed to contain the rage, she couldn't be sure. She would not accept his scraps.

"Eat, lass, you'll need your strength for what lies ahead tonight."

She lifted her chin and shook her head. "I'll not be

treated like an animal. I'd rather starve." The flash of anger in his eyes was quickly concealed, but it gave her a moment's pause.

"Very well then, lass, you canna say I dinna give you fair warning."

He turned away, and she curled and uncurled her fingers. The bastard would suffer dearly, she would ensure it. Various ideas of the punishment she'd like him to endure flashed in her thoughts.

A hand on her shoulder drew her from her murderous plans, and she looked up into sparkling blue eyes. A woman with dark red hair smiled sadly at her. She held a full trencher.

"Here you go, lass. You need your strength." She offered the trencher, but before she could place it in Marissa's hands, Ian tore it away.

"Fiona, I warned you once. I will see to my slave's needs. Not you." He stood and faced the crowd at the table. "All of you take note. The lass is my slave, and only I will see to her care."

The solemn agreements that followed birthed still more dread. Ian would not stop until he had completely humiliated her. She would ensure 'twould be the hardest task he'd ever faced.

\* \* \*

Ian waited until he had complete agreement from everyone, including Fiona, before he turned and gathered up the chain to Marie's collar. He tugged on it, forcing her to stand. She swayed unsteadily, and when Fiona made a move to aid the girl, Ian held her back.

Likely her legs were sore and cramped, and she'd eaten almost nothing all day. Guilt speared him. He took her hands and quickly sliced through her bonds. She gave a yelp and rubbed her wrists, her face twisted with pain. Another stab of regret knifed into him, sharp and ragged. He wanted to ease her discomfort, wanted to hold her as he had on their journey. He couldn't. He had to remain firm and follow this through.

Without another word, he turned toward the stair, leading her by the chain. He pulled her behind him, until he reached his chamber. While he normally shared it with Jamie, tonight he knew he would be alone. With Marie.

He closed the door and turned to face her. If her eyes were daggers, he'd be dead right now. He held back a smile. He so enjoyed her fire. Yet the glimmer of apprehension dulled his excitement.

He glanced at the large bed. Longing to be there, sleeping heavily, rose swift and sharp. He couldn't indulge the need, not yet. More than anything, he needed to take Marie again, to show her what he expected from his slave.

Her stomach rumbled loudly. Mayhap he'd been too cruel to deny her meal. He strode back to the door, opened it and called for his sister. Fiona appeared with the trencher, saying nothing, but giving him a knowing smile. He scowled and slammed the door in her face. Heaving a deep breath, he turned to Marie.

Once again, her stomach noisily protested the lack of food; surely the scent of the meat and vegetables had to be torture for her. He held the trencher before her.

"Go ahead, lass, eat."

She hesitated when he offered the trencher, finally giving in to her hunger and accepting the food. He let her sit at the small table while she ate, amused at how she devoured every bite with gusto, yet daintily sipping at the ale in her mug. When she finished, she lifted her gaze to his.

"Thank you."

He nodded, then tugged on the chain. "Come, lass, you have a long night ahead of you. I wish to begin."

Her eyes widened, sparking with outrage when she was forced to stand by the pressure on her neck. He stepped closer, quickly undoing the plaid covering her and baring her completely. His cock hardened under his kilt and he barely stifled a groan. The mere sight of her naked charms so easily made him forget all else, no logical reason why forming. He led her to the bed, securing the chain on her collar to a hook in the wall before stretching her out on the feather mattress. She had very little range of movement, but he wasn't finished. He quickly secured her arms above her head, then stood back to admire her body, bound and ready for whatever he chose.

"I won't fight you; you don't have to do this."

"You have no choice, slave. I decide how you are to be taken. I canna yet trust you not to attempt to kill me in my sleep."

The way her face reddened told him she wished to do exactly that. He chuckled and stripped off his clothing. Her eyes widened to see his erect cock. He stroked it, cupping his balls, noting the eagerness which crept into her tawny eyes.

"You'll get your taste of this, lass, soon enough. I find I have the urge to teach you exactly what your position will be."

He knelt between her legs, spreading them wide with ease when she tried to resist. A quick slap against her inner thigh drew a surprised yelp.

"Hold still, lass. Dinna fight me, or 'twill go much worse for you."

She glared, her only sound harsh ragged breaths and she tugged again on her bonds. Another slap to her thigh, another squeal. He repeated the strike once more, and again, until she shrieked.

"Please, stop!" Tears choked her voice.

"Then obey and you will avoid punishment."

She nodded and gulped, her eyes shiny. Her legs went limp around him.

"That's better."

He ran his fingers soothingly over her reddened skin, savoring the sigh of relief she tried to hide. He continued the little movements, noting the way she trembled. The sensation of her muscles tensing around him hardened his cock painfully. Her response to his touch delighted him. After he'd collared her, he'd worried she might not respond to him. Yet, here she was, chained and enslaved, and she still desired him. She might not want to, but she did. Her nipples peaked hard and red on her breasts, the sweet scent of her arousal filling the room.

Slowly, he moved higher, and her sighs turned to high-pitched gasps as he neared her sex. With soft touches, he ran his fingers over the curls hiding her secrets and she gave a delightful quiver. He drew away, but heard the protesting moan she couldn't quite conceal.

Resting himself on his elbows above her, he focused his attention on her breasts, lightly patting and caressing until she arched toward him. He made no move to caress her nipples, content to watch the hardened buds strain as he neared them, then drew away.

"Ian, please."

Satisfaction at hearing her beg poured through him, but he held back his smile. Instead, he gave her breast a light slap. She cried out.

"Nay, please, don't hurt me anymore."

Her husky plea almost undid him. Still, he hardened his resolve. "You don't call me by my name, lass. I am Master to you."

Fire flashed anew in her eyes, but when he lowered his head and licked her nipple, she gave a strangled moan.

"Tell me who I am."

Her eyes snapped open, focusing on him. He read the defiance there a moment before she spoke.

"You are Ian. My kidnapper."

He slapped her breast again. "Try again, slave."

She pressed her lips together. So be it. He grabbed her nipple and pinched it hard. She gave a strangled cry.

"What do you call me, slave?"

She remained stubbornly silent, and he pinched her again, harder this time. Sobs garbled her shriek.

"What do you call me?"

"M-Master," she sobbed, tears streaming from her eyes. He brushed them away and she turned her head, as far as the chain would allow. Still, her body trembled.

One hand slid down her belly and over her mound, cupping her sex. He drove a finger into her. Her pussy was soaked with her cream, and he gave her nipple another pinch. Her sex clenched around him, even though she groaned and sobbed again. So, the minx liked a little pain with her pleasure.

When her gaze turned to his once again, passion clouded the golden depths. Yet, he also sensed despair in her, and it tempered his earlier need to be cruel. He continued to stroke her pussy until she moaned and writhed beneath him. Her panting breaths and soft cries warned him she was close to a release, so he withdrew. Marie gave an agonized protest, her hips thrusting against him.

"Easy, lass. Remember what I told you. Your pleasure depends on my whim."

"You are a cruel bastard."

"Aye, but I think you like it." He arched an eyebrow at the red flush creeping into her cheeks. Her words said one thing, but her body told him another. The truth. She couldna hide her passion for him, no matter how hard she tried.

He pinched her nipple hard again, and her back arched sharply, a sharp hiss escaping her clenched teeth. He lowered his head, using his tongue to soothe the tormented flesh, and her soft panting cries changed in pitch. He continued to tease her with his lips and tongue, moving to her other breast to begin anew. He had the odd thought he might never get enough of her body, her responses. He forced it aside, concentrating on exploring the lass chained to his bed.

* * *

GIANNA SIMONE

Marissa no longer possessed the ability to resist the
fire of lust Ian stirred, his hands and mouth driving her,
scattering her concentration. The thought he would
ultimately deny what he stoked in her hovered in the back
of her consciousness, giving her the small strength to
hold out just a little. When his teeth scraped over her
tender nipple, the battle was lost, and she tossed her head,
trying to stem the rising swell of need. Her sex ached, her
thighs trembling as Ian held them far apart.

"Bastard," she choked out, her fingers clenching as
he bit lightly on her breast again. The discomfort seared
her, his teeth tightened and the pain flashed white hot
through her, settling with a throbbing intensity in her core.
Her clit pulsed and she jerked her hips toward him, trying
to convey her want.

A sharp smack on her thigh drew a strangled cry, but
the sting added to the tempest overpowering her. He
slapped her again, the sensation shooting straight to her
needy sex, and she moaned, offering herself once more.

"Aye, lass, you do like it."

Another slap to the other thigh, another and another,
and Marissa panted, her body alive with desperate hunger.
Each strike brought a shock of pain that intensified the
longing. Her vision hazy, she still made out the slight
smile hovering on Ian's lips. He leaned back, his
expression contemplative. She barely had time to consider
what that meant when he suddenly drove his cock hard
into her. The delightful sensation of being filled
consumed her, and her desire shot ever higher. He pulled
back, hesitating before impaling her again. She moaned,
meeting his thrusts, the pleasure both maddening and
exquisite. When he lifted her legs, sliding them over his
shoulders, the position drove him still deeper. She wanted
more, the only thought clear in her passion-clouded mind.

He bent her near in half, his face close to hers, his
warm breath an added torment to the upheaval he incited.
His mouth took hers then, one hand kneading her breast,

flicking at her nipple. When he gave her a hard pinch, she exploded in white hot heat, her heart thundering wildly, her body bucking under the waves of delight crashing and breaking over her. A faraway shout echoed in the room, and she realized it was Ian's, as he pulsed inside her, his seed spilling into her in a hot torrent.

Several minutes passed before he moved, and by then, the roaring in her ears had been replaced by their mingled harsh breathing. She tugged at the bonds holding her arms above her, desperate to wrap them around him and hold on, to steady herself against the storm of unknown emotions threatening to choke her.

He raised himself up, his keen gaze sharpening on her. When he pulled free of her body, she held back her moan of disappointment. It wouldn't do for him to know how much she liked having him inside her. She was a fallen woman, to have liked the pain he'd inflicted, leaving confusion and a lingering desire for more in its wake. She hated the way it had enhanced her pleasure, making her need more potent and harder to fight. She was weak. Foolish. She was a slave. His slave. She closed her eyes against the threatening tears.

"Marie?"

She'd almost forgotten the false name she'd given. With hesitation, she dared to look at him. The concern in his stare almost loosed the sobs she held at bay. He said nothing, reaching to free her arms. She bit her lip against the ache of movement, shocked when he gently rubbed her shoulders to chase the discomfort. The constant change from cruel barbarian to tender lover left her dizzy. A few short hours ago, he'd humiliated and shamed her before his entire clan, now he seemed genuinely concerned. Which was the true man?

She stared at him silently, her thoughts whirling with the pieces of the puzzle that made up Ian MacCallum. Why did she so desperately want to solve it?

# chapter NiNe

When Marissa awoke, she noted no one in the room with her. Sunlight flickered through the narrow window. She started to rise, but the heavy collar around her neck and the chain attached to it reminded her of her position. Memories of the night before tormented her, flashes of Ian waking to take her again and again in the night. Her body still tingled, sore in several spots, but the discomfort was oddly pleasant. She stretched as best she could and wondered where he had gone.

As if her thoughts had conjured him, the door opened and he stepped in. Once again, he wore the same emotionless expression, nothing even in the depths of his dark eyes. She didn't know whether to be alarmed or excited to see him.

"'Tis about time you woke. Come, there is much to be done today. I've tasks for you to see to, and I expect you to make haste."

Tasks? Would he set her to hard labor, humiliating chores usually left to the lowest level of villagers?

"What sort of tasks?"

"The women need help in the kitchens. You will do whatever they tell you, and if you disobey, I'll know."

She held back a scowl, though supposed it could be much worse. "May I... I need to relieve myself."

He nodded, and unhooked the chain from the collar. "I'll wait outside the door. Dinna dally."

He closed the door behind him and Marissa quickly tended her ablutions and reached for the tartan she'd worn until last night. The fabric was stained and she grimaced. He'd given her nothing else to wear. Surely he didn't expect her to work naked?

She struggled to wrap the plaid around her when Ian's

hands on hers stopped her. She hadn't even heard him come in.

"Nay, lass, I have a dress for you now." He held out a bundle of gray cloth.

She took it with trembling fingers and unfolded the dress. It was a simple kirtle of coarse wool, with no decoration. She sighed. The garment of a slave. She would hold her tongue, for now. She turned her back, his amused chuckle bringing heat to her cheeks. His humor was understandable, since she had no secrets from him any longer. Somehow, she needed this small measure of privacy while she slipped into the kirtle.

She frowned. Without a chemise to protect her, the itchy fabric already irritated her skin. How she longed to shout at him, rail against his cruel treatment. 'Twould do her no good now. She had to bide her time and wait for her chance. For surely, it would come.

When she turned, he refastened the chain to the collar and led her from the room. As they went downstairs, the sound of voices from the hall grew louder. When he led her into the room, the conversation stopped. All heads in the room turned to her, their gazes like a physical touch on her body. She held her head high, even though the collar and chain betrayed her current position. She was no slave. She was noble born, and would survive this ordeal.

Whispers rose, and she made out a few words here and there.

"Ian... all night."

"Heard her screams."

"Sounded like a hellcat."

"... in *my* bed."

Heat flooded her face, but she stood tall. These barbarians' opinion meant nothing to her. When she was saved, they would all pay for aiding Ian in this cruel game. Mayhap with their lives. She shook her head. How could she be so bloodthirsty? She was no better than Ian if she took revenge in that manner.

He led her outside, behind the keep to the kitchens. Inside, several women worked, some kneading dough, others stirring massive pots over the fire pit at the open end of the kitchen.

Several of them turned to stare when Ian led her to his sister. The sight of Fiona's kind eyes brought a rush of relief to Marissa, near weakening her knees.

"Feed her then set her to whatever tasks you need," Ian said. He took the end of her chain and stretched it out, fastening it to a bolt in the floor. The length gave her enough room to move about, but she could not unhook it. Any hopes for escape now evaporated.

Ian spared her barely a glance as he turned away. When he strode away, another woman stepped before him.

"Ian, I've missed you while you've been gone." The woman was tall and slender, with soft blonde curls falling down her back. A twinge of jealousy stabbed Marissa when the woman placed a possessive hand on Ian's arm and pressed closer.

"Elizabeth, I'm sure you have even more suitors than ere I left." Ian's voice held a note of amused warmth.

Hurt, swift and sharp, knifed into Marissa's gut. The soft smile he gave Elizabeth knotted her stomach. She watched while they continued to speak, their voices now too low to allow Marissa to make out their words. The flirty way Ian bantered with the other woman caught her heart in an icy fist. Why should she care?

A hand on her shoulder drew her attention from the troubling sight. She looked up to find Fiona, who gently took her arm and led her to a table. A hunk of bread and a piece of cheese were placed before her, beside a mug of ale.

Marissa ate, but her gaze kept moving toward Ian and Elizabeth. The bread tasted like dust, the cheese a sticky glob she could barely swallow. 'Twas obvious Ian cared for the woman. The realization forced home her own place in his life. Why did it hurt so much? He'd taken her against her will. Then why did she long for him to look at her with such tenderness and affection? Why couldn't he show her just a little compassion?

She hated herself for wanting more from him than he would ever be capable of giving. To him, she was nothing more than a piece of property, to be used for revenge and his own sadistic pleasure. He'd hurt her, yet even as she recalled the pain he'd caused her, her sex warmed and swelled, growing wet.

What depraved desires had he created that she could like such things? 'Twas bad enough he'd taken her innocence, he'd turned her into an animal, reduced to mad longings, in just three short days.

She pushed the bread away from her and washed what she'd eaten down with ale. Ian had headed for the door, Elizabeth staring longingly at him. When he had left, the other woman turned to Marissa. The sweet smile she'd given Ian twisted into a menacing glare.

She stalked closer, and Marissa lifted her chin.

"Dinna get any ideas about Ian," Elizabeth said. "You're nothing but a slave to him, less than a dog."

"Get you gone, Beth, afore I tell your father who you've been meeting behind the fens while Ian's been away."

Fiona stood between Marissa and Elizabeth, and Marissa's regard for Ian's sister grew. Mayhap the other woman could be swayed into helping her.

"The English slut may warm his bed now, but he'll destroy her and come back to me."

"Silly lass, he left your bed years ago. If he wanted to be back there, he would have been by now. Dinna fool yourself into thinking you can win his favor again."

Elizabeth scowled, but turned to her tasks, muttering under her breath. Fiona leaned over Marissa.

"Dinna let her bother you, lass. She means nothing to my brother."

"I don't care what Ian does with other women. I just want to go home."

"You will, lass, you will. Now, come, I need some help peeling these vegetables."

Marissa was thankful for the busy work, and Fiona chattered away. Marissa discovered 'twas easy to talk with the other woman, and soon found herself discussing her training and skill in swordsmanship in swordplay. How her twin brother, Rowan, had treated her as an equal, practicing with her, and teaching her many tricks. He'd not been fostered out like her other brothers. She'd often wondered why, but had never asked, just glad he'd stayed with her and their family.

She bemoaned the fact her skills in running a household and needlework lacked, but Fiona just laughed. If it hadn't been for the collar around her neck, Marissa might almost think she was at Montchester and free, and talking with her sisters, except she hadn't been involved with such chores at Montchester.

Hours passed, and Marissa assisted Fiona with many preparations, setting pots of water over the fire, plucking fowl, and sweeping up the ash from the fires that had spilled to the floor. Her initial surprise to see all of the women, including the wife of the laird, working so hard had sparked a curiosity about this clan. While she noted several scullery maids, they also seemed to be a welcomed part of the family, rather than the servants in her own home, who were nothing more than villeins in debt to the manor in various ways.

This keep was much smaller than Montchester as well. The women all seemed to enjoy working together. Though time and again, Marissa felt as if she was being watched. More often than not, when she looked around, she found the hostile glare of Elizabeth focused squarely upon her.

Fiona approached just as Marissa finished plucking the last of three chickens. "Let me take those, lass, and you sit here and rest."

Marissa hadn't realized how much her legs ached until she perched upon the stool Fiona provided. She wondered how much longer to the next meal. Her meager breakfast had not filled her. A shadow fell over her and she turned, a lump lodging in her throat.

Colin.

\* \* \*


Ian headed toward the kitchen. Marie would likely be near exhaustion, if he knew his sister. Fiona would work the lass hard. Good. She'd be too tired to fight him later, when Jamie would join them. He had told Jamie of Marie's reception to pain, and Jamie had been eager to participate. Ian wanted to see how far he could push her. He was disappointed the smith hadn't yet finished the new collar, but soon enough, he would savor the night when he could place it around her neck.

His stride slowed at the realization that Elizabeth would likely be there again too. His stomach knotted. He'd long ago ended his association with the woman, but she'd apparently set her sights on him once more. He'd tried to dismiss her nicely, not wishing to hurt her, but she'd failed to recognize his intent. While she was pleasing to the eyes, he found any desire he may have had for her previously had long since vanished completely.

A shriek greeted him. Marie!

Another scream, followed by a man cursing loudly. Several other women's voices reached him and he ran to the kitchens. He stopped short to see Colin holding his upper arm, blood seeping between his fingers. Marie stood a few feet away, a dagger tipped in red in her hand. Fiona shrieked at Colin, who glared murderously at Ian's slave.

Sensing what was about to happen, Ian moved toward Colin, but too late. The man had already advanced on Marie, reaching out with his good arm to grab her. She evaded the attempt, thrusting the dagger before her like a sword. Even while Ian ran toward the pair, he admired Marie's skill, dodging each of Colin's attempts to grab her. All too soon, the chain fastened to the collar went taut and her evasive maneuvers ceased. An evil grin split Colin's face.

"Gotcha now, lassie. You'll pay for stabbing me."

He lunged. Marie sidestepped, slashing the dagger out before her. Colin howled. She'd landed a blow to his other arm. The man recovered quickly and clamped a hand on Marie's wrist, squeezing until she released the dagger, sending it clattering to the floor. He raised his other hand, but Ian reached him then, catching Colin's fist.

"You dare strike my slave?" Ian yelled.

"She tried to kill me!" Colin wrenched his arm free. "I'll have the debt repaid. Now."

Ian looked at Marie, her angry, wide eyes telling him all he needed to know. "Did you try to kill him, lass?"

She shook her head, her lips twisted in a sneer. "Nay. He attacked me. I merely defended myself."

"The bitch lies, Ian." Colin's voice took on a worrisome tone.

"Nay, I dinna believe she does. I know you've wanted her since you stole her away, but she is mine."

"Look at me! The little whore deserves to be whipped for slicing me!"

Ian held back the urge to pummel the man for calling Marie a whore. Instead, he nodded. "Aye, she will be punished."

"I want to do it. Give me the whip!"

"Nay, Ian, he attacked me! You cannot let him -"

He held up a hand to silence Marie. "You are a slave, and you took a weapon to one of the men. You must be punished."

Ian knew she spoke the truth, and his fury at Colin simmered dangerously close to release. Her lowly position allowed her no chance at defense, regardless of the circumstances. Damn that fool Colin for creating this situation. Ian needed to speak with Donal and do something about the Crawford clansman.

She shrieked in outrage. "You will let him whip me? You are a monster!"

"Nay, slave, I will punish you. You were warned last night what could happen. Now you will learn."

He ignored Fiona's angry protests, unhooking Marie's chain from the wall. He wanted to punch the smug grin from Colin's face.

"Nay, you cannot! 'Tis not fair, I did nothing wrong!" Marie insisted.

He knew she was right, but her position demanded payment for her actions. He had to find some way to appease Colin without having to use a whip on her. While he did admit the thought of striking her body with the leather excited him, he wanted that to be for their mutual pleasure, not in true punishment. What Colin demanded would be brutal, vicious and could cause serious harm. 'Twas the last thing Ian wanted to allow to happen, yet he held no doubts Colin would not rest until he had received recompense to his satisfaction. He prayed Donal Crawford's fair mind would be enough to hold Colin at bay.

Marie resisted him. He turned. "Dinna make this worse on yourself, lass. Come with me now."

Her pale face and frightened eyes tore at him, but he couldna show weakness before the others. Instead, he ignored the curious stares and led Marie to the keep. He hurried up the steps and shoved her into his chamber.

"Ian, please, don't do this! I did nothing to deserve it."

"Calm yourself, lass. You stay in here while I try to appease Colin another way." He kept his tone soft and gentle, trying to reassure her.

She slumped. Somehow, he fought the urge to take her into his arms and further soothe her worry. Instead, he hooked her chain to the bolt over the bed and out of her reach. He said nothing more when he left the room, thoughts whirling with ways to save his reputation and keep Colin satisfied as well. Wouldna be easy, but Donal Crawford was a wise and just man, and knew well Colin and the man's sadistic tendencies.

An hour later, he walked away, pleased with the conversation. Fiona and the other women affirmed Colin had indeed attacked Marie and her use of the dagger had been in defense alone. As such, Ian was to pay Colin no more than ten shillings. As a slave, Marie had no right to wield the weapon against any in the clan, no matter the circumstance. Donal had agreed 'twas not fair to whip the lass for protecting herself. Ian had agreed to see to further punishment in private, as much or as little as he deemed fit. He trod the stairs slowly, thinking about how he could incorporate her punishment into tonight's plans. A smile curled his mouth. He knew just the way. No matter how much she might protest, he knew Marie would enjoy the coming events.

\* \* \*

Marissa paced as much as her chain would allow, too nervous to try to seek comfort in the bed. Would Ian really whip her? She shivered, fear tightening her throat. The damn metal bit into her neck, and she tugged at it, wincing when it scraped along her skin.

Could he really be that cruel? Aye, she knew he could. She hoped he could see reason. She'd done nothing but defend herself, surely there was no crime in that. She frowned. Likely Ian wouldn't perceive it that way. He seemed to derive great pleasure from humiliating her. Here was a perfect chance for him to do so again.

But whipping? How would she survive such brutality? Fear snaked through her veins, chilling her. She'd almost rather he killed her. No matter, she would endure, survive and not break. When she had her freedom back, she would repay him for all he'd done.

The door swung open and she spun about, her heart set to racing once more. Ian stood in the doorway, his mouth set in a grim line. There was her answer. She lowered her head, trying to gather her courage. His shadow fell over her and she lifted her gaze to his, determined not to show fear.

"I've paid Colin ten shillings for the damage you caused."

So he would take it out of her flesh then. How she knew, she couldn't be sure, she just did. "So when will you whip me?"

His humorless smile sent another slice of panic along her spine.

"I'll not whip you, but you will be punished. Jamie is to join us tonight, and he will witness your punishment and report it back in the morn."

A strange combination of relief and excitement took over her limbs. She trembled at the thought of being at the mercy of the two MacCallum clansmen again tonight. Despite her reservations, her sex clenched in anticipation, her clit pulsing with eagerness. She fought against the sensation, hating herself for wanting what she knew they would give.

"I see." Her voice held steady, bolstering her courage. She would endure. The words repeated over and over in her thoughts, calming her. She would endure.

"Do you, lass? Do you know what we will do to you?"

She shook her head, though truly, she had some idea. All of the various things they might subject her to flashed in her thoughts, spurring enthusiasm, instead of dread. Somehow, she managed to suppress a shiver of excitement.

"Aye, I can see you're anticipating. Dinna be so eager."

"Did you treat your wife this way?" A brief moment of satisfaction passed over her at the shock on his face.

For an instant, bleak agony darkened his eyes before he shuttered it.

"'Tis none of your concern, lass."

"I believe it is. You have kidnapped and abused me, and caused me to suffer."

"I willna discuss my wife with you."

"Did she like it when you bound her? Did you torment her as you do me? Did you force her to perform despicable acts?"

He sighed. "Aye, lass, my Sheila did enjoy a hard spanking as much as she enjoyed my attentions. I dinna have to force her. She knew her place and accepted it willingly."

Marissa's voice eluded her for a few moments before she recovered her senses. 'Twas madness to enjoy such depravity. Yet, her own enjoyment of Ian's attentions marked her as mad as well, did it not? Swallowing hard, she met Ian's steady gaze.

"So you did abuse her!"

He shook his head, his eyes hot and hungry as they moved over her. A tremor of excitement rippled through her.

"I didna abuse my wife. She knew I loved her. She enjoyed our play. As I know you do."

"Nay, I do not." Even to her own ears, the denial rang false. Marissa knew he did not love her; and took great pleasure in hurting her. What did he plan to do with her tonight? Another flare of wariness sprouted, but she fought to keep from revealing that to him.

"Dinna lie, lass. I can see your anticipation already. Have no fear, this night will not only serve to teach you your place, but you will give in to the lust, as you always do."

The flash of alarm faded as quickly as it rose. He stepped closer, and ran his finger along her jaw. She remained motionless, but couldn't contain the sharp intake of breath at his touch. A smile parted his beard.

"Aye, lass, you like what I do with you." His voice had lowered, thick and rough. "It pleases me to see you respond."

He leaned over and brushed his lips lightly across hers. Her heart pounded, his beard against her chin inciting the uneven rhythm. She swayed against him, and he caught her, gathering her close, but kept the kiss light and seeking. Her fingers curled into his shirt. He finally drew away, his eyes unreadable as he stared at her. He gently brushed a hair from her face, pressing another kiss on her forehead.

As quickly as the tender side of him emerged, it vanished when he righted her, his expression suddenly a cold mask. He said nothing more, simply turned his back and walked out of the room, leaving her alone once more. His kiss had hinted at his emotions, but she refused to consider any notion that her abduction was more than a sadistic game to him. On the heels of foolish hope came brutal reality. She would be punished tonight, and shared, by both men.

No matter how she tried to force the memories out of her mind, the recollection of the night Ian and Jamie had taken her remained strong and clear. Despite her uneasiness of what lay ahead, anticipation easily outmatched the wariness. With unsteady legs, she lowered herself to the bed. What had she become?

\* \* \*

Ian returned belowstairs, asked Fiona to bring Marie a meal. With the task done, he sought out Jamie. His clansman lingered outside the keep, staring into the night sky.

"Are you ready?"

"Aye," Jamie said, not turning to face Ian. "Are you sure this is the way you want to punish her?"

Ian sighed. "Colin willna rest until he thinks Marie has been penalized to his satisfaction."

"She defended herself. You wouldna punish

anyone else for such a deed."

"Nay, but I claimed her as my slave. She doesna have the right to wield a weapon."

"Ian, you need to show her more kindness. Why must you break her?"

"'Tis revenge, Jamie, you know that. For my wife and my son."

Yet, he found his conviction had weakened when he thought of his vengeance. If he had not taken Marie, his attack on Montchester would be imminent. Now, he realized his urgency seemed to have weakened.

Jamie shook his head, a disapproving frown creasing his bearded face. "Verra well, when shall we begin?"

"Soon. I've had Fiona bring her a meal, she'll need her strength. But, Jamie, when you see how she reacts to pain, you'll understand this willna be a real punishment." Where had the urge to convince Jamie of that come from?

Jamie cocked his head. "She likes it?"

"Aye. I tested her last night. She responds to pain as well as pleasure." The recollection of her lust-glazed eyes when he'd reddened her skin shot through him like a bolt.

Jamie grinned, obviously seeing his reaction. "Well, then, mayhap I will have to test the theory on her pretty little arse."

Ian grinned back. "If you choose."

He clapped Jamie on the shoulder and the two men headed into the keep. Several people watched them climb the stairs to the chamber.

"Best make her scream," Jamie said in a low voice. "So they'll believe she's truly being punished."

"She'll scream, for sure. There will be no doubt to any who overhear that she is facing justice for her crime."

"Colin, you mean?"

"Aye. Likely he'll listen to us tonight. Might as well give him something worth overhearing."

Jamie laughed as they stood outside the locked chamber. "I expect 'tis a good thing he canna get in the room."

"You have the right of that."

# chapter ten

Marissa's fear left her frozen standing near the bed when the chamber door opened. Ian strode in, followed by his clansman. Jamie turned to bar the door as Ian walked over.

"Remove the dress." The softer man who had kissed and held her tenderly earlier had vanished.

She swallowed past the lump in her fuzzy and dry throat. "Am I to be punished now, then?" She glanced at Jamie, who now stood beside Ian, hands on his hips.

The two men could almost be brothers, adorned in their kilts, dark wavy hair falling to their shoulders, neat beards that highlighted strong jaws. Dark flashing eyes that seemed to see right into her soul. Knowing she would be at their mercy tonight both excited and frightened her. Ian still meant to punish her, of that she was sure, but what role would Jamie play in the event? Still, the idea of both of them touching her, taking her, as they had done before, set off tremors of eagerness she couldn't deny. Keeping it concealed from the two men became a struggle, but she could at least be honest with herself, no matter what she told them.

"'Tis not your place to question. Remove the dress, or I'll remove it for you."

She sighed, reaching behind to undo the laces that kept the garment tied around her neck. Her fingers brushed the metal collar, and a renewed flash of annoyance at its meaning stirred. She glanced at Ian, who stood watching, waiting, arms folded. How she longed to let loose her frustrated irritation, but didn't dare. Not with the two of them standing over her. Chained and unarmed, she stood no chance of besting them.

Laces freed, the rough gray wool slipped off her

body, leaving her bared before them. She lifted her chin. The delight sparking in their eager gazes suffused her with pride. They found her attractive. They wanted her. Despite her situation, the heady sensation of that knowledge spurred her excitement.

Her nipples hardened in the cool air, and a moment of embarrassment washed over her. She fought the urge to cover herself with her arms, as she probably should. Instead, she issued a silent challenge with her eyes, and a hint of a smile.

"Ian, the lass is bold," Jamie finally said, the thickness of his voice starkly evident in the otherwise silent room.

"Aye." Ian's voice, just as husky, revealed his desire as well.

Marissa's heart raced, knowing she was the cause of their lust, and as much as she worried what was yet to come, she knew these two handsome men would give her that glorious pleasure they'd introduced her to. As long as she remained at their mercy, she might as well enjoy it, consequences be damned. There was no escape, but also no need to make her circumstances any more miserable.

"Time for your punishment, lass. Come." Ian turned and whispered something to Jamie, then sat on the bed. He waved her toward him.

Marissa's step landed more hesitantly than she preferred, but she soon stood before Ian. He grabbed her wrist and tugged her down across his lap, his legs pinning hers between them. Jamie took her wrists and held them tightly in his lap. Her hands rested on his kilt, and the hardness there left no question to his reaction to her. The wisp of pleasure ignited in her core.

Each breath shuddered through her as Ian's hand lightly stroked her arse. This she could bear, and would survive, and she relaxed in the hold of the two men. When Ian's hand came down hard on her bottom, she gave a sharp gasp.

The bite of the strike and the warmth that followed both hurt and thrilled. She hadn't expected the jolt of pain to turn to pleasure, her pussy swelling with the next stinging slap. She jerked against his hold, barely a chance to catch a breath when the next hit landed, and she realized he used both hands now, one sliding between her legs to tease her sex.

"She's wet, Jamie. See?"

Marissa's face heated and she kept her head down when Ian withdrew his hand. She knew he showed it to Jamie and her shame at finding pleasure during such a degrading act brought the sting of tears.

"Aye," said Jamie. His finger under her chin forced her to look up at him, her wrists still held tightly in his other hand. "'Tis nothing to be ashamed of, lass. For some, pain can feel as good as the tenderest caress."

Somehow bolstered by his words, Marissa barely flinched at the next strike, biting her lip to stifle a gasp when Ian's fingers once more found their way to tease her pussy. Jamie's finger ran along her lip, pulling it free of her teeth.

"Dinna hide your cries, lass, we want to hear you."

God's bones, how did they make her feel like she might combust? Another strike of Ian's hand ignited a low moan. The blows came faster now, and she gasped and cried out with each one, twisting against the sting. The licking fire, starting in her bottom, grew impossible to refuse. Ian's hand in her cleft still moved slowly while Jamie continued to hold her chin, forcing her to look at him while she endured this exquisite torment.

When the blows stopped, Ian gently ran a hand over her flesh. She sobbed with a combination of agony and relief, his touch an explosion of heat in her skin, as if fully released by the now soft touch. Yet, despite the deceptively soothing manner, his calloused fingers stirred a ferocious yearning.

"Feel."

At Ian's command, Jamie released Marissa's chin. Her head slumped down but when his cool hand slid lightly over her burning skin, she arched back, not sure which sensation was more intense, the discomfort or the wicked delight..

"Hot! And such a pretty shade of red."

The gentle motion of their hands sent the heat deeper into her. She writhed against them, their captive hold hopeless to fight off, though admittedly, her efforts were weak at best.

She found herself suddenly upright and swayed with the sudden change in position. Jamie's hands on her shoulder steadied her and she was soon guided to the bed. The moment her sore arse touched the mattress, she cried out and tried to rise, but two set of hands had already secured her wrists and ankles to the bed.

Her eyes widened when she took in her position. Arms were tied above, as they had been so many times since she'd been kidnapped, but the position of her legs brought a tremor of alarm mingled with her excitement. Spread open, with no way to prevent them from doing whatever they chose. Just like that night in the forest. She raised her gaze to Jamie, pleading silently, hoping he might be swayed into freeing her. He merely smiled.

Both men lay down beside her, and she gulped, turning to meet Ian's hungry gaze. Something there calmed her, but powerful wariness remained. She knew how cruel he could be, yet recalling the delicious way he tormented her spurred her current desire, chasing the last remnants of her unease.

Each man slowly caressed a breast. Marissa tossed her head. This situation was madness, shameful, but so delicious, such a pure pleasure, she didn't care. As their fingers swirled around her nipples, pinching and stroking, pressing and patting, she gave in to the delight, and savored the escalating need in her body.

In tandem, they left her breasts. She almost protested,

except the path they took proved more thrilling.

"God's teeth, you're killing me," she cried out when they meandered slowly down her sides and belly, closer and closer to her hungry sex, the yearning to be touched there growing almost painful.

Ian chuckled and lowered his head to take the hardened nipple nearest him into his mouth. She nearly screamed at the scrape of his tongue against the sensitive skin, but it came out a strangled moan when Jamie mimicked the action on the other side. Her head pounded with the furious rush of passion, and when Ian's fingers danced lightly in the curls protecting her sex, she barely realized the cries echoing in the chamber were her own.

"I think the lass is enjoying her punishment too much." The nonchalance in Jamie's tone brought a note of alarm, which seemed to heighten her yearning.

"Aye. She needs something to remind her this isna just pleasure."

Marissa gulped, then screamed. Ian's hand landed hard on her sex. A jolt of pain on her sensitive clit spread with ferocity and echoed with the sharp bite of pleasure. Sensing his gaze on her, Marissa met his stare. She couldn't be sure, but suspected he knew just how much she wanted him to repeat the startling action. He held her motionless with his eyes, her breath caught just as she anticipated. He didn't make her wait long, bringing his palm down harshly on her again. She wailed, writhing against the jagged and raw pleasure, in stark contrast to the gentle way Jamie's mouth moved over her breasts. Her body hung on the edge of release, but Ian must have sensed this, for he stopped, and motioned to Jamie to cease his attentions as well.

Marissa wanted to weep with frustration. The shocking strikes on her pussy had heightened her need. Sweat beaded her brow. Her clit, hard and tight with desire, throbbed incessantly, in time with the pounding of her heart.

"You see, Jamie, how she responds to pain?"

Heat flooded her face. She closed her eyes, briefly shamed by her wanton behavior. Ian's fingers on her cheek, gently caressing, sprouted tears.

"Lass, 'tis no disgrace, just like Jamie told you before. 'Tis a delight to see you respond to my touch, any touch."

She refused to open her eyes, so Ian's teasing fingers at her sex stole her breath with the unexpected touch. Once more, two mouths latched onto her breasts, and she forgot her embarrassment, giving in to the inferno the men stoked.

They tormented her flesh for what seemed forever, the mouths and fingers working her into a frenzy. Her focus narrowed to the waves of pleasure they wrought in her body, and she writhed against her bonds, wishing she could somehow hurry them along, drive her to that awaiting peak of bliss, the pleasure she craved.

Another jolt struck when Ian slapped her sex again. She gave a keening moan, on the verge of begging him to repeat the action. He must have read her mind, for he did as she hoped. The release burst over in a thousand shooting stars, her entire being attuned to the white-hot pleasure roaring through her. Every muscle in her body throbbed with delight. As the roaring in her ears died down, she realized the screams she'd heard were her own. Sated, she fell limply against the bed.

"Now that was a glorious sight for me tired eyes."

Jamie's husky voice sounded like a shout beside Marissa's ear. His tongue caught her lobe, sparking a shiver when he drew the soft flesh between his teeth for a nibble that sent more quivers through her pleasure-weakened body.

"Aye, she responds nicely to the pain." Ian's voice sounded muffled, his mouth still teasing her sensitive breast, teeth catching her hard nipple in a flare of delight. She couldn't think to form any words of response, even as their fingers and mouths continued to play over her body, drawing fierce tremors of ecstasy.

After several moments, they left her. She shivered, this time with a chill. Hands at her ankles soon freed her bound legs, though they left her arms tied. Before she could ask their intentions, they turned her over on her belly. Firm hands lifted her hips, and before her hazy mind clear enough to concentrate, she found herself up on her knees, which they spread very wide. She tried to turn her head, but again, hands lifted her chin, forcing her to look up into Jamie's amused glance.

"Time for you to see to our needs, lass," he whispered.

A sharp slap on her ass told her Ian's position, and his cock brushed her entrance. She moaned as the head slid along her damp folds, her sex clenching in anticipation. When he filled her with one long stroke, she gave a deep sigh of pleasure, and found the tip of Jamie's cock poised at her lips. She didn't hesitate to open, savoring his hot, hard flesh as it filled her mouth, his musky taste combining with Ian's thrusts, driving her body back to the fever pitch of moments ago. Once more lost in passion, the two men filling her body so perfectly, she bucked against Ian; at the same time, sucking hard on Jamie's hard cock, her tongue and lips drawing groans that added to the maelstrom. Knowing she pleased them spurred her escalating lust, and she licked and sucked fiercely, liking the way Jamie's shaft throbbed in her mouth.

A sharp slap on her still-tender arse startled her before the now familiar warmth washed over her, adding to the tempest, and making her desperate to reach release. 'Twas as if she hadn't just come so ferociously before, she needed to feel it again. She redoubled her efforts and pulled harder on Jamie's flesh, moaning when Ian spanked her again, timing each slap with his thrusts.

'Twas too much; she screamed, the sound muffled, and she came apart again. Her body had become merely an instrument the two men played to perfection, knowing just what to do to bring that fierce pleasure over and over.

Behind her, Ian stiffened, just as Jamie gave a low groan, his hot seed spilling into her mouth. She sucked harder, savoring the salty taste, while Ian bathed her sex with his. When the storm finally passed, and the men drew free of her body, she fell to the bed, panting heavily. Her arms were released, and she found herself cuddled between two solid bodies.

Sleep threatened, but Ian's hand brushing the hair from her forehead held it at bay. She wanted nothing more than to stay like this forever, cocooned between the two men and feeling as if they truly cared for her. Tears burned her lids. She just wanted Ian to love her as she did him.

She stiffened, the realization drawing her instantly from the haze of warmth. She shivered against the icy chill now invading her body, even as Jamie idly stroked her hip and breast.

"What is it, lass?"

She couldn't answer, didn't want to answer, so she shook her head, her eyes remaining closed. Though she couldn't see, she sensed both of them watching her curiously. Ian pulled her tighter against him, turning her so she lay with her head on his shoulder. Jamie snugged up behind her. She was helpless to move away while they held her like this. Trapped.

The collar at her neck suddenly seemed to sear her skin. Ian ran his fingers along the metal encircling her throat. Was he reminding her of what she was to him? The idea burned, but she refused to rail against him. She would show no weakness. When the time came, she would escape this madness. A madness that threatened to take her very soul.

\* \* \*

Ian stared at the lass in his arms, her now stiff body confusing him. He caught Jamie's questioning gaze and shrugged. A few minutes ago, Marie had been as needy and desperate as they, allowing them to do whatever they chose. From her reactions, she had enjoyed the play as much as they. Then why her sudden coldness, her refusal to look at either of them?

He remained silent, studying her. The tightness slowly left her body and she gave in to the need for sleep. Her breathing turned slow and steady, every now and then, what sounded like a sob breaking through. He pressed a kiss to her head. He didn't want to see her like this, wanted the wild wanton girl who had been as untamed as he.

"I think she regrets it," Jamie whispered. He lowered his head, pressing his mouth against her shoulder.

"Nay, she enjoyed all of it," Ian insisted. Of that, at least, he was sure.

"Mayhap she feels tarnished. Much as I enjoyed your sharing her with me, mayhap I shouldna do this again."

"Nonsense. She liked having us both and we will do so again."

"Ian, are you sure 'tis wise to keep at her like this? Have you given any thought to the fact we could be wrong? She was an innocent until we took her. Now ..."

"Now she is my slave and there isna anything she can do to change it. My actions are just." Yet even as he thought it, he didna want to ever let her go. Was that why he refused to consider any possibility he could be wrong about the attack on his clan? Deep in his heart, the realization sparked that he didn't want her to remain as a slave, and found himself wondering what 'twould be like to have her bound to him for always. As his wife.

He shook his head. Madness lay in those thoughts; the girl was merely a means for revenge. His vengeance was justified; he refused to believe any other alternative, would stand by his claiming her as his slave. As such, she had no rights, and would do well to remember that. In the morn, he would again remind her of her position.

\* \* \*

Royce read the parchment and crumpled it in his fists. This news, along with Edward's response to his latest request, would devastate Gillian.

"Father?"

Royce turned to his eldest son, Rowan. While not his natural child, he loved the young man as if he were truly his own. Part of him had been glad for the necessity of keeping Rowan in his household, while fostering out the sons Gillian had borne him. While he missed his children, having Rowan always beside him had soothed that emptiness. He stared at the dark-haired young man, who so strongly resembled his true parents.

Few knew the truth of Rowan's lineage. The son of a Welsh rebel and his mistress, he had almost been put to death as an infant, to prevent anyone in Wales from using him against Edward and England. Gillian's plea to spare the boy had resulted in the promise that Royce would never allow Rowan any opportunity to rebel against the English king. Raised as Marissa's twin., Rowan had grown to be as much, if not more of a son than his own flesh and blood.

"What is the message?" Rowan asked, studying Royce intently. The green eyes reminded him of the day years ago when Rowan's mother had died shortly after birthing him. He recalled how his wife had pleaded with him to help save the innocent babe's life and how he'd almost refused. He'd long ago buried any remaining guilt, but every so often, his son's appearance would bring recollections of those troubled days. He feared the trouble to come when Rowan learned the truth of his lineage, which he eventually would.

"Edward has refused my petition to continue my search. He is camped at Burgh by Sands, and expects me to join him anon."

Rowan reached for the parchment. "There is another message."

Royce nodded. The second note held the potential for disaster. "From Warwick. Apparently Edward has fallen gravely ill. There is suspicion he will not last the sennight. 'Twould explain the strange wording of the king's orders."

"Then you are free from your obligation. We can continue our search."

Royce shook his head. "Should Edward be unable to continue on, I may be expected to assist in leading the men against The Bruce."

"When did the messenger leave Edward's camp?"

Royce admired his son's continued strategic thinking. "Yesterday morn."

"Then we hope Edward recovers. His battle with The Bruce will give us the distraction we need to search other areas in Scotland. If the king does not regain his health, and you are needed, I will lead the search for Marissa."

"It may be our only option. I must send my response. The messenger is in the hall while his mount is being seen to. Come, I could use your help in my reply."

He knew Rowan would do well to lead a party into Scotland, though 'twould be the first time he would have the responsibility. Besides, Royce wanted to be the one to find his daughter.

# chapter eleven

Marissa stretched, her tight muscles protesting the movement. Her arm came up against a broad chest and she froze. Another chest snugged up tight against her back. Recollection bombarded her, recollection of two devilish men pleasuring her. Or hurting her, she thought, a memory of Jamie's harsh spanking flashing through her sleep-addled thoughts. Yet, even that stirred a shivery thrill.

No wonder her muscles ached. The two of them had used her thoroughly, over and over again. Not that she'd minded. Her "punishment" had evolved into several spankings and being forced to repeatedly suck each of them to a groaning release, but she hadn't resisted anything. An image of being bound and spread on the bed as they had used their mouths on her, tormenting and teasing until her release had left her wrung out and weak, seared into her consciousness.

If only she could feel as safe and wanted in the daylight hours as she did in the darkness of night. She knew once Ian awoke, he would return to humiliating her, and reminding her of her position in his home. A lump lodged in her throat. She wondered why she so desperately wanted Ian to want her as more than just a lowly slave. The hard muscle under her hand twitched and she looked up at Jamie. A regretful smile curved his lips.

"You are delightful, Marie." He pressed a soft kiss on the tip of her nose and eased out of her embrace. The sudden chill left by his absence drew a fierce shiver. In her ear, Ian chuckled.

"I'll warm you, lass," he murmured, his lips sliding along her shoulder. Another shiver, this one of excitement, slithered along her spine.

She watched Jamie wrap his kilt around his waist, covering his cock. Why did that action disappoint her? He paused and winked, as if he knew her thoughts, just as Ian cupped her breast. She gasped, her sex growing hot and wet. Another finger pushed into her, and she held Jamie's gaze while Ian used his hands to drive her quickly to the point of release. Just as suddenly, he withdrew his hands, and she cried out, her eyes still locked on Jamie. The corners of his mouth twitched and his eyes gleamed with deviltry, watching her as she squirmed against Ian, using her body to urge him to continue.

She found herself flipped on her back, Ian looming above her. That feral smile that always sent sparks of excitement through her revealed his hunger. Her heart raced and she reached to wrap her arms around his neck. He stopped her, and placed her hands on the bed.

"You dinna get to touch lass. Hold still."

The order came through clearly in his tone, and somehow, she managed to hold back her moan of frustration. She wanted to hold him, touch him, explore him as he did her, his fingers sliding through her hot, wet folds and finding her clit. He swirled around it slowly, not really touching it, then tickled at it lightly. She cried out, over and over, her words unintelligible moans.

"I canna hear you, lass. Did you want something?" Ian's teasing voice added to the tempest as he continued to toy with her sex, knowing exactly where she wanted to be touched, yet avoiding it.

A hand on her breast drew her attention to Jamie, who'd returned to sit on the bed beside them. These two would wear her out, leave her limp and sated in a puddle on the bed. She didn't care. When they held her, touched her, took her, like this, she always found herself wanting it to last forever.

Ian's teasing fingers grew more insistent, and he slipped three inside her, twirling them, and she bucked, a ragged wail escaping her clenched teeth.

"Ian, please!" she cried.

A slap to her thigh cooled the fire briefly, but the sting and ensuing warmth stoked the heat back to a ferocious blaze. She held back a sob, not caring how cruel he could be. She took a deep breath, desperate to steady herself in the whirlwind, but it didn't help.

"Please, Ian ... I beg you, don't stop."

His pleased smile intensified the flashing heat. Jamie now had both of her breasts in his hands, massaging, squeezing, and pinching her nipples. Each touch sent another bolt to her core, her pussy clenching on Ian's fingers, still buried deep.

"That's it, Marie, give in to what your body wants," Ian crooned. She couldn't answer, could only buck onto his hand, her back arching to thrust her breasts more fully at Jamie.

"Come for us, lass, let the sweet pleasure take over." Jamie's words startled her. She hadn't realized he had moved so close to her ear, his lips brushing against her skin yet another delight. Her surprise evaporated as Ian continued tormenting her sex, pinching her clit, her gaze held by Jamie's intense stare.

The climax burst over her in rapid, jarring spurts, obliterating all thought except the joy that sang in her veins. Ian continued manipulating her, Jamie's seeking fingers squeezing her flesh harder. She barely had a chance to catch her breath when another wave of yearning washed over her. She couldn't protest, her voice abandoning her, and all too soon, she once more straddled the edge between need and ultimate pleasure. She gave a silent prayer both would continue, and held her breath.

Ian gave her a curious smile and for a moment, she panicked, thinking he meant to leave her on the edge again, but he never stopped his attentions. When Jamie's hot mouth enveloped one hard nipple, Marie nearly screamed from the force of the orgasm tearing through her. She felt as though she were being tossed about like an empty flour sack, and she rode the fury, savoring each explosion of bliss as they occurred.

Finally, they released her. She had trouble lifting her drowsy eyelids, but managed to look up at the two eagerly smiling men. She recognized that expression, and knew both men planned to take her now. Already her body jerked back to life, vigor seeping back into her passion-weakened limbs.

Ian didn't wait another moment, filling her with one hard thrust, accompanied by a strained groan. Jamie straddled her shoulders, his erect cock hanging right before her mouth.

"You know what to do, and what I like."

That she did, he'd taught her well last night. Recalling his instructions, she opened her mouth, sliding her tongue along the warm flesh throbbing in front of her, then sucking the tip of his cock between her lips.

"Dear Lord in Heaven, lass, you are gonna be the death of me," Jamie ground out. She let him sink further into her mouth, swirling her tongue around him and lightly scraping her teeth along the underside of his cock. His musky taste overwhelmed her senses.

Ian's fingers tightened on her hips, driving furiously into her and making her squeal.

"Keep doing that Ian, she sings nicely around my cock."

She could barely breathe, but somehow managed to maintain her rhythm on Jamie, while Ian continued to drive into her with a breathtaking pace. When he pinched her clit, she cried out, the sound muffled by the cock in her mouth. Ian did it again, drawing a similar response, moments before Jamie released his seed down her throat. He pulled away, his softening cock sliding along her lips. She caught the tip with her tongue.

"Behave, slave," Jamie scolded. But his tone held laughter. He leaned back, content to watch as Ian continued to thrust forcefully into her. She remembered to keep her arms at her sides, her fingers clenching in the bedcovers as Ian increased his already-wild rhythm.

Marissa's core tightened, she grew close to release again, and didn't want Ian to leave her with pent-up frustration. She couldn't do anything to aid herself, at the whim of Ian, should he decide to grant her pleasure. She forced away the despair at the unfairness, instead focusing on reaching her orgasm before Ian could deny her.

His thrusts grew more insistent, his fingers digging into her hips to hold her still. Each stroke of his hard cock spurred her hunger, and she rapidly climbed toward the peak of delight. Jamie's hands once more tweaking her nipples, she came apart in a blinding fury, unable to stop the cries from escaping her as the pleasure tumbled over her, again and again. Somewhere in the distance, she heard Ian's shout, felt his cock pulsing within her, his seed filling her.

By the time she'd regained a steady breath, Ian was already pulling away and rising from the bed. She held back a moan of disappointment, wishing she could stay here with them like this, debauched as it may be.

"Up, lass, there's work to be done." His cold tone told her he'd reverted to the cruel slave master once again. She sighed, forcing her weak and trembling legs to rise. Jamie stood silently when Ian tossed her the gray kirtle, then dressed himself. Still, she caught his intense study of Ian's clansman, and wondered what thoughts he dwelt upon.

"Tend your needs, lass. I'll wait for you outside the door," Ian said gruffly.

And she was alone. She held back a great shuddering sob. How did the two men turn her into a wanton whore, eager for whatever depraved activities they inflicted on her? She used water from the basin to wash her face and wipe away the tears that had broken free. Once her needs were relieved, she strode to the door and opened it. As promised, Ian stood outside, though Jamie no longer remained. With dismay, she held still while he affixed the chain to the collar. The glimmer of hope he would leave her unbound flickered out. Still, she'd remain vigilant. One day soon, he would make a mistake and she would be ready for it.

She followed Ian belowstairs, already numbed by the frantic morning. Just like yesterday, he brought her to his sister, who provided a quick meal to break Marissa's fast, then disappeared, leaving her chained in the kitchens. By the time he returned to gather her, she was exhausted and wanted nothing more than to sleep. She let Ian lead her back to the keep, where many of the clansmen had gathered.

Ian sat in a chair beside Donal Crawford and pointed to the floor beside him. Gritting her teeth to hold back her angry response, Marissa knelt on the cold stone floor. She lowered her eyes, lest he see the venom she directed at him. Her weariness soon had her slumping, until something in the conversation drew her out of the haze of fatigue.

"Word's come that Longshanks has fallen ill. The Bruce may have won before the battle has even begun."

Marissa strained to determine who spoke, but could not be sure. The king was ill? What did that mean?

"The English king is foolish and stubborn," Ian said. "And has an uncanny way of surviving what would fell most other men."

"Aye," Donal said. "'Tis true. But if he is truly ill, without a leader, Longshanks' troops will have none to lead them. His son is weak, and will be easily routed."

"'Tis not the son Bruce is worried about," came another voice. Marissa thought it was Jamie, but didn't dare lift her head to see. She wanted nothing to give clues to Ian that she absorbed every word.

"Aye, 'tis the king's warriors we need to fear," Donal agreed. "The Prince of Wales canna command an army as his father can, but Longshanks has many others who can lead men into battle."

Marissa thought of her father and wondered if he would be tasked with continuing Edward's battles. 'Twould mean he would be in Scotland, possibly nearby. Hope soared in her chest, but she forced herself to remain still.

"I am sending some warriors to The Bruce," Donal said. "Ian, your plans to return to Montchester must wait some more."

"I understand. There is time before I undertake that part of my plan," Ian replied.

A tug on her chain forced Marissa to look up at him. She kept her face free of expression, not wanting to reveal her optimism that her captivity could soon be at an end.

"Are you listening, lass? The English king will soon fall. As will his men. Vengeance is at hand."

"You hope one of those men is my father."

A hint of a smile appeared in his beard. "Mayhap. 'Twill make my siege on Montchester easier when the time comes."

"You filthy bastard! You would still attack my home, even if my father were to ... fall in battle with The Bruce?" Voicing that thought left the taste of bile in her mouth.

"My vengeance has nothing to do with The Bruce's plans. I will see Montchester destroyed as my village was."

"Even if you know there is a strong chance you are wrong?"

Several gasps sounded around her, but she held his now stormy glare.

"I am not wrong, slave. You would do well to remember that!" His eyes darkened with anger, but she did not let the sight intimidate her.

"But what if you are? If you attack my home, my family and you are wrong about who attacked yours, you will be responsible for their murders!"

"'Twill not be murder, 'twill be justice."

She shook her head, hating the way the metal on her

neck chafed. The odd thought she would bear marks forever from the collar poked through her anger.

"You are a cruel, sadistic man. I will see you burn in hell for this!"

She couldn't contain her shout, and a rush of murmurs rose in the stunned silence. The anger on Ian's face grew lethal, and she swallowed the lump that had suddenly appeared in her throat. She refused to back down, lifting her chin and daring him to do his worst.

"The slave dares defy you, Ian? How do you plan to punish her?"

Marissa's stomach rolled at the sound of Colin's voice. Ian ignored the Crawford clansman, his gaze still focused squarely on her.

"Methinks 'tis time to retire for the night," he said, his voice low and calm.

A shiver passed along Marissa's spine. Calm his voice may be, but she sensed the rage lurking beneath, could almost feel it. It was all directed at her.

She wasn't afraid. He could do anything by now, and she would survive it. She had so far. She was strong, could hold her own. God help Ian when she got her hands on a sword. By the time she finished with him, he would regret even being born.

"Come, slave. 'Tis time for me to seek my bed."

He stood and tugged on her chain, forcing her to rise. She held back a sneer, but narrowed her eyes, letting him know just how much she hated him.

*You don't hate him.* The voice in her head taunted, and she refused to acknowledge the truth in the thought. Even now, angry as she was, the sight of his hands curling the chain around them, drawing her closer, set her stomach to flipping, her core to tingling. Her nipples poked against the rough wool of the kirtle, even the irritating fabric an enjoyable sensation. His grim glare did little to calm the rising excitement, her sex growing damp and hot. Already she throbbed, even though she knew he would stoke this fire and then likely deny her any relief from the pulsing torment.

He turned toward the stairs and she followed. What else could she do? Every step furthered the heat in her pussy, swelling and clenching on emptiness. The thought of his hard cock filling her sent the sensations into a high-pitched hunger. God's blood! How could just a glare weaken her resolve? She should fight him, seek a weapon to use against him, and refuse as best she could any advances he made. Instead, she followed meekly, and anticipated, with more eagerness than she should, whatever he might do through the long hours of night.

When they reached his chamber, she stood quietly until he had closed and barred the door. Somehow, that action set her heart to racing, her mouth suddenly dry. Nevertheless, when he turned to face her, she let loose her rage, not willing to let her other emotions have any control over her actions.

"You vile, cruel bastard! You continue to exact more vengeance from my innocent body, and still 'tis not enough! How far will you go in abusing me to reach your ends? You're a sadistic animal, and when the tables are turned, you will be begging for my mercy!"

He chuckled and stepped closer, drawing her near, still wrapping the chain tighter and tighter around his hand. He finally stopped when she stood inches away.

"Lass, someday that tongue of yours will get you into real trouble. For tonight, though, I've better uses for it."

The thought of taking his cock in her mouth excited her, even though she tried to be appalled by the thought. No matter her attempts, the anger slowly gave way to something else she recognized all too well. Desire. Hunger. Lust.

She'd become a slave, all right, a slave to her body and the needs Ian stirred in her. The brief moment of despair was chased by his hand cupping the back of her head, drawing her near for a hungry kiss.

Royce and Rowan strode to the keep, the silence between him and his son heavy and thick.. This latest news had filled him with dread and hope. Edward had passed days earlier, leaving his army in disarray. Royce mourned the loss of his childhood companion, his trusted king, and the friend he had been these past many years. While this latest turn would make things between England and Scotland even worse, what concerned him most was still his daughter. He could not now venture across the border to seek her, not until after he received word on what plans Edward may have made for this occurrence. Warwick's message had not held as many details as Royce preferred.

"Father? I am not needed in Burgh Upon Sands. I can begin the search for Marissa."

"Nay, Rowan. The Scots will be celebrating, and 'tis too risky to allow you to lead a small party into hostile lands. Edward's son will continue, though Warwick is truly leading the army. I expect word from Montchester's captain shortly with the status. I don't know how long Edward's vigil will last. With luck I will be in London before his body arrives. If all appears well and settled, I will return and we will set out to Scotland."

"Mother will not be pleased about the delay."

"There is no hope for it. I cannot risk Montchester by standing by, or refusing to meet the king's procession in London. The son is unstable, though he intends to stay in the north for now. I do not trust his wife or her lover in his absence. If given the chance, they would seize any opportunity to take not only my lands, but those of their perceived enemies. Those who supported the king will be most suspect. I must be in London to maintain the peace among the nobles while the prince continues to Scotland."

The politics he worked so hard to balance looked now to possibly come undone. Edward's son was an ineffectual leader in war, and though Royce knew the prince needed his aid, he needed to safeguard the realm by ensuring no internal politics escalated into serious strife among the nobles. The Prince of Wales had many of the king's men beside him, they would do what was necessary to win the upcoming battle.

The real trouble lay in the fact that many others would seek favor from the new king through his wife. Royce did not trust the woman, or any of her advisors, not to steal whatever possible. He didn't dare risk his family's well-being, and in order to protect all of them, he needed to make sacrifices. Sadly, his daughter would be the first, much as it ripped his heart to pieces to think of what she endured. If only he had some word to know if she still lived.

Would his wife understand? Mayhap, but more likely not. He dreaded sharing this decision. Her sorrow would turn to rage, and even Edward had once cowered under her fierce anger.

"Would you like me to tell her? Your neck may be safer."

Royce smiled at his son. Despite the hopelessness of the situation, the much-needed attempt at humor eased the tightness in his chest. He gave silent thanks once again to have such a fine young man beside him during this difficult time.

# CHAPTER TWELVE

Another week passed and Marissa's routine remained mostly unchanged. Each night, Ian, and often Jamie, had shown her more of their wicked sexual games. Her response defied logic. She knew she should resist in some way, but the slightest glance from Ian set her body ablaze, desperate to feel more of that soul-stirring delight.

Most of her days were spent helping Fiona in the kitchens or with the laundry. The Crawfords were not an extremely large clan, but they required large amounts of food and had an abundance of laundry on a daily basis. Most of the women did not speak to her, and she suspected Elizabeth was behind the many hostile looks she received. She didn't care.

Her thoughts now focused largely on the state of the war between Scotland and England. Edward's vigil at Burgh Upon Sands continued, according to a messenger who had come yesterday, but there had been no further word as to what would happen next. The king's son continued to march toward Scotland, though no one really knew if he intended to engage the army. The uncertainty had many tense and uneasy.

She had to put her plan into motion now, and gather as much information as she could. She looked around and seeing no one nearby, drew closer to Fiona. What she was about to do was dangerous, but so many facts remained hidden. 'Twas time to uncover them and learn all she could.

"Fiona? May I ask you something?"

"Aye, lass, what troubles you?"

Marissa bit her lip, hesitating. With a deep breath, she asked, "When was your clan attacked?"

Fiona stared for a few moments, before

understanding lit her bright eyes. She nodded heartily. "I see what you're about, lass, and I admire you for it, but 'tis a waste of time to ask questions about things you know nothing about."

"I know in my heart my father could never have done the things Ian said. I intend to prove it. Now is my chance, with the battle between England and Scotland in abeyance, and possibly never to happen."

Fiona smiled. "I see you're as stubborn as my brother. Verra well. 'Twas two years ago at shearing time. We had just finished with the sheep, getting the wool ready for market, when a messenger from The Bruce arrived with word about the massacres, and we were warned to be prepared to defend ourselves."

Marissa tried to recall if she had heard of any attacks during the time Fiona had indicated. With Montchester so close to the Scottish border, word of events as far as the Uplands reached them often, especially if that news happened to be bad. There had been nothing. But she recalled one important detail.

Two years ago, her father had been at Lyndon, her mother's ancestral home. He had spent a good part of the summer and autumn months there, aiding her Uncle Simon with some sort of disturbance. Marissa knew because that was the time her brother, Rowan, had taught her how to properly wield a broadsword, a skill she had yet to master at the time, due to the heft of such a weapon. Hope glimmered, hope she could finally convince Ian her father had done nothing to harm his family. 'Twas impossible, if Fiona's statement about the timing was indeed true.

"Did the messenger say who committed these attacks?" she asked.

Fiona shook her head. "Only that they bore the pennant of the English king. There were no survivors, so no one knew for sure."

"See? It could have been anyone, one of Edward's

men, or even other Scots! Anyone could have led the attacks. I know it could not have been my father."

"Lass, you canna really be sure."

"Aye, I can. Without any doubt, because he was in Wales at the time."

"Are you sure, lass? Your father's banner was seen. We lived to tell what we saw."

Marissa shook her head, excitement growing at this first clue which could clear her father's name and perhaps win her freedom. "Fiona, you are wrong, and Ian is wrong. All of you."

"Hush!"

"Nay! Listen to me!" Marissa insisted, relieved when Fiona fell silent and waited. "I know because two years ago this spring, my brother taught me to use a blade my father had always forbidden me. My father would not have allowed the lessons had he been at Montchester. Surely you realize leading an attack from the Welsh border would be impossible. So you see? He could not have done it."

"Lass, do not speak of this. 'Twill only get you in trouble with my brother."

"What will get Marie in trouble with Ian?"

Marissa spun about to see Jamie behind them, fingers hooked in his sword belt. When had he arrived? Had he heard any of what Marissa had shared? If she could convince him she had information to exonerate her father, would he help her?

"I was asking about the attacks." She raised her chin defiantly.

"Aye, that will give Ian a sour temper. Best you not speak of it again, lass. Now come with me." He bent to unfasten her chain from the bolt in the floor. He wound the length around his arm, until she had no choice but to stand before him.

"Where are you taking me?" Myriad emotions swirled about her, muddying her thoughts.

"Ian has something for you, lass." He turned and headed back to the main keep.

Fear gripped her heart. "For me?" She had no illusion 'twould be a gift. What did the man plan now?

"Aye. I think you will be grateful when you see."

Too many questions rang out in her thoughts for any one to keep her focus. She decided she should take her chance with Jamie, before she had to wait.

"Jamie, I know my father could not have attacked your clan."

He paused and tuned to look at her. "You are foolish and stubborn, Marie. You will do better to not speak of it ever again. Accept your fate."

She shook her head. "I cannot. I know 'tis impossible for my father to be responsible. He was on the Welsh border at the time your village was destroyed."

He tilted his head, eyes narrowed. He scowled, even as he rubbed at his bearded chin. "Are you sure, lass?"

She nodded. She repeated what she had told Fiona about the broadsword. His studious expression clearly revealed he gave her words serious thought.

"All right, lass. I will give your words consideration, but you are not to speak of it to Ian."

"Will you?"

"Mayhap. I must think on it further before I bring him more nonsense that will anger him."

'Twas not an agreement to help, but he had agreed to consider her theory. Her hope continued to grow. She could see in his expression he believed her words had merit. As Jamie was not as blinded by Ian's need for vengeance, he could be more objective. With enough time, she could convince him. In turn, he would help her convince Ian. She hadn't felt so cheered in weeks. Still, she needed him to understand her time to uncover the truth quickly approached its end.

"You have until nightfall tomorrow, Jamie, or I will share what I know with him myself."

"You have no right to make demands, lass." He didn't bother attempting to hide his smile.

"'Tis not a demand. 'Tis a promise."

He grinned broadly. "Lass, not one flicker of your fire's been doused. I see why you've got Ian tied up in so many knots. Now, come."

"What about you, Jamie? Do I affect you the same way?" She bit her lip, wishing she could call the question back.

"Aye, lass, you do."

His lowered voice sent a shiver along her spine. He tugged on her chain and led her into the keep, through the great hall and up the stairs. She barely noticed the leering stares of the Crawford men, her excitement over what she'd learned taking over most of her thoughts. She could barely even focus on what lay ahead when she faced Ian once more. Nothing he did would dim her hope, and her surety she would soon be saved.

* * *

Ian waited for Jamie to bring Marie to him. He ran his fingers over the slender, highly-polished metal collar. It had taken longer than he'd liked to have this new collar made, and every time he saw the bruises on her neck from the one she now wore, he had tried to hurry the smith along. The man had been busy making new weapons for the upcoming battle, but Edward's death had caused a delay while Donal waited for word from The Bruce. Ian used the time to pressure  the smith to finish this piece. The man had done a masterful job, and this elegant collar appeared to be like fine jewelry. 'Twould look lovely around Marie's neck. He hoped she would agree. Most slaves were not so lucky to have such a fine collar.

His fingers clenched around the steel. 'Twas still the mark of a slave, and each day that passed, increased his guilt over what he put the lass through. More than a dozen times every day he gave thought to freeing her, but found he didn't want to let her go. His vengeance had turned into something more, something he refused to face.

He ran a hand over his face and sighed. He'd come to care for her, and could no longer deny it. She had a fire that called fiercely to him, made him anxious to taste her, touch her, take her. He used his claim over her to take what he wanted, no needed, from her. In return, he gave her pleasure as well. He knew it, had seen the longing in her gaze when she thought he wasn't watching her. That she responded so eagerly to his desires, debauched as she'd declared many time, fed his passion for her. Even watching her with Jamie inspired a desperate burning that never fully went out.

He knew Jamie felt similarly. He'd seen his clansman watch her with hunger, and the easy affection Marie shared with Jamie soothed Ian's guilt a little. He couldna show her such tenderness, but was glad she received it from Jamie. 'Twas much the same with Sheila, though Jamie had never shared their bed. But his clansman had shown Ian's wife an understanding of her husband Ian had been unable to completely allow her to see.

Ian had adored his wife, all knew that. In their home, he was her lord, and she obeyed him and tended to his needs. Sheila had loved him, had told him several times every day. She'd borne his son and stood proudly by his side while he ruled his clan beside his father. She had never questioned him, utterly devoted in every way. Ian knew she'd been saddened by the part of himself he'd kept separate, the part that had wooed the young lass when they had been barely old enough to ride a horse. As they'd grown, and his responsibilities grew, he'd cut off that playful side, to tend to more serious matters. Sheila had understood and stopped pining for their earlier carefree days, often turning to Jamie for light-hearted conversation and silly fun. Without the duties of a laird taking his time, Jamie could easily tarry about with no pressing business.

Why did Ian think of this now? He was about to present Marie with a beautiful new collar, and his thoughts should be on her. After he had placed the metal around her neck, he planned to spend the evening in furthering her instruction. He'd been anxious to bury himself in her arse, and tonight, he and Jamie would do just that.

The door opened and Jamie entered, followed by Marie. Something about her seemed more animated than before. For a few moments, Ian wondered at it. He turned his attention to his clansman. Jamie responded to the silent communication with a shrug. Ian crooked his finger at Marie and she stepped slowly closer once Jamie unhooked the chain.

Ian pointed to the floor. "Kneel, slave."

She hesitated, the fire he'd come to adore sparking in her tawny eyes. But she obeyed, falling to her knees before him. He caught the wince as she came in contact with the stone floor.

"Jamie, bind her hands behind her."

"Nay! Why?" Her protest, shrill and sudden, echoed through the room. She tried to resist Jamie as he pulled her arms back and bound her wrists. Apprehension now mingled with the anger in her stare.

"You will thank me for this, lass." He crouched before her and unlocked her collar. Her eyes widened when he pulled it from her neck.

"You ... are you freeing me?"

He shook his head and lifted the new collar. The hope in her eyes had faded, her gaze now focused on the shiny metal in his hands.

"Jamie, lift her hair." Ian watched her, anticipating she might try to resist, but she held herself motionless as Jamie lifted her long black hair. With quick movements, Ian settled the new collar around her neck and locked it. With a finger under her chin, he tilted her head back.

"It looks lovely, lass. And it must surely be more

comfortable."

She nodded, but the tears shining in her eyes squeezed his chest. He fought the urge to draw her into his arms; instead, he stood and looked down at her, forcing a stern expression to his face.

"You should thank me, lass, for giving you such a lovely collar."

"Thank you."

Her whisper barely reached him, and intensified the twisting of his gut. He leaned down and helped her to stand. He debated whether to free her bonds. Her emotions were clearly too raw at the moment, and he suspected if he freed her, she would fight him. He longed to feel her hands on his flesh. He would. Soon. He knew how to reach her.

He turned her about and sliced through the thong holding her wrists together. His supply dwindled. He'd spent two long years preparing the leather strips and he'd used nearly half already. Oddly, he didn't feel any urgency to make more in replacement.

He guided her to the bed and sat, positioning her so she stood facing him. He motioned to Jamie who took a stance beside him. Marie's head remained down. Ian reached out a finger and tipped it back, forcing her to meet his gaze.

His heart splintered to see the despair in the depths of her tawny eyes. Yet, she remained silent, and he recognized a resignation that alarmed him. Without taking his gaze away, he said, "Jamie, I'd like to be alone with Marie tonight."

"Aye." Jamie stood, hesitating beside Marie. He ran a gentle hand along her hair. "It'll be all right, lass."

He leaned over and pressed a kiss to the top of her head. A tiny sound escaped her, and Ian was suddenly, inexplicably, jealous of the tenderness Jamie showed her. Yet, through it all, her gaze remained focused squarely on his. No doubt she longed for the same tenderness from him.

He remained still and silent until the door had closed. Marie continued to stare, saying nothing, though she gave another hitching sound. With a groan, he pulled her into his lap, holding her close and breathing in the sweet, fresh scent he'd come to recognize as solely hers. This little slip of a lass had wormed her way into his heart and he could fight it no longer.

"Why must you hurt me?"

Her tiny-voiced query pierced his soul. He set his jaw, thinking of all he had made her endure in the last weeks. Mayhap 'twas time to gentle his approach.

"'Tis for my pleasure, lass. But also for yours. You canna deny you like it."

She shook her head. "'Twas not what I meant. Your touch, no matter how you give it, does incite ... feelings in me. But why must you shame me, humiliate me? Revenge? You know I don't believe what you say. I want to prove it. Let me."

He didn't know how to respond, because he knew she was wrong. Yet, the doubt that lay below the surface of his need for vengeance poked up again. He knew, with his very soul, who had killed his wife and son.

Didn't he?

What if he had erred? The nagging whisper echoed again, taunting him. The sounds of Sheila's screams, the sight of his son being cut down, rose in his thoughts. He allowed the rage to remind him of his goal.

"You canna prove anything. I saw the pennant."

"Do you care nothing at all for me?"

Another question that left his head spinning and his thoughts stumbling in another direction. He couldna tell her the truth, 'twould give her power over him. He refused to yield. In answer, he tangled his hand in her hair and tilted her head back. Her eyes widened, excitement flaring in their tawny depths and her breath caught, realizing his intention. Her lips parted, but before she dared protest, he covered her mouth with his, stunned when she didn't resist in any way. Instead, she responded with a ferocity he hadn't expected, her arms wrapping tight around his neck.

He gave his vengeance no further thought and lowered her to the bed. The feel of her trembling beneath him made him crazed with lust. He shoved the rough gray dress up over her hips. His hands moved rapidly over her body, the heated feel of her skin like velvet. Whimpering moans escaped her and her hips moved toward him, as if seeking him to fill her. He leaned back and swept the hair from her face.

Her golden eyes slowly opened, clouded with passion. The sight hardened his cock further. His control weakened, he shoved her legs apart, cupping her sex with one hand. Her heat scorched his fingers, her pussy slick with desire. Her fingers tightened in his hair as he stroked her molten folds, savoring each gasping cry. He found the swollen and hard nub of her desire. Her entire body bucked wildly as he teasingly circled it. Her head thrashed and he lowered his mouth to the slender column of her neck. The new collar had warmed against her skin, and the glint of the metal stirred a further sense of possessiveness. She was his. He wouldna let her go, not until he'd sated this boundless need. Her response to his touch had become an obsession, as had the need to drive her to this maddening delight. His heart pounded and he continued to stroke her heat slickened flesh. Her gaze held his, the sight of the adoration he read there making his head spin.

*Jesu,* how had this English lass created such hunger in him? He pinched her clit, covering her mouth to swallow the screams, her body rippling with waves of pleasure. The sensation of her bucking against him almost made him spill his seed before he'd even had a chance to bury himself in her body. He drew away to study her once more, savoring the sight of her flushed cheeks, her chest heaving with each gasping breath. A surge of pride that he'd caused this reaction fed his desire. His cock throbbed, he could wait no longer. He pulled the dress over her head and spread her legs, settling between them.

\* \* \*

Marissa shivered in the sudden chill, despite the fire that had just claimed her. Residual pangs of pleasure still rippled with a fierce echo. The hunger in Ian's eyes held her on the edge of delight. She clung tightly to his shoulders, needing his solid body to help ground her against the wild desire that held her in thrall.

When he held her and touched her like this, with tenderness and desire, she could almost pretend she was not his captive. Or she could admit she didn't mind belonging to him in such a way. His touch had a way of reducing her to nothing but need and heat.

His fingers skimmed along her collar. While lighter and more comfortable than the previous one, it still made clear that, to him, she was merely a possession.

"Mine," he growled.

She held his dark stare, her heart thumping heavily. Something about the way he claimed her verbally said so much more about her position than the metal encircling her neck. Twining her fingers into his hair, she pulled his head down, sealing her mouth against his. 'Twas enough to distract her from the odd emotions stirred by the single uttered word.

His hands on her thighs, spreading her open, sent her spiraling once more into the abyss of pleasure. His rough touch stoked the heat to fever pitch, his fingers filling her in preparation. She buried her face in his neck, not wanting him to see how much she needed him to take her, fill her, drive her to the joyful heights he'd taken her to before. 'Twould only give him more power over her if he knew how much she needed his mastery.

She gasped when he buried his hard cock in her with one swift stroke. Her legs wrapped around him, holding him close. He gave a sharp laugh as she easily met his rhythm. In and out, his hard, hot flesh stroked her inner walls, sending her into a frenzy. Flames, scorching and searing, licked at her skin, feeding the riot upending her senses. Yet, in the center of it all remained a strange calm, an acceptance of his possession.

All thought fled as he lifted her legs, sliding them along his shoulders. The change in position gave him a different angle, and he drove still deeper, until she felt as if they were one, moving at a frantic tempo, yet completely in unison. The pressure in her core intensified with each rough thrust, and finally broke over her in blinding delight, her body tossed in the maelstrom of sizzling sensation. Over and over, the waves of pleasure shocked through her, and above the roaring in her ears, she heard Ian's gruff shout a moment before his seed bathed her sex.

Their harsh breathing mingled and they lay in a heap, the dampness of Ian's body a comforting warmth. When he withdrew from her, she moaned in protest, then sighed in relief as he merely pulled her close and tucked her against his side.

A tear rolled free at the realization she never wanted to leave the haven of his embrace.

# chapter Thirteen

Summer sun warmed the land. Marissa's monotonous task of peeling root vegetables neared an end when she picked up the last. This morning, her thoughts dwelt on her family, and trying to find a way home. Word had come that the prince intended to continue to march north, even though his army slipped into disarray. Would her father be obligated to join him? Suspicion lingered the battle would ultimately be abandoned.

This meant several things to Marissa. If the battle were to be abandoned, 'twould mean the Crawfords had no need to send any men to The Bruce. That left all the warriors in the clan available to Ian. Which meant the possibility strengthened he might return to his plan to attack Montchester.

The possibility also existed her parents would be away from home, likely in London attending to political matters. Her father's opinion and guidance would be sorely needed. 'Twould leave Montchester and her sisters and Rowan at risk. If she could not dissuade Ian from his intentions, she needed to escape and warn Montchester, as well as defend it. But how?

In the last few days, something in Ian's demeanor had changed. The night he had given her the new collar, he had been strangely intense, taking her as though he would a lover. Even now, her heart swelled with the recollection. She no longer made any attempt to deny her love for him, but reality remained clear. He did not share those feelings, despite his recent kinder treatment. More reason she needed to escape.

Her most important reason for fleeing remained her

father and clearing his name. She must prove her father's innocence. Yet, she couldn't do that chained here as she was.

A shadow fell over her and she lifted her head. Jamie smile sent her heart into a racing rhythm. Despite her fierce longing for Ian, his clansman inspired a similar need in her body that nearly matched what she felt for Ian in intensity. He'd been able to wrest reactions and emotions from her with his simple and easygoing charm. Besides, Jamie had been more receptive to her insistence about the attacks. An idea formed, even though she hated using him in such a way. The regret rankled. Why should she care for their comfort? They had none for her.

If only her body could forget their touch. Why did she still crave it? 'Twas a curse she'd bear for a long time.

"How are you this morning, lass?" Jamie asked, taking a seat on the bench beside her. "Did you sleep well last eve?"

Heat bloomed in her face at the recollection of the pleasure she'd shared with him and Ian the previous night. "Aye. Like a babe."

He chuckled and the sight of his warm and affectionate smile set her heart to racing. "Other than that, then, how do you fare today?"

"For a slave, you mean?" Marissa fixed a fierce glare on him, and ignored the way her heart fluttered when he grinned. "How do you think I fare?"

"My guess is, other than your collar, you are faring verra well."

And she had thought him more understanding? "You are as foolish as your clansman then. I am chained here, made to perform chores of a servant, and must endure the hostility of the women. And do not forget Colin, who enjoys taunting me with my position."

She shuddered at the recollection of the loathsome man's leering insults. He'd taken to seeking her out each morn to do so. So far, she managed to ignore him, and kept the fact of his visits to herself, but she knew 'twas only a matter of time before the man grew bolder.

"He still dares to come near you?" Jamie's frown grew positively menacing. "I will put an end to that. Else he'll face the consequences."

"Nay, you will just make it worse. He seems content to shout his insults and leave."

"Ian willna like it."

"Ian doesn't care how I suffer."

Jamie fixed a steady gaze on her. "He cares, lass, more than he'll admit."

She wished Jamie spoke the truth, but knew otherwise. If Ian cared, he would free her, or listen to her. Believe her. She shook her head.

"Nay, I am but a means to revenge. He won't stop until he has broken me. I won't break, Jamie. He'll not have his satisfaction." She slammed her fist into her open palm.

He chuckled. "You are a fierce one. I think 'tis one of many things Ian likes about you."

"If he liked me, he would listen to reason and free me!"

Jamie sighed. "He has no choice, lass. He must keep his pride."

"Pride? At my expense? I've done nothing to goad him into the way he treats me like I'm an animal. I will be free, Jamie. I can't say when or how, but I will. I did nothing to deserve being treated like this. I can prove his need for vengeance is focused on the wrong man. You know this."

"I only know what you told me, lass. You have no proof."

"But I can get it. You spoke to him, and he's still as stubborn as an ass!"

Jamie avoided her gaze for a moment, then met her stare directly. "He's lost a lot, and he needs to find vengeance for that."

"His wife and son. I know. But my father did not do it. If Ian would just listen to me, I can help him find the real murderers."

"I was there, Marie. I saw the knights. The pennant."

Marissa shook her head, even as she recognized the doubt in his gaze. A surge of triumph spiked in her heart. "You also admitted, you didn't see it clearly. I know my father was in Wales."

"He served the Hammer of the Scots. The English king ordered many raids. Your father obeyed him."

"Nay. Not in something like this. My father is an honorable man. He is often credited with making Edward see reason. I *know* this. I will make you all see."

"You will have a difficult time convincing Ian. He's still sworn to destroy your father."

"By using me."

"Mayhap at first, 'twas his intention. Now, he has different reasons for wanting to keep you. I canna blame him." He gave her a sly smile and a wink.

Her core tightened in response, and moisture dampened her sex. She forced the sudden and sharp desire back and tried to concentrate on his words. Not the sight of his fingers as he rested his hand on his knee. The recollection of those hands roaming her body drew a shiver. She looked away.

"What do you mean he wants to keep me?" The hope Ian truly possessed kinder feelings for her grew stubbornly stronger. Those thoughts were no safer than dwelling on her desires for Jamie. God's teeth, she'd worked so hard to give up the longing to be wanted for herself, and not as a tool for vengeance, yet it still held her in its tenacious grip. Fighting it left her so tired.

"He does care for you, lass. You have turned him on his ear."

The solemnness of his voice convinced her Jamie believed his words. She stared for a moment, still not sure she had heard correctly. Or dared to believe.

"Nay, you are mistaken."

"I'm not. Afore Colin kidnapped you, Ian was poised to strike your home."

"I know that. But I don't see how that has anything to do with -"

"The moment he saw you, his plans changed. His need to destroy Montchester fades, a little each day. He's seen to your protection more than once, if you recall."

"You call seducing me and tormenting me, and spanking me protection? You Scots have an odd way of seeing things."

Jamie threw his head back and laughed. For a moment, Marissa wondered what Ian would be like if he ever allowed himself to laugh that way.

Jamie leaned in close, his voice low. "Lass, you have a liking for the darker side of desire. 'Tis nothing wrong with that. You're lucky Ian shares your tastes."

"So that's why he didn't attack my father? Because he likes to cause pain while lying with a woman?" She hoped he didn't notice the way her words faltered. That very pain enticed her, even now.

"Nay, because he saw something in you that called to him, and 'twas stronger than his need for revenge."

"As for that, Jamie, I think the pleasure he gets out of hurting me is part of his vengeance." Still, heat rose within her.

"Never forget, lass, you like what we give you. Your body responds to the wicked sensations. I saw the proof myself, lass, and I see it now, just the way you're trembling at the mention of our play."

Heat flooded her face. She looked away. His low chuckle sent shivers along her spine. He leaned in close, his breath against her neck. She squeezed her eyes shut, but not before she caught sight of Elizabeth glaring menacingly.

Jamie's mouth near her ear started sparks of longing, and though she tried to ignore the sensations, she trembled, her longing intensifying.

"He has asked me to give him the night alone with you. Again. I'm not happy with that, I had plans for you tonight. Methinks he is tired of sharing. His possession of you has turned into your possession of him. But I'll be back tomorrow, lass, of that you can be sure."

He was gone when she turned to face him. Ian wanted to be alone with her again tonight? 'Twas the third time in five days. The blood rushed in her ears, and she shook her head to clear the haze of desire Jamie's nearness had inspired. Ian wanted her alone again. Surely that meant something. But what?

"Sassenach slut! Soon, you'll be spreading your legs for all the Crawford men, won't you?"

Marissa looked up at Elizabeth. Anger quickly replaced the wispy yearning. "Leave me alone."

She moved to place the last of the cut potatoes into the basket. When she stood to step past Elizabeth, the other woman tugged on the chain, bringing Marissa up short.

"Listen well, whore. Ian was once mine, and though he toys with you now, he will eventually tire of you and return to me. You'll be sold or traded, or killed."

"I think not." Marissa straightened her spine and jerked the chain from Elizabeth's grasp. "If he'd wanted me dead, I'd already be long buried. He keeps me because I give him what he wants. And needs."

Elizabeth once again yanked on the chain, wrenching Marissa to her knees. "You are a slave, nothing more. When he tires of you, you'll wish he'd killed you long ago."

Marissa's fury consumed her and she caught sight of the dagger on the table. She shouldn't, though she longed to slash the blade along the other woman's snarling face. Elizabeth yanked again on the chain. Any restraint fled. Marissa's fingers closed around the knife and she picked it up, snatching the chain free and standing. Within moments, the tip of the blade rested near Elizabeth's chin. The other woman froze.

"Get away from me before I give in to the urge to slice your throat," Marissa growled the threat, pleased with the way Elizabeth paled and backed away.

"You will pay for this." She looked around, but found only Fiona. "You saw! She attacked me."

Fiona shook her head. "Nay, I saw you attack her."

Elizabeth narrowed her eyes. "Ian will hear of this."

"He willna believe you, Beth, so dinna waste your time." Fiona shooed her away and turned to Marissa. Her angry expression softened. "Dinna fash yourself, lass. Ian knows how she is. He will see her lies for what they are."

Marissa prayed Fiona was right. Just as hard as she prayed Ian cared for her, even a little bit. Her hands shook as she accepted the cup of ale from Fiona, and drank deeply to soothe her jangled senses. Fury and fear mingled and left her knees weak and her stomach rolling. What sort of punishment would she be made to endure over this?

\* \* \*

Ian didn't understand Marie's quiet demeanor. Not once had she glared at him from her seat on the floor at his feet. He'd spoken with his sister, before Elizabeth had cornered him. He'd told the shrew he didna believe her lies, and to stay away from Marie. Mayhap 'twas what bothered the lass. He needed to tell her he didna blame her for her actions in defending herself.

He sighed heavily. The guilt seemed to intensify more each day, each trial that she faced because of him. He'd brought her here and thrust this whole mess upon her. His constant concern for her had grown to a fierce nagging he couldn't silence long enough to pay attention to Donal's words. At least this afternoon, his gift had been completed. He would give it to her tonight. He couldn't tell her he cared, 'twould weaken his position over her, but he could certainly show her signs of affection. He no longer felt anything akin to hate, and somehow, the need for her to know had grown impossible to resist.

"Ian, are you listening, lad?" Donal's voice cut into Ian's concentration.

"I'm sorry, I wasn't."

Donal gave a sly smile, his gaze sliding briefly to Marie. "I see that. I was saying Longshanks' death gives The Bruce a great advantage."

Ian forced himself to nod in response, though he didn't care one whit about the coming battle between the English and Scottish armies. He glanced at Marie, who still knelt silently, head down, hands folded in her lap. Was this some game or did she truly fear what might happen this eve?

"Ian, you're not listening again."

Ian looked at Donal, and shrugged apologetically. "I'm sorry. What did you say?"

"He said The Bruce will not need as many men as first thought."

Ian recognized the sneer in Colin's voice, but chose not to respond directly. He kept his gaze level with Donal's.

"Dinna worry about my plans," Ian said. "I havena decided when I will return to Montchester. With the English king now dead, I expect his son willna be able to manage the army."

"Aye, but Edward has many earls at his command, men who can lead an army." Donal's gaze flicked again toward Marie.

"Are you saying I should seek out The Panther on the battlefield?" Though he didn't look at her, from the corner of his eye, he noticed Marie's head lift.

"It may be an easy way to achieve your vengeance." The Crawford laird fell silent, giving Ian a meaningful look.

"I will think on it." He drained his mug of ale and placed the tankard on the table. "I will speak with you on the morrow. Come."

He directed the last to Marie, tugging on her chain until she stood beside him. She stared brazenly, and he recognized her struggle to keep from voicing the questions the conversation had certainly spurred. He held back a smile and he turned to the stair.

As soon as he closed the chamber door and barred it, the barrage began.

"Do you truly think to face my father on a battlefield? You stand no chance against him. Do you think you can even recognize him? He won't be flying his pennant, you know. You shouldn't go. The English army will lay waste to The Bruce and his men."

"Do you worry for me, lass?" He folded his arms.

"Nay, of course not. You can't be planning to drag me into battle with you. What if you get yourself killed, then what happens to me?"

He chuckled. "I'm sure Donal and Jamie will work something out." He kept his tone light and carefree, rewarded with her muted growl of annoyance.

"What makes you think I won't be gone long before your body is carried back here?"

"Because Donal will take good care of my property while I am at war."

Why did he continue to belittle her? Why could he never remember to use kindness with her, instead of dominance? He sighed.

"I heard what happened today in the kitchen."

She paled, her throat moving. "And what were you told?"

"That Elizabeth attacked you and you defended yourself admirably."

Her lips twitched. "Aye?"

He nodded and grinned. "My sister told me all of it before Beth could. She willna try to hurt you again."

"So you believe I didn't attack her?"

"Aye."

"Thank you."

The fondness and warmth in her eyes stirred a wealth of sensations he couldn't name. He gave a thought to the gift, but decided to wait.

"Ian?"

"Aye?"

"Will you please listen to me? About my father?"

Her words shredded his hope to get through this night without a fierce confrontation. He should have expected she wouldna let go of her theory, but he didna like the way her insistence weakened his. She was *his* slave, she was to obey him.

He shook his head and undid his belt, quickly unwinding his kilt and shirt. When Marie remained still, he waved a hand toward her. She folded her arms and lifted her chin.

"Dinna think to refuse, lass. Remove the dress, or I'll do it for you."

She hesitated, then shook her head. "You will have to tear it from me. I'll not submit to you this time, you mule-headed oaf! You don't have the decency God gave a pig. You are an animal, and I should've known better than to try to use reason with you."

He grinned at her insults. So she wanted to fight? He would grant her wish, but she would soon realize she couldna best him.

"Verra well, lass."

She backed away when he stepped toward her, but his grip on the chain prevented her from fleeing too far. He pulled her close, grinning at the defiant anger lining her face. When she stopped barely inches from him, he placed his hand in the neck of her kirtle and yanked. The fabric tore easily, the threads shredding apart oddly loud in the silent chamber. She gave a gasp and tried to shove him away, but he merely hauled her against him. She pummeled him with her fists, but he simply lifted her and hoisted her over his shoulder.

She shrieked, now pounding his back, all manner of insulting names spilling from her lips. "Bastard! Maggot! Half-witted pig! I will see your heathen arse swinging from the gallows!"

She gave a cry when he tossed her to the bed. A moment later, she scrambled to her knees, her dark hair flying around her head like a wild storm cloud, tawny eyes flashing like lightning. Her hands, still balled into tight fists, remained at her sides, but he sensed her readiness to fight.

He shook his head and reached for her. As he suspected, she lunged, but he easily caught her wrists and yanked them together, holding her still with one hand while he reached for the tattered remains of her dress. Pulling her arms behind her, he wound the torn fabric around her wrists. She stilled, but her eyes maintained the fire of her fury, as well as the heat of desire. He saw it clearly, despite her anger. He grinned.

"I will have such fun with you tonight, lass."

He paused, running a finger along her jaw. She jerked away, but he merely slid his hand around to cup her head, holding her still while he devoured her mouth. With his lips and tongue, he finally coaxed a shuddering response from her, despite her obvious attempt to remain unaffected. When he drew away, she gasped for breath. Aye, she wanted him. No matter what else came between them, this passion never seemed to fade.

\* \* \*

Marissa stared at Ian, breathing heavily. Her cleft quickly grew wet, throbbing with anticipation. Damn him, and damn her treacherous body's response. His eyes glazed with passion. The sight, as always, set her heart into an uneven rhythm.

"Do you see you canna fight me, lass?"

She lifted her chin. He chuckled and the sound excited both her desire and anger.

"I won't submit to you again."

He ran a finger down her cheek again and despite her resolve, she shivered. His smile broadened.

"You like what I do to you. Your words say otherwise, but I see how your body responds to my touch."

"Nay." The whispered protest sounded hollow even to her own ears.

His finger continued its path, down along her neck to her breastbone. Heat flared from the point he touched her and her nipples hardened painfully in the cool chamber. He moved lower still, just his finger, circling her breast, until the tip throbbed. He pulled his finger away and brought it to his mouth, his gaze holding hers as he licked the tip. He moved back to her breast, and placed his finger directly on top of the pebbled peak and gently rubbed.

Marissa sucked in a deep breath, her legs trembling. She clenched her fingers, and her jaw, but the moan escaped anyway. She wanted him to stop, she wanted more. She bit her lip, unable to resist the need growing stronger with each second. He continued to tease her, until she swayed and nearly fell against him.

He lowered her to the bed, her wrists still caught behind her, in the remains of her only clothing. She might be able to pull free, but oddly, she didn't attempt to. He loomed over her, but instead of alarm, only eagerness pulsed through her. His hard cock brushed her thigh, his flesh searing her skin. Her sex swelled and heated, and she gave up the last remnants of any intention to resist. She let her legs fall open, telling him without words what she wanted.

He grinned, clearly recognizing her submission, but shook his head. She knew then he meant to torment her all night. Her body tensed in preparation. In eagerness.

She closed her eyes briefly, to steady the torrent of emotion. She wanted this, wanted the way he would drive her to pleasure, yet hold it back, over and over, until she begged for release.

Recognizing his delight in her torture stung as well as pleased her. She liked knowing he enjoyed her responses, even if he humbled her with his wicked ways. He could be cold and demeaning in front of others, but when they were alone like this, he revealed his hunger. For her.

The knowledge soothed her distress. When his fingers glided toward her cleft, she arched toward him, seeking more of his touch.

"Aye, lass, you do want this." He slid into her sex, his fingers finding her clit and teasing it to further hardness. She tossed her head, her legs straining as she strove for more of his touch.

"Dinna rush me." His scolding words were tempered by the husk of his voice, revealing his own intense desire. He continued to touch her lightly, until her entire being focused on the center of her body, and Ian's gently caressing fingers.

"Ian, please," she moaned.

"Hush, lass, and let me see to you. 'Tis my decision to allow your pleasure. Or not."

She cried out against the last words, her hips moving in time with his ghostlike touch. Fire radiated outward, until she tasted the bitter flames. When he lowered his mouth to her breast, his tongue circling the tight nipple, her world shattered into shards of blinding light, her body tossed wildly with the force of the release. When Ian bit into her breast, she cried his name, and pressed more of her flesh into his searching mouth, savoring his fingers still moving over her wet sex making her body dance like a puppet. When the tempest passed and she could hear again, she opened her eyes.

"You come so nicely for me." His thick voice drew a shiver, her sex clenching in an echo of her climax. The pleased note of his voice suffused her with a warmth she enjoyed far more than she should.

She curled into him, his arms coming around to hold her, even while he tore the fabric holding her wrists together. His fingers lightly stroked along her arms and back, soothing the ache. Soon, she again pressed against him, his hard cock nudging her entrance. She raised her leg, sliding it over his hip and driving her sex against the tip of his erection. He groaned and took her mouth in a bruising kiss as he thrust, filling her with one stroke. She gasped against his lips, already trembling toward another powerful release.

Ian kept his movements slow, just enough to tantalize but not enough to send her spiraling into delight. He pulled his mouth away. She stared into his dark eyes, loving these moments when he let his guard down and showed her his true self. The hunger, the wanting, in his stare was for her. She clung to him as he rocked within her, steady and deep, each stroke intensifying the heat until she panted his name.

He pressed her closer, grasping her hip and angling her so he could penetrate deeper.

"Feel how I fill you, lass," he growled, pinching her nipple and thrusting harder. She arched against him, incapable of words. Her nails scraped along his shoulders, and she moved in time with him, until a hoarse groan and a wild, deep stroke preceded his release, his seed pulsing into her. The world faded to white around her, his name torn from her lips in a hoarse cry as the pleasure overcame her. Her body rocked against his, the pleasure escalating to an explosion that curled her toes.

When her senses returned, she became aware of Ian studying her. The affection in his eyes suffused her with a powerful surge of satisfaction. His soft cock slid free of her body, drawing a moan of protest. He chuckled, tucking her against him and pressing a tender kiss to her forehead.

"Ah, lass, you soothe my soul."

She remained silent, the lump in her throat leaving her unable to speak. His words strengthened the fondness he'd already wrested from her. Her eyes burned. She was doomed.

# chapter
# fourteen

Marissa woke with a start. Her body tingled; recalling the way Ian had loved her last night filled her with contented warmth. Jamie's words from yesterday morn echoed in her thoughts. Was it truly possible Ian cared? The way he had looked at her this time almost had her believing it to be true. She recalled his last words before sinking into slumber.

Not an admission of love or any other affectionate feelings. A statement of possession, one that held a hint of affection. Or did it? If she were honest with herself, she might admit she wanted him to care, even if only a little. *Fool. You're nothing but a means to revenge.*

She shifted, trying to resettle herself. Something seemed different. Realization stole over her. He hadn't refastened the chain! Heart pounding, comprehension came into startlingly clear focus. Her chance had come! She glanced at him, sprawled on his back, sound asleep. She lifted the blanket and slipped out, shivering when her bare feet hit the stone floor. With careful movements and stealth she had learned from her brother, she silently pulled the only remaining itchy gray kirtle over her head. Her soft boots followed and she wrapped her hair in a knot at the back of her head.

For a moment, she stood quietly, watching Ian sleep. Her heart ached, then raced, then ached again, at the recollection of all that had happened between them in the last several weeks. How much she'd changed. Her core tightened to recall his frantic lovemaking this very eve. She closed her eyes at the sting of tears.

He'd kidnapped her, ruined her. She would do well to

remember that and look forward to her revenge. She turned away, slowly creeping to the door. Recently, he'd gotten careless. Her heart squeezed at the idea his oblivion might be due to other reasons. Could it be because he had grown to trust her, even just a little?

He *was* beginning to trust her. She paused, her fingers clutching the door handle. The implications gave new life to the absurd thought she'd had not more than a few days ago. The idea of being by Ian's side as more than just a slave sliced into her already raw emotions. She shook her head and opened the door.

The sting of tears angered her. Why should she be sad? An image of Ian's face, intense in pleasure, along with one of Jamie's laughing countenance, remained firmly in the forefront of her thoughts. Damn them to hell and back! She needed her freedom. Their wicked treatment had robbed her of sense. 'Twas time to get it back.

It took some time to make her way out of the keep and to the stables. Every snore, every creak, every rustle in the night air, gave her pause. Luck certainly had worked in her favor this time though, for she soon stood outside the keep's main doors.

She approached the stables, the sight of one of the Crawford men perched in a chair against the wall giving her pause. She hesitated before realizing he too slept. How would she get one of the animals past him? Or anyone else for that matter? Much as she didn't like what she must do, she had no choice.

Spotting a heavy shovel, she quietly moved toward it, her fingers curling around the handle. Once more, her training aided her when she crept up silently to the man and, closing her eyes and offering a silent apology, brought the shovel's blade down on his head. He slumped out of his seat and fell to the ground. Marissa laid a hand on his chest. His heart still beat strong. Relieved she hadn't killed him, she hurried into the stable and quickly spotted Ian's mount. It didn't take long to saddle the beast, and on her way past the unconscious Scotsman, she knelt and took his dagger from its sheath. His sword lay across his hips, the odd angle caused by his fall. She slid it free, hefting the unfamiliar steel in her hands. 'Twould do, was made of fine steel and crafted with care. For a moment, she admired the skill of the Crawford's smith, then turned her attention back to the task. She needed the sheath, as well.

"Ugh!" Rolling the man over, she quickly divested him of the belt and sheath, and climbed into the saddle. Adjusting her weapons, she headed the animal toward the south, in the general direction of England and Montchester.

She didn't look back.

\* \* \*

Ian stirred, reaching for Marie. Finding the place beside him empty, he forced heavy lids open, expecting to see her tending her needs. His vision adjusted easily to the darkened room, owing to the dying fire, A quick perusal of the chamber knotted his gut. She wasna here. A panic he'd never known sliced into him. At the same time he threw back his blankets, a loud cry of alarm echoed about the castle.

He wrapped his kilt around himself and hurried from the room. Arriving arrived belowstairs, he was greeted by the sight of one of the Crawford clansman, rubbing his head, his stance unsteady as he was led to a chair by the hearth. Ian began to put the pieces together in his head.

"I was struck!" He groaned and leaned heavily over the table. One of the women pressed a damp cloth to his head.

"By who?"

"Your slave, Ian! Couldna be anyone else. She attacked me, stole my sword, and your horse!"

He stared at the man for a few moments, thinking. Wishing. Praying, he'd misheard. Donal Crawford's voice cut through the growing anger turning his vision red.

"She's escaped, lad. You best find her. She could get hurt out there alone."

Ian's fingers clenched and unclenched. She'd escaped. Stolen his horse and a weapon and left. Left *him*. He didn't want to acknowledge the pain stabbing through him, twisting his innards, feeding his rage. How could she have left him?

He gave Donal a curt nod. "Aye, I'll bring her back. And make her regret stealing my horse." He'd make her regret more than that. When he found her, he would punish her for committing such crimes. For leaving him. A thread of despair tinged his anger.

"Ian, the lass has only done what you yourself would have in her position. Dinna be too hard on her when you find her."

"Donal, I will handle her as I must." He didn't want to acknowledge the reality of Donal's words. His own thoughts were too scattered to make much sense. The only thing he remained aware of was that he must get Marie back.

Donal heaved a sigh. "Very well. Who will you take with you?"

"I go alone."

"Are you daft, man? Willna be an easy task finding a lass who doesna want to be found. You'll need others to help you."

Ian shook his head. "She hasna been gone more than a couple of hours. I willna have any trouble finding her."

Donal seemed to want to say something more, but kept silent. Ian turned, and went back upstairs to gather his sword and dagger. He picked up the small sack with his gift. He opened it and took out the bracelet. Polished to match the collar around Marie's neck, he'd also taken the few stones of the MacCallums he'd managed to save, including Sheila's emerald pendant and had them added to the cuff, so it looked like a fine enough piece of jewelry for a queen. The emerald glinted in the rising sunlight, seeming somehow a mocking taunt. He'd planned to give it to Marie, but he'd forgotten it in the explosive moment they'd come together. He should've known he couldna trust her. He shoved the metal back into the sack and fastened the pouch to his belt. He strode back belowstairs, coming face to face with Jamie.

"I'm coming with you."

Ian shook his head. "Nay. I do this alone."

"I can help."

Ian stared at his clansman, and shook his head again. "Nay. I will seek her and bring her back. Await me here."

Jamie sighed. "Verra well. But dinna hurt her, Ian. She just wants her freedom."

"Dinna tell me how to handle my slave, Jamie." His pride had been wounded, he wouldna admit to any weaker feelings toward Marie in front of the staring Crawfords.

"I care for the lass, too, dinna forget. Heed my words, and dinna be a fool."

Ian scowled and moved toward the door. He caught Colin's smug grin. His fingers itched with the urge to land a rain of blows on the other man. This 'twas all his fault to begin with.

"You have something to say, Colin?"

Colin shook his head, his grin widening. "Nah. No need to tell everyone what they already know."

"And what would that be?"

"That you canna handle one wee lass."

Ian clenched his fists, holding back his rage. "You dinna know what you speak of, Colin. Now stand aside lest I force you to."

Colin gave a sarcastic wink and moved over to let Ian pass. While he strode to the stables, he toyed with the idea of not returning here once he'd found Marie. He couldna do that. Jamie and his sister needed him, and he still had his vengeance to mete out. And a slave to punish.

His cock hardened at the thought of Marie over his

lap, her bottom reddening as he spanked her, before tying her to his bed and taking her fiercely, reminding her of her place. He smiled. He would find her and when he finished with her, she'd never want to leave him again.

He stopped mid-stride. Where had that come from? Why did he care if she wanted to stay or not? The choice wasna hers to make. She would remain with him, as his slave, until he saw fit to release her, whether to freedom, or to someone else.

"Ian!"

He turned to see Jamie jogging toward him. He scowled. He didna need another lecture. "What is it, Jamie?" He turned back to the barn.

"Dinna sulk, 'twill not help you think clearly."

"What the hell is that supposed to mean?" He scanned the barn, determining which horse to use. Jamie's mount would do nicely.

"You're angry. And you're hurt."

"Hurt? Are you daft, man?" Yet, he couldn't deny deep inside, to himself, he did feel pain. This type of pain he knew, and it fueled his anger once more that he endured it yet again. "The lass needs to be reminded of her place. She is nothing more than a slave."

Jamie shook his head. "Dinna be so stubborn. Is it so terrible to admit you could be wrong and that you care? Your family died, Ian. But you didn't. You survived. You canna keep living as though you are dead as well."

"You don't know what I feel!" Ian turned back to his horse, adjusting the leather.

"Mayhap not completely. I didna lose a wife and a son, but you, and Fiona, are my only family. And for you I keep going and live my life. Here is your chance. 'Tis clear to me how you feel. The look on your face when you realized she fled ... it told me more than any protests you'd make. You want to keep her, slave or no."

"You dinna know what you speak of."

"Aye, Ian, I can see it. The way you look at her, the

way you touch her. You might share her with me, but 'tis obvious to all she is special to you. Believe me, I understand how you feel. I feel the same. She's a special lass, and if you treat her well, she'll care for you in return. I think she already does, despite her flight. You can make her want to stay. I want you to make her stay. Willingly. You have the power to do so."

Ian shook his head. Yet he knew Jamie was right on some level. Hadn't he just thought of having her back beside him, no matter what role she took? He preferred she agreed to return to him. He scowled, and Jamie chuckled.

"Treat her with kindness, Ian, and she will stay with you until you're both wrinkled and gray. If you dinna take care, I'll steal her away."

"Dinna threaten me. She is a slave, Jamie. You'd best remember that." He knew 'twas his anger speaking now, because letting the agony out in place of his rage would leave him bleeding and raw. Aware of the many eyes watching the exchange, he left the anger in control. He would not show any weakness before the Crawfords.

Ian finished cinching the horse and mounted up. Checking his sword at his side, he gave Jamie a nod and rode out without another word. He would find her ere long, and then he would see she never escaped him again.

\* \* \*

The ebony blackness of the night slowly gave way to a dusky gray as the sun began to rise. Marissa looked around, taking note of the landscape. Based on the rising sun, she headed in the right direction.

She patted the horse, wishing for the chance to make him run, but didn't dare until she had more light. As soon as the sky brightened further, she'd give the animal his head. She had to put more distance between herself and Ian.

Had he awakened yet, did he know she was gone? Was he looking for her? Her heart gave an odd jump and her stomach tightened at the thought of his reaction when he realized she'd escaped him. Likely, he'd be furious.

*You'll be punished. Publicly.* His words from the first night they'd arrived at his home echoed in her head. The very thought of how he could punish her drew a quiver and a corresponding tingle in her core. The recollection of the times he'd spanked her, sending heat and desire flooding through her body came at her with blinding speed. An image of him and Jamie looming over her intensified the hunger, her pussy swelling, getting wet. She shook her head. He may have introduced her to the pleasures of sex, and the pain he inflicted on her, but she refused to let that rule her needs. Once she'd returned home, safe behind Montchester's walls, she would forget, put the memories of these last weeks behind her.

With a heavy sigh, she knew she'd never forget. For the rest of her life, she would hold the memories of her time with Ian in her heart. While she hated the way he'd humiliated her, she couldn't deny she still loved him. She'd seen glimpses of his tender, caring side. That part of him had touched her as deeply as his wicked sexual games. She ached for his loss, knowing the agony he'd endured drove him. She wanted to soothe that pain for him. The only way she knew how was to make him see he was wrong about her father and help him find the real culprits. She didn't want to deny him his vengeance, she wanted to ensure he exacted it against the right people. As long as she remained enslaved by him, she could never do that.

The sky grew pink, then orange, and finally the sun rose higher in the sky, and Marissa squinted against the brightness. Seeing nothing but flat fields ahead spurred her excitement. She tightened the reins and urged Ian's horse into a run. The slow frustrating pace of the nighttime hours faded and she leaned low over the horse's neck, covering great lengths of terrain. She had to keep moving. At the same time, the need to be vigilant, alert to the possible presence of others while still in Scotland. Once she crossed into England, she could seek refuge with English citizens. How long before she reached there? The danger of running into other Scotsmen, possibly even The Bruce spurred her need to hurry.

Montchester lay an entire day's ride beyond the border. Thinking back on the journey to the Uplands, she guessed she still had another full day and night before she reached England. Possibly more. She couldn't afford to waste a single moment.

The thought of home and safety, her mother's warm embrace, her father's proud smile, sparked a burst of sorrow. Would they still welcome her? Would her father seek to avenge her honor? She honestly didn't know, even though she hoped they would want her back. Her parents loved her, she knew that. Just as she knew her father would want Ian to pay for his crimes.

Why did the thought of turning Ian over to her father cause a knifing pain in her heart? She forced herself to focus on her journey, continuing south, each stride of the animal beneath her taking her closer to home.

She slowed the horse to rest him, once more studying her surroundings. She'd seen that stand of trees before, on the journey north. 'Twas where Ian had first shared her with Jamie. Her stomach knotted at the recollection, her body aching for their touch. She held back a despairing sob, shamed at how she wanted to be between the two men again, while they drove her body to unimaginable pleasure with their wicked and depraved games. With a shake of her head, she urged the animal past the grove and on to the edge of the forest.

Another hour passed. Marissa wiped her brow. Her stomach rumbled, reminding her of the unplanned haste of her flight. The sun grew warm and she would need to stop soon, find water and rest before setting off again.

How long had she been riding? How much closer to England had she traveled?

By now, Ian knew she'd left. Did he search for her? Her heart raced. Part of her wanted him to forget her and let her go, but the other part of her, the more insistent part, wanted him to come after her. Why? Little doubt lingered he would simply let her go; she'd stolen weapons and his horse. For that alone, he would follow. She wanted him to seek her for other reasons, reasons she didn't want to examine.

She needed to cover more ground, put more distance between them before he caught up. She didn't want to run the horse again yet. He'd carried her a long way already and he deserved the rest. She'd ridden along the edge of the forest for a while now, but perhaps now 'twas time to lose herself in the coolness of the trees. Mayhap she would find a stream where she could water the mount.

While she rode, her thoughts drifted again to Ian, the way he could make her feel with just one touch, or a glance. Damn it, she couldn't be missing him! He was a kidnapper, a heathen Scot, and not fit to grovel at her feet. He would pay for what he'd done to her, her father would ensure that. Immediately after that thought, a despair took hold of her.

The nights and days of passion she'd shared with Ian assailed her with a ferocity that left her breathless, her flesh heated and aching. No one would ever make her body sing like that again, not that she would ever let another man touch her that way again. After the delights she'd enjoyed with Ian, no one could ever compare.

The horse suddenly perked up, easing into a slow trot. He must smell water. She let him go at his own pace, smiling when they rode up to the banks of a small stream. While the horse lowered his head to drink, she slipped from the saddle with a relieved sigh.

Her legs wobbled a bit, but she soon steadied herself. She knelt beside the water, cupping her hands to sip some then splashed her face. She adjusted her dress, wishing she had something more suitable to wear. With the damned metal collar around her neck and the drab kirtle, she would have difficulty convincing anyone of her noble birth. She would deal with the issue should it arise. For now, she had to remain hidden and alert to anyone who might be near, though she hadn't seen a soul since her departure.

She should be glad of that, for anyone she might encounter would certainly pose danger. She stood, stretching, and walked slowly as the horse munched some grass. She removed the sword from the sheath and held it before her, testing its weight. She smiled, thankful she had convinced her brother to teach her how to handle such a heavy weapon. Even so, the unfamiliar blade remained difficult to swing. She re-sheathed the sword and looked to the sky.

The sun had risen higher, 'twould be noon ere long. She must continue. After a few more minutes, she mounted and guided the horse southwest. How much longer before she reached England?

The sound of hoofbeats, coming up fast, drew her from her thoughts. She guided the horse toward the trees, determined to hide.

She dared a glance over her shoulder, her eyes widening. It couldn't be! She kicked at the horse's flanks, but he didn't pick up his pace.

"Move, you beast," she urged. Another glance over her shoulder confirmed who approached. Ian. How the hell had he found her so fast? He must have discovered her flight within an hour. Else he wouldn't have caught up so quickly. She kicked the horse again and he thankfully broke into a run. Behind her, Ian gave chase, having obviously seen her.

"Damn! Run, you beast, run! Faster."

A loud war cry split the air. To her horror, the sound brought the animal to a complete stop. Unprepared, she found herself flying over his head, landing with a heavy thud on the ground. She gasped, her vision blurry, and she struggled for air. Ian approached and she forced herself up, pulling the sword from its sheath and taking a stance.

Ian still neared, drawing his own sword. The amusement on his face angered her further, but she held it in check, needing to keep her focus. Her chance had come and she didn't intend to waste it.

She twirled the blade in her hands, the unfamiliar weight of the steel settling into her grip while she tested the sword.

"Well now, lass, didna get very far, did you?"

"I'll get farther once I dispatch you."

He laughed, the sound angering her. She swung the sword toward him, a flicking motion that quickly had him lifting his own steel. The amusement faded from his face and he blocked her blow, the blades making an unholy scream as they slid against each other. She drew away briefly then forged on, driving him back under a rain of strikes. He blocked each one, easily twisting away from her reach and making her charge for him again.

With a scream of rage, she lunged, withdrew, lunged again. Over and over, until she finally sliced past his block and landed a glancing blow on his opposite shoulder. The calm that came over his face alarmed her. She readied herself for another attack when Ian glanced at his wound.

He turned and shrugged. "Barely a slice, lass, surely you can do better."

She recognized his taunt as a way to make her angry. Careless. She gave him a grim smile and focused all of her concentration on taking down the man before her.

She approached slowly, moving from side to side, careful not to betray her intentions. With a quick feint to her right, Ian moved with her, prepared to block. At the last moment, she lunged in the opposite direction. Only his speed prevented her from landing a deeper blow, her blade once again going wide of her target. Her frustration grew. She was tired and wielding an unfamiliar weapon, and Ian's skill easily surpassed hers. She curled her fingers around the hilt, studying his stance, looking for a weak spot to drive at.

His gaze dropped to her chest, and she took her chance, lunging forward once again. Ian blocked the strike, this time catching her arm and sliding his blade along hers with a screech that echoed in the otherwise still glen. A quick twist of his wrist, and the sword was wrenched out of her grasp, sent to the ground several feet away. She screamed her outrage and reached for the dagger still tucked in the belt. Ian anticipated her move and disarmed her again, a quick twist of his arm sending her flying to the ground on her back.

He stood over her, his broad shoulders blocking the fading sun. She barely had a chance to register the ominous clouds rolling in overhead. She wanted to howl in frustration but couldn't take a deep enough breath to do so. Instead, she pounded the ground with her fists and rolled over, still trying to steady her gasps for air. Ian's hands were on her shoulders, pulling her up. She fought as best she could, but still weakened by her inability to breathe steadily could not fend him off when he bound her wrists before her. She swung her fists at him, but he caught her by the arms before she made contact.

"Damn you!" she shrieked, her breathing still as erratic as her heartbeat. "You bastard, let me go!" She kicked at him, but he evaded her foot, his expression erupting into fury.

"You will make your punishment that much worse if you dinna stop."

"Will you whip me this time, you heartless heathen? Go ahead, do your worst. I'll be free of you one way or another." She recognized the lack of conviction in her words. At that moment, she knew she was truly damned.

"You stole a horse and nearly killed a man. You attacked me and drew blood. A whipping is the least of your worries. Were I in your place, I'd be more worried about losing a hand. Or worse."

She gulped. He wouldn't! Would he? She barely had time to think about it before he hauled her into his arms then tossed her over his shoulder. She pummeled his back with her bound hands, earning several sharp swats on her bottom.

"You will pay! I will have your head! You will regret everything you've done to me!"

Her words were met by three more blows to her arse. She gasped, her body responding with a clenching in her core. She squirmed, trying to assuage the sudden fire, and hold onto her anger at the same time. Another spank, followed by his chuckle, turned the simmering heat into a fiery torment. He would dare laugh at her? She'd see how amusing he found it when he knelt before her, and she held his life in her hands. She'd be as ruthless as he. Yet, even as the thought solidified, it faded, lost in the tempest escalating in her body.

"Concentrate on what lays ahead, lass. You'll have a difficult few days."

"Why, are you going to give me to all of your clansmen? I won't break, you know. No matter what you do to me, I will keep trying to escape you until I am successful." Thankfully, her voice held steady and strong and she managed to conceal the depth of her yearning.

Thunder rolled overhead and, for a moment, Marissa had the odd thought God confirmed her vow. She bit back a hysterical chuckle, knowing her fury and despair made the storm's timing seem like a divine comment on her situation.

"Damn!" Ian swore. He tossed her onto his horse, and climbed up behind her, holding the reins of the mount he'd ridden to follow her.

She squirmed, but he kicked his stallion into a run, just as rain started, slow and misty at first, but quickly gaining in force. She tucked her face into his chest, hating the way her body came even more alive, eager and anticipating, at Ian's scent. The familiarity inspired a thousand memories, each one another reminder of how his touch could make her beg for more. Her sex swelled and clenched, the rhythm of the horse's gait intensifying the need growing within.

She had no idea where he took her until they came across a tiny cottage situated just outside a grove of trees. Where had that come from? She barely had a chance to think on it further when Ian slipped to the ground, pulling her with him. He led her inside.

The cold dark cabin held a musty odor, and a thick layer of dust coated the table and floor. Ian shoved Marissa into a chair, freeing her wrists before retying them behind her, then to the chair back.

"I'll be back after I've seen to the horses."

# chapter fifteen

She remained silent when he left her alone. She tugged at her bonds. She hung her head, willing herself not to cry. She'd been so close to escaping! How far had she gotten before he'd found her? She couldn't be sure, unclear on exactly what time she'd fled. It had merely been a few hours since the sun rose. How the hell had he caught up so fast?

Her thoughts circled around to what sort of punishment Ian intended to mete out. Would he whip her? Or cut off her hand, as he'd warned? *Jesu*, she had stolen a horse and wounded a man to do so. She had no idea about Scottish law. They were barbarians, anything was possible. She could even be hanged.

He wouldn't do that. Or mayhap he would. She tugged once again at the leather binding her to the chair. Panic stole her breath. She had to get free before they returned to Crawford Keep. Slowly, her eyes adjusted to the dim light and she looked around, wondering how to escape this worsening nightmare.

The door opened and Ian, soaked through, stepped inside. The rain hit the thatch roof of the small cottage with tiny thuds. Despite her efforts to avoid looking at him, Marissa's gaze focused steadily in his direction, his dark hair plastered to his head, water drenching his shirt and making it cling to his solid muscles. Her mouth went dry, her heart racing. He looked like a wild animal and, to her consternation, her body responded with ferocity.

"You better hope the horses don't turn up lame after that run through the muck. 'Twill be another crime added to your growing list."

"So you will whip me then? What else? Hang me? Cut off my hand?"

"Imagine what you will, lass. I havena time to think about you yet." He stripped out of his shirt and kilt, and no matter how she tried, Marissa couldn't look away when his fine chiseled shoulders and back were bared, followed by his firm arse and powerful legs. She held back a moan, knowing the responses that body could coax from her. Already her nipples hardened in anticipation of his touch. She lowered her head, willing her thoughts to anything but how much she still wanted him, even though she hated him for capturing her again.

When he was fully naked, he turned to her. His cock stood out hard and erect, revealing his own desire. For her. The thought brought heady pleasure, even though she wanted to deny it, with a desperation that near matched her fatigue.

"I see you want me still then, lass, despite your foolish attempt to steal my horse and escape. You didna get far, you know. I was able to find you quickly."

She remained silent, determined to hide her response. He chuckled again and she had the sense he knew how she fought to keep her focus on escaping him, not throwing herself into his arms. He stepped behind her, cut her loose from the chair, but just as quickly retied her hands before her. She doubted he would let her be unfettered by the bindings anytime soon. Her suspicions were confirmed when he affixed the cursed chain to the collar.

"This was me first mistake. I'll not make it again."

He tugged on the chain, forcing her to stand. She had an inkling of his intentions when he took the seat she had just vacated. Once more her guess had been accurate when he jerked her down over his lap. She kicked and fought him, cursing him as loudly as she could. He merely caught her flailing legs between his and pressed hard on her shoulders, forcing her head down and holding her immobile. Quick movements had the kirtle lifted, her arse bared to him.

"You beast! If I still had a sword, you'd be gutted

right now!"

"Well, you dinna have a sword anymore, do you, lass?"

With that, his hand landed hard on her bottom, harder than he'd ever done before. The burn that followed each smack grew, the discomfort soon a sharp and jagged pain. Again and again, his hand came down, until finally a choked cry broke free through her clenched teeth. Nay, she would not cry. But he never stopped, and soon great heaving sobs tore from her. Still, he continued, until she wailed and pleaded.

"Please, Ian, stop!"

"Still you show no respect."

Damn him, he would humiliate her as well? Fine, she would give him what he wanted. This time.

"Please, I beg you! Stop!" She choked on her tears, gasping when he continued to spank her.

Finally, he ceased. She barely noticed, the fire in her arse so powerful, it overwhelmed her senses. She seemed to be floating, her vision blurry and dim. Ian raised her up and she moaned, an odd numbness settling through her body.

Before she could gather her thoughts, Ian's mouth was on hers, brutal and hungry, and her fingers curled as he drove his tongue deep into her mouth. Her tears continued to fall, the saltiness adding a new and fierce dimension to his kiss. Marissa whimpered when he cupped her head and held her still, his other hand catching and squeezing her breast. She shoved into him, no longer caring that she should be fighting him. Her body wanted this too badly, and she had no hope of overcoming the powerful need.

His touch was rough, harsh and so very pleasurable. He pinched her nipple and she moaned again. The reason for her flight quickly disappeared from her thoughts, replaced with a hunger that consumed all else. When Ian pushed her to the floor, lifting her dress and shoving her legs wide apart, she reached her bound hands to him, eager to have him fill her. He paused, staring at her with a curious expression, before shoving into her with one fierce thrust. Her back arched against the sensation, delight exploding through her, making her feel more alive than she ever had before. He held her still as he pounded into her, and she didn't care about the hard floor scraping under her back, burning against her tender bottom. All that mattered was this intense lust, the need to be taken as Ian took her. The fire in her veins grew hotter, more potent, until she felt as though flames licked at her body.

Ian stiffened above her, his seed bathing her sex, a hoarse groan escaping his clenched lips. He remained motionless for a few moments, though Marissa thrust toward him, urging him to continue. He didn't, merely opened his eyes, fixed an angry glare on her and pulled out of her body. She whimpered, her need still extreme and so close to rapture. He merely stared, then jerked the chain. She resisted momentarily, but the pressure on her neck grew too painful and she slowly rose, her legs shaking. He led her to a corner and tossed the end of the chain over a rafter. Silently, he urged her to kneel in the corner, adjusting the chain so she didn't hang herself. Once satisfied, he circled the chain over and over the rafter, until she could not reach the end.

"That should hold you. Now keep quiet, I meant to get some rest before we return." With that, he turned away and left her kneeling in the corner.

"You bastard! You're going to leave me like this?"

"'Tis where a slave belongs. Chained and on her knees." He didn't even look at her when he answered, merely finding his way to the opposite corner of the room, laying out a pallet. She stared wide-eyed while he settled in, paying her no more attention. He truly meant to ignore her in this position. All too quickly, the discomfort in her knees grew painful, the sharp ache spreading through her legs. She tried to lower herself, but the chain proved too taut. The bastard had set her this way apurpose! One more crime to be added to the list of acts he would someday pay for.

And yet, her hungry passion intensified in the silence. Tears welled in her eyes. How could she still want him after all he'd done? He had no care for her, no concern or regard for her discomfort. A soft snore reached her from across the room. He slept? The tears fell now, fueled by rage and her determination to be free of him and to exact her vengeance.

* * *

Ian woke from his doze. How long had he slept? Not long, judging from his grogginess and the sight of her. Her lips pressed together in a grimace. The guilt surprised him. He should be pleased she suffered, her discomfort should mean nothing to him. But it did. She held herself erect on her knees, and he wondered why she hadn't at least slumped down to ease her sore muscles. His gaze moved over the chain wrapped around the rafter. She'd hang if she lowered herself.

Damn it! He should have realized. He didn't want her dead. At the very idea of Marie's body, lifeless and limp, his heart tightened. Why should he care? Her death would destroy the man he'd vowed revenge upon. Wasn't that Ian's ultimate goal? Marie was merely a tool to achieve that end, nothing more.

*You lie.* He ignored the voice in his head and rose from his pallet. He strode over to her, hating the way she cowered away from him. Yet the defiant fire in her eyes seemed to intensify.

He held back an amused smile. Now would not be the time to reveal any tender emotions toward her, be they amusement or concern. She was merely a slave and did not deserve any such consideration, not after her actions of the last hours.

He remained silent as he uncurled the chain from the rafter, taking care not to strike either himself or Marie with it. When she was free, he urged her to stand, noting the way she did so, shakily. When she rose, she swayed and he caught her before she could fall. Her muscles had likely cramped. With an oath, he bent and lifted her into his arms, settling her in the chair before the still-empty hearth.

"The rain's stopped. We head back to the keep now."

He turned away and gathered his pallet, then turned to her. She sat limply, her head bowed. He frowned. Where was her fire, her defiance? He'd expected her to resist him, but she didn't. Why did he so badly want her to?

"Come. You need to be cleaned."

She lifted her chin, an angry sniff her only sound. He bit the inside of his cheek to keep from laughing. The tightness in his chest eased to see signs of her rebellion. That was the Marie he'd come to ... He stopped himself from finishing the thought, his humor souring. He couldna feel such things for her. She was his enemy. Somehow, he kept losing sight of that simple truth.

Yet, the sight of her highborn attitude, combined with her disheveled and dusty appearance, seemed at odds. Lack of sleep explained why he found the sight almost comical. He'd arisen before the sun and his fear and anger at Marie had made his rest just now little more than a fitful catnap.

Once outside, he took his first good look at her. Dark smudges under her eyes betrayed her own weariness. Her slow and uneasy step tugged at him. He still couldna be sure how much of a head start she'd gotten in her flight this morning, but 'twas clear exhaustion would soon claim her, no matter how she might fight it. He longed to pull her into his arms and hold her as she gave in to sleep, but reminded himself of his goals. Loving her didna change that.

He stiffened. Nay. He could not love her. He had loved his wife, not this slip of a lass who was key to his vengeance. He would never love again, had vowed that when he'd held Sheila's lifeless body in his arms, when he had buried her beside his small son in the cemetery behind the burned out church.

Yet, this English lass stirred him in ways he'd never thought to feel again. Her response to his desires had been beyond what he could have hoped for. His wicked yearnings had not broken her, they'd enhanced her natural passion, one she'd felt for him right from that very first night Colin had brought her to the caves. Ian should have known then his plans would veer drastically from his intended path.

He shook his head, the troubling thoughts making him dizzy. He wanted to get Marie home, where he could resume his plans for siege, and remind her of her place. After discovering her gone, he realized he didn't ever want to release her. He needed to make that perfectly clear to her, as quickly as possible.

The sky had cleared, the fast moving storm long gone, the afternoon sun warming Ian's back. He looked behind him at Marie as he led her to the stream he knew ran nearby. She very carefully avoided looking at him, though he could feel the waves of anger rolling from her. He sighed. 'Twould be a long time before his slave was willing for him again. His cock stirred at the thought of showing her how her body could want him, need him, even if her logic told her otherwise. Soon enough, she'd be in his arms again, while they rode back to Crawford Castle. He had a few hours to enjoy her, make her tend to him. Mayhap, he would give her pleasure as well. He found himself anxious to watch her eyes glaze over in bliss, to hear her cries and feel her body shudder beneath him.

* * *

Marissa wondered what thoughts ran through Ian's mind. She didn't dare look at him, for fear of seeing his fierce anger, or revealing her hurt. This pain, though, was more than just the aches in her back and legs. This pain cut through her like a hot blade, slicing her heart into tiny shreds. Why should she care how he treated her? Why should she want him to look at her as more than a means for revenge? She wanted the tender way he gazed at his sister, or that hateful shrew, Elizabeth. She wanted his touch to be one of caring, not one of hated ownership.

Yet, the thought of his possession eroded her determination to hate him. When Ian took her, she felt as if nothing else in the world could ever matter. The pleasure he gave her was more than just a physical satisfaction. From the very first time, she'd sensed a deeper bond between them, something that transcended the realities of their opposing goals and lives. He wanted to destroy her father. She knew without doubt her father had not killed so many innocent villagers. She wanted to prove it. Ian would not allow it.

And yet, she knew, somehow, if she could truly prove her father's innocence, she and Ian might be able to forge something from the disastrous relationship they currently shared. *At least, I hope so.*

She sighed, catching sight of the stream they approached. Aware of Ian watching her, she strode past him, grateful he at least gave her enough slack to kneel by the bank. She splashed water in her face. 'Twould have been nice to do more, but her bound hands left her little freedom, and she refused to beg him to release her. She would endure whatever he had planned. She would not break, no matter how hard he tried to do so. He *would* respect her for it.

He knelt beside her, but she steadfastly stared at the stream rushing furiously through the field, aided by the additional water of the recent rains.

"Marie."

She held her tongue. All of her concentration focused on not turning to him.

"Look at me."

She recognized the order in his tone. With a weary sigh, she finally faced him, careful to keep her expression bland and filled with disinterest.

"Would you like to bathe?'

She shrugged, looking away again. His fingers on her chin forced her to look at him.

"You need to bathe."

She merely nodded, refusing to give in and rail against him, even though she desperately wanted to. Let him think he'd broken her, let him think she cared naught how he treated her. She knew she'd taken the right approach when he huffed in exasperation and produced a dagger. A split second of fear he might stab her evaporated on a wisp. He sliced through the leather binding her wrists, then yanked the dress over her head, leaving her naked.

A moment of fury that he would dare vanished. Hadn't he done far worse already? Whatever was still to come, it couldn't be as bad as this. At least they were alone.

"Will you drown me then?"

He recoiled as if she'd struck him. She held back a pleased smile. So there was a conscience somewhere in there. She would play to that, but she had to do it carefully. 'Twouldn't do to give away her methods. Let him think he broke her. She knew better.

He wrapped an arm about her shoulders and guided her to the water. She wanted to sink into him, have him fully embrace her, but she held herself stiff, forcing him to push her along. The cold water had her gasping for air, but she quickly savored the flow and lowered herself into the stream. Ian released her, backing away to sit on the bank.

She had no soap, but still managed to enjoy her time

in the water. All too soon, the temperature had her shivering. Ian helped her out, then wrapped a fresh cloth from his saddle bag around her.

"Come. You'll be sick if you dinna dry off."

Silence hung heavily over them while he secured the tartan, leaving her hands free. That changed as soon as he finished packing the horses. A leather thong once more held her wrists together, and she found herself in the same position as her initial kidnapping. In front of Ian, her hands secured to his saddle, and no way to defend herself from his seeking hands.

When he guided the horses north, his hand crept up to casually cup her breast. 'Twould be a difficult ride. Yet a growing part of her looked forward to it.

*** 

Several hours later, Ian held Marie nestled against him. She slept, thankfully. She would need her strength tonight when they arrived home. He tightened his embrace around her, pressing a kiss to her head and inhaling her sweet fresh scent. Once more, his arms tightened.

The first moments when he'd awoken and discovered her gone still tormented him. The fear had almost frozen him, until he realized what her absence meant. The knowledge felt like a rusted blade slicing into his chest, slowly, causing the most agonizing pain. He'd let his anger take over and rule him after that, and it still did to some extent. The rage had cooled somewhat. Especially once he'd found her.

Her anger, the despair in her voice when he'd caught her poked at the edges of his own still-ragged hurt. What had he expected? That she would run into his arms? He hadn't expected her to fight as she had, though. He recalled Jamie showing how she'd managed to slice his sleeve. His clansman's claim that Marie possessed skill with a blade had proven true today. A solid admiration for her ability took hold. She'd been a worthy adversary, despite her unfamiliarity with the blade, and her exhaustion.

Her vehement loyalty in defending her father roused more respect. She was so sure The Panther could not have destroyed his village, he could almost believe her. He knew she believed it, insisting the man had been in Wales at the time. She must be mistaken.

Even though he swore to himself she was wrong, he realized he wanted to believe her, wanted to believe her father had been far from Scotland when the MacCallums were attacked. Maybe he *should* give her words some thought. Jamie had urged him to think on it several times, but Ian's plans for revenge consumed him so thoroughly, he'd refused to give the idea he erred any consideration. Sometime today, he'd realized how important Marie now was to him, how he could never let her go. With that, his anger at her attempt to leave him faded and his doubts about the attack had grown stronger.

The cuff in the pouch at his belt hung as heavy as a sack of barley. The gift he'd planned to give her had become yet another reminder that she wanted to escape him. He couldna blame her; after all he'd done, he would think her mad if she didn't try to flee. Then why did her flight slice so deeply?

His confused thoughts left his head spinning when he finally guided his horse into the village, drawing immediate notice and welcomes from those in the bailey. The clamor didn't even rouse Marie, still slumped against him in slumber. He pressed a kiss to her temple then lifted his chin. He wished he could have snuck inside without being seen.

He neared the keep and his sister ran out. Fiona's expression changed from concern to fury, and he knew exactly who she intended each emotion for.

"Ian, you heartless bastard, you should have let her go."

"And mayhap let her be caught by others? You know

verra well what sort of dangers roam the lands. The Bruce and his soldiers could have found her. What do you think they would have done to her? She's lucky I found her alive."

Marie stirred in his arms and he glanced at her. "Easy, lass, we're home now."

She gave a little tremor, and he wondered at it before Fiona reached for Marie.

"Give her to me, Ian, you've done enough."

"Nay, Fiona. The lass is mine to see to." Nevertheless, he accepted Fiona's assistance in helping Marie down, then dismounted.

"And punish."

Ian turned to the voice, knowing Colin taunted him. Sure enough, the other man approached.

"She stole a horse. She should be hanged for it."

Marie froze in his embrace. He ran a reassuring hand along her arm, holding her close against him.

"Nay, lass, I willna let that happen." His eyes narrowed on Colin. "'Tis none of your business how I discipline my slave, Colin."

"I found her first, damn it. She was mine to claim." Colin's eyes darkened in fury, his fists clenched at his side.

Ian rolled his eyes. This again? Marie's entire body went tense and she shrank back against him. He wanted nothing more than to comfort her. He squeezed her hand, and the gesture seemed to settle her. Ian shook his head.

"Spoils of war are decided by the leader. 'Twas me. You ruined all my plans by taking her. I claimed her, as is my right, and I will handle her."

"I demand you return the wench to me, or fight me and win her fairly, as you should have done at first."

A fierce trembling overtook Marie and Ian once again squeezed gently in reassurance. He wouldna allow Colin to take her, no matter how many attempts the fool made. The idea of the English lass at the whim of Colin's vicious tending sickened Ian.

"Nay, Colin, you willna do any such thing," Donal cut in. "Ian, by my order, had the right to claim her as leader of the mission. He speaks the truth that you ruined all he's worked for by stealing the lass away. In doing so, you forfeited any claim you may have had on her. She is Ian's to keep, or release, or sell, as he sees fit."

"But 'tis not –"

"Colin, hold your tongue, or you'll regret forcing my hand." Donal stared the younger man down, and Colin relented, lowering his head and stepping back.

Ian heaved a sigh and turned to the clan laird. "Thank you, Donal. I've been thinking on what you said this morning. In three days' time, Jamie, Marie and I will be gone from your village. This fight with the Panther is my own."

"Are you sure, Ian? You canna attack an English castle without men. We are your clan as well, and wouldna deny you."

Ian nodded. "Mayhap 'tis time to start over. Attacking Montchester no longer seems to be the right path. Keeping the lass is a far better revenge."

He didn't miss the way she twisted in his embrace, trying to look at him. He tightened his grip, keeping her in place. Her exasperated huff almost drew a chuckle.

"If you insist, Ian, then I willna hold you back. I will do everything in my power to see you are not found should any make their way here seeking her."

"Thank you, Donal. Now, if you'll excuse us, I have a slave to see to."

"Aye. 'Tis glad I am you've decided not to whip the lass, especially out here, for all to see."

Ian looked down at the dark-haired girl standing silently in his embrace. "She still faces punishment for her crimes. I'll not have her pleading for help from any onlookers. She can be convincing, as you've noticed my sister already has a soft spot for her."

Marie elbowed him in the ribs. He held back another smile. Did she not realize he would ensure she fully enjoyed her punishment? He couldna wait to show her.

"As do you, Ian, if you'd only see it." With those softly spoken words, Donal turned and walked away. The small gathering of clansmen dispersed. Except for Fiona, who stood hands on hips, and glared at him.

"You are a cruel man, Ian," she said. "Losing your wife and son was a terrible blow, but you canna take it out on the poor lass."

"Fiona, I dinna want to hear any of your pleading for the girl's sake. She stole a horse, injured a man and tried to kill me. Any punishment she receives, she's more than earned." He had to maintain his appearance as a leader, while so many eyes and ears focused on him. Marie squirmed again in his embrace.

"Let go of me, you have no right!" she cried.

"Aye, lass, I do. Now stop fighting!" He turned her enough to meet her angry gaze. After a few moments of staring fiercely at her, he recognized the moment she chose to abandon the battle. He wondered if she'd understood his unspoken message.

Fiona shook her head. "At least let the poor lass rest before you beat her."

Marie jumped, but Ian didn't allow her attempt to flee his embrace. Instead, he drew her still closer, until each breath that rasped through her jangled through him as well. He lowered his voice and leaned over to his sister.

"I willna beat her, Fiona." *Not that any of the rest will know otherwise, anyway.* He straightened, and louder, said, "Now, let me tend to this matter without your interference."

Fiona moved in close to Marie's ear, and whispered something. Ian tried, but couldna make out the words. Whatever she'd said, the message had a calming effect on his slave. Her trembling eased and the tension coiled within her stiff body loosened. The urge to know what his sister said warred with his need to act like he didna care. With a scowl at Fiona, he pushed Marie toward the keep.

She did not resist, for which he was grateful. As they made their way to the stairs, he caught Donal's eye and nodded his thanks once more. If he planned to leave in a few days, many tasks needed his attention. First, he had to determine where to go. He didna want to abandon his plans for revenge, but that would have to wait while he focused on immediate concerns.

They reached his chamber and he pushed Marie in, eyes narrowing when she stopped short just inside the door. He followed her startled stare. Jamie sprawled on the bed. Ian suspected whatever his clansman had in mind would not be good.

* * *

Marissa wondered why Ian seemed so upset at the sight of Jamie. For herself, her body did her thinking for her. Her pussy heated, and she clenched her fingers in an attempt to resist the longing.

"Why are you here, Jamie?" Ian asked, as he propelled her further into the room. Her knees trembled. A silent prayer of thanks was offered to God that she didn't fall to the floor in a heap. Ian continued to guide her, past the bed and toward the wall. She didn't want to think about what he intended.

"I didna want to say anything in front of the others."

"About what?"

Marissa didn't miss the frustration in Ian's tone. Clearly, Jamie's presence bothered him, but why?

"I fear you will need all of the Crawford warriors, no matter your change of plans," Jamie replied.

Marissa turned to stare at him. Ian roughly turned her back to face the wall. She held still, listening. Jamie's words made no sense yet, but she would soon decipher his meaning.

"Jamie, have you nothing better to do than come in here with talk of a fool?"

"'Tis not just talk. I overheard Colin saying he sent a messenger to Marie's father. The earl will soon be made aware of his daughter's location."

Hope swelled in her heart. Her father would come for her! A whoop of joy threatened to escape and, though she tried not to betray her excitement, Ian's low chuckle told her he'd noticed her reaction.

"Dinna get your hopes up, lass, we'll be long gone afore your father gets near this village." He released her shoulders and turned to face Jamie, who had stood and approached them.

"You still plan to leave then?" Jamie asked.

Ian nodded and Marissa's hope sank, replaced by despair. If he took her away, her father might never find her. She had to find some way to get him to remain in the Crawford village.

"I thought you wanted revenge? Why not stay and wait for my father?"

Ian regarded her with narrowed eyes, rubbing his beard-covered chin. "I dinna think we should discuss this now. I have a punishment to mete out. Would you care to join me?"

He directed the last to Jamie, who grinned. Marissa's heart pounded. She'd thought earlier that perhaps Ian meant to forego this punishment, but that hope was quickly dashed. Yet, the sight of the two men looking at her as though they were starved and she a succulent roast spurred a riot of eager sensation in her belly.

She didn't even care how the wantonness inside her rose so quickly, obliterating every other awareness. She merely waited until they surrounded her with warmth and gave herself over to them.

Ian tilted her head back, his eyes moving over her face, as if seeking the answer to some unspoken question. Before she could make any sense of it, his mouth crashed down on hers and the hunger in his kiss obliterated every other thought. She swayed, and Jamie stepped up behind her, holding her still while Ian devoured her. Hands slid over her body, but she could barely tell who touched her where. All she knew was the heat built quickly, consuming her senses. She vaguely recognized they drew her toward the bed, Ian's lips still on hers, his hot tongue searching her mouth, teasing her, making her moan with abandon. When he drew away, she whimpered in protest.

"Easy, lass. I still need to punish you."

If he'd dumped a pail of cold water over her, it would not have chilled her as much as his words. She stared wide-eyed, trying to ignore the sensation of Jamie's hand sliding up to cup her breast.

"But I thought ..." She closed her eyes against the bitter and familiar sense of betrayal. For a little while, she had truly believed he would not beat her. How could she have been so wrong? "Look at me."

Despite her intentions, she obeyed Ian's stern order, surprised to see his smile.

"I willna whip you, lass. I find I don't have the urge or the strength to do so now. But the others must think I am."

A wave of relief so intense swept over her, she might have fallen if Jamie's arm around her waist didn't keep her upright. Ian gave her a grin.

"When I strike, you are to scream as loud as you can," he said.

"I don't understand." Her words drifted into a low moan as Jamie slid his mouth along her neck, addling her wits. His warmth intensified the tumult of emotions and sensations, and momentarily, her world tilted. She gripped Jamie's arm to steady herself.

"Look."

Ian lifted a small thin whip and smacked it across his palm. The sound of the contact echoed in the room. She flinched at first then understood. With a smile, she nodded.

Ian laid the whip into his hand several times. After each one, she dutifully screamed, though by the fifth blow, she had to fight to resist the laughter bubbling inside her. Through it all, Jamie held her, caressed her, kissed her, his touch reverting her humor to something much more urgent. When Ian finally laid the whip aside and reached for her, she thought she'd never been more excited about anything ever before.

She stood between them, all three breathing heavily. Ian wasted no time devouring her mouth. Thankfully, Jamie's position still kept her upright while his hands roamed her fevered skin. She moaned, desperate to find some way to hold onto each of them. Ian drew away, studying her intently. She wanted to drown in the dark depths, and Jamie's mouth skimming the curve of her neck intensified the sensation of floating. Her body had become weightless, only their hands holding her down.

"You are a lovely sight, lass." Ian cupped her cheek. "The fire inside you burns bright." Jamie murmured in agreement, his voice against her skin a caress of its own. She panted, unable to look away from Ian's seeking stare. What did he think to find?

He held out a hand. "Come."

She placed her fingers in his and let him lead her to the bed. Jamie helped guide her. In moments, she lay atop the mattress, a man kneeling on either side of her. Her chest heaved with excitement. They settled beside her and she closed her eyes in bliss when their hungry and searching caresses moved over her.

\* \* \*

Ian leaned back to study Marie. In the light from the hearth, her soft skin glowed hot. Her eyes sparkled like fine topaz and didna mask the depth of her want. She moaned when Jamie slid his hand between her legs. His clansman's dark head stood stark against her pale flesh.

The sight sent a jolt of need to his already hard cock. He stroked himself, but knew wouldna soothe the intensity. He rose above her, pushing her legs open. For several moments, he remained still, watching Jamie's fingers move over Marie's heated cleft. She moaned, her hips moving in time with the man's touch, her cries growing sharper.

"Jamie, stop."

When his clansman drew away, Ian once more pumped his cock and positioned himself. Her moist heat stroked his erection like velvet, and he gritted his teeth to hold back, wanting this to last longer. Marie's moans grew muffled and he looked up to see Jamie over her face, his cock encircled by her red lips. The sight snapped his control and he exploded within her, the tension in his balls released in a furious rush. Jamie's groans indicated he was near, and Ian panted, barely managing to open his eyes to see the other man stiffen in pleasure. He couldna see Marie's face, only her mouth around Jamie's cock visible, but Ian knew she savored the man's flesh in her mouth. He stroked her clit and she shuddered, giving a muffled shriek.

Ian withdrew, and Jamie did the same. Marie stared, her expression still tight with frustration. Her tawny gaze pleaded silently and he nodded to Jamie. Still holding her gaze, Ian lowered his head to her cleft, sliding his tongue along her folds. Her back arched and she gave a tiny cry as Jamie sucked the tip of her breast into his mouth at the same time. The sound of her moans, punctuated by sharp cries whenever one of them bit a little harder, soon had Ian wound tighter than a ball of twine once more. He forced thoughts of his own desires from his mind and concentrated on making Marie scream in pleasure. He swirled his tongue around the hard button as it pulsed under his attentions, the flesh hot and slick and sweeter than ambrosia. Her fingers were in his hair, pulling, the motion in an even tempo with the rolling movements of her hips.

He nibbled at her cleft and she gave a keening wail, her body tightening before erupting in tumultuous shudders, her cries echoing throughout the chamber. He continued until the fierce tremors passed and she lay weakly beneath him, eyes closed, her face soft in satiation. He glanced at Jamie and realized his clansman suffered as he did. He rose and motioned for Jamie to take his place. He stretched out beside Marie, taking her hand and guiding it to his cock. Her eyes fluttered open and she smiled as he guided her, until she had found a satisfying rhythm. She paused briefly as Jamie entered her, but soon resumed, setting a tempo with Jamie's thrusts.

Ian savored her hand sliding on his shaft, her grip tightening as Jamie stroked into her. All too soon, he was ready to explode again. He didn't bother to fight it, easily giving in to the consuming release. When he'd regained his breath, he resumed watching Jamie take Marie. His clansman clearly enjoyed her, as she did Jamie. When Jamie gripped her hips and raised her, she cried out, arching into Jamie, her scream mingling with Jamie's groans. She writhed against him. Ian could barely breathe watching the raw passion between them. Knowing she responded to him as eagerly soothed any hint of envy.

Jamie eased away and flopped to the bed beside her. Marie remained limp and motionless, but a small smile hovered on her lips. Ian grinned and drew her near, pressing a kiss to her forehead. She sighed and snuggled into him and Jamie drew the blankets over them, settling on her other side.

Ian grinned at his clansman and lowered his head to the pillow. He caught Marie watching him. Her cheeks reddened and she curled her face into his shoulder. He stroked her hair, wondering how his feeling for her had grown so deep.

\* \* \*

"Messenger at the gates!"

Royce paused on his way to the keep. He used his hand to shield his eyes from the sun's glare as he looked up at the guard positioned on the walk. What could this mean? He needed to depart for London immediately, and the delay irritated him.

"From the prince?" Royce called.

"Nay, sir. I cannot tell."

Did he dare hope 'twas word about Marissa? Ceasing his search for her had been one of the hardest things he'd ever had to do, but mayhap now he would know if she still lived. 'Twould give him, and Gillian, some peace. He might even let Rowan take a regiment to seek her.

Royce sighed. "Raise the gates."

"Royce! Is it Marissa?"

He closed his eyes at the sound of his wife's voice. The idea of Gillian's heartbreak increasing felt like a dagger in his heart. He turned, her hopeful expression cutting even more. At least she no longer glared at him with anger.

"Nay, 'tis not."

She sighed and her step slowed, some of the optimism fading from her violet eyes. The strands of gray in her dark hair seemed overabundant today. She leaned into him as the gates opened.

A bedraggled Scotsman rode into the bailey, hand on the hilt of his sword. Royce strode over, his own sword at the ready.

"I hear you seek your daughter," the man said before Royce could question him.

"Who sent you?"

"No comfort for a weary messenger?" The man offered a tentative smile, but did not receive a response in kind. "Ah well, no surprise there. I know where you can find your daughter."

"You'd best tell me what you know, lest you find your head on a pike."

"She's with the Crawford clan. Colin Crawford stole

her first, but she belongs to Ian MacCallum now."

A white-hot rage consumed Royce, he could barely hear over the roaring in his ears. Fists clenched, he moved toward the Scot, but strong hands held him back, his wife's scream cutting through the haze of fury.

"Royce, no! Hear him out! He knows where Marissa is!"

The desperation in Gillian's voice spurred a need in Royce to ease her fear and heartache. He nodded, composing his anger and motioned the Scotsman down from his mount.

Hesitantly, the man complied, clearly not sure he was safe in the English castle. Royce merely ordered a stableboy to tend to the Scot's horse, and waved him toward the keep.

"Come inside and rest. And tell me everything you know."

# Chapter Sixteen

Marissa woke with her head tucked securely on Ian's shoulder, his arms tight around her waist. She gave a wry smile. There would be no slipping from his bed this night. Mayhap any other. Since her failed flight, she hadn't been more than a few feet from him. He'd kept her beside him at all times, kneeling beside him at each meal, and held tightly in his arms while he slept. She didn't really mind. His attentions had changed, from cold and demanding to warm and caring. The constant close proximity had given her the chance to listen when he discussed his plans to leave the Crawford village and head north. He either did not notice how closely she heeded his conversations with Jamie or Fiona, or Donal Crawford, or he didn't care how much she overheard.

The idea of being dragged even further away terrified her. If he wouldn't release her, then she had to convince him to remain here, with the Crawfords. Jamie understood her frantic plea for help and tried with no success to dissuade his clansman, though at least the younger MacCallum had been able to convince Ian to postpone the journey for a few more days. When she'd listened in on their discussions, Marissa knew her suspicions had been accurate. The Crawford village was not terribly far from England. Certainly a shorter ride than the journey north had been. She now recognized Ian's machinations, delaying their travel by stopping more than he needed to. Had he done it to confuse her or for another reason? Her body tingled when she recalled the events during each of those stops. She shook her head. For now, she had more important matters with which to concern herself. She prayed her father still sought her. If so, her best chance of being found was if Ian stayed here, with his adopted clan.

She lifted her head to study him, his face calm and relaxed in repose. She ran a finger along his well-trimmed beard and recalled the sensation of those whiskers scratching her thighs while he'd feasted on her sex. Even now, the recollection stoked another fire inside her, and her pussy ached to be filled with his hard cock.

She sighed. More thoughts of her ruined future taunted her, but she forced them aside. Someday, some way, she would rebuild her life. And keep the memories of Ian's passion close to her heart.

"Lass, do you never sleep?" Ian's grumble stirred a giggle.

"I'm sorry. I didn't mean to wake you."

"Well, you did and for that, I just may have to punish you."

His words did as much to send her need surging as his hands. She barely had time to consider what her body's response truly meant when his fingers found their way to her cleft, stroking her lightly.

"You're an insatiable wench. Feel how wet you are already. You're going to wear me out."

A slide of his fingers around her clit stifled any response and she arched into his seeking touch. The chain on her collar clinked as he flipped her on her back, rising above her, his hand still moving over her pussy. He lowered his head, nipping one hardened nipple, drawing an agonized groan. She desperately wanted to hold onto him, to touch his skin as he did hers, but remembered to leave her hands at her sides. If she was to have any pleasure, she had to wait for him to allow it.

But that didn't mean she wouldn't enjoy what he did in the meantime. One finger, then two, dipped inside her, curling and twisting, until she moaned and panted, her body tossed in the tempest.

"You may touch, lass, I need to feel your hands on me."

Exhilaration soared over her and she slid her fingers

along his powerful shoulders. The muscles flexed and twitched under her seeking caresses, and she relished the sensation before grabbing fistfuls of his hair when he lowered his mouth to torment her breasts with his tongue and teeth.

"Ian, please." The plea escaped her before she even realized. He raised his head and pierced her with his dark stare.

"What do you want, lass?"

"I want you. Please, Ian, don't deny me."

His answer was a bruising kiss, his tongue driving into her mouth, the flames licking hotter than ever. Everywhere he touched seared through her and she moaned into his mouth when he once again teased her pussy, driving her to the bliss she knew only he could give. She wanted it, needed it, so badly, her mouth watered as if she sucked on a sugared almond.

He roamed her body almost carelessly, his rough caresses driving her wild. She writhed beneath him. He slid his fingers along her sex, roughly searching out her clit and teasing it to hardness. She cried out, begging for more of his gruff touch. Her thoughts had narrowed to only him, his body, his touch, his scent. Even the soft noises of approval he couldn't hide spurred her, and her hips moved in time with the rhythm of his caresses, her vision blurring, the passion overpowering her, the only thing she focused on.

"That's it, lass, move for me. Show me how bad you want me." His words surrounded her, and she cried out, white-hot pleasure tearing through her in ferocious waves. Her body bucked under him, dancing to his command. His fingers never stopped moving, driving deep inside her and making her scream his name.

When the riot finally calmed, she huffed a deep breath and opened her eyes to find Ian smiling smugly down at her. Too spent to care, she nodded eagerly when he moved between her legs, his hard cock brushing her damp folds. She twitched around him again, finally finding enough sense to reach down and curl her fingers around his hardened flesh. The warmth and softness of his skin set her longing rushing anew as she stroked him, savoring the feel of velvet and steel. He gave a harsh groan, but didn't stop her and, emboldened, she grew more playful with her strokes, using her nails to scratch lightly. The action drew another groan and Ian trembled violently, his fingers tightening on her hips. She barely noticed the discomfort, too intent on toying with his cock, knowing her touch undid him as fiercely as he did her.

All too soon, he tore her hand away. She would have protested, but when he drove into her with one thrust, her complaints evaporated and she wrapped her legs around his waist, holding on tight. She matched his tempo, keeping up with his furious pace, each stroke both teasing and satisfying. She looked into his face to find him staring intently at her while he pounded into her with such speed, it left her dizzy, yet wanting more and more.

His fingers once more found her clit, pinching, and sending her soaring over bliss's edge once more, her body rocking with the waves of passion breaking over her.

"Ah, lass, you squeeze me so nicely when you come."

His words barely filtered through the haze and she found herself soaring toward another peak, Ian's cock and fingers keeping the pleasure coursing through her. Another blinding release left her gasping his name, her back arching, forcing him still deeper inside. He gave a harsh groan, his hot seed filling her and sending her into another spinning release, her cries accompanying his satisfied moans, the combination making an odd sort of music that left her exhilarated and content.

Ian soon pulled free of her, and the empty feeling left her bereft, oddly so. Tears burned her eyes, but she held them back as he rolled and pulled her near, tucking her against his side. The feel of his hand gently gliding along her back soothed her. Even though he'd never said the words, his soft touch revealed that he did care for her, even if just a little bit. The sensation of belonging slammed into her, stronger than ever before. How could this be? He'd kidnapped her and tortured her, and she found herself delighting in being with him more each time he claimed her. Fighting him any longer now seemed a useless waste of her strength.

What madness lay in her soul to want to stay here for always? The sex had addled her thoughts, 'twas all.

\* \* \*

Marissa ate the last of her bread and washed it down with ale. Fiona watched her closely, and it seemed as if the other woman had something she wanted to say. She remained silent. Didn't matter. Marissa had a request of her own.

"Fiona, I need a favor."

"Ian will kill me if I help you, lass."

Marissa sighed. "Nay, he will not. I want to send a message to my father."

Fiona's face paled. "Lass, you canna!"

"I need to ask his help. He will come for me, but Ian lays a trap for him, and I cannot risk that, not until I have the proof I need. The only way is for my father to find it before he attempts to rescue me."

"But I thought you wanted to be free of Ian."

The very thought squeezed Marissa's heart. While she wanted her freedom, she was no longer convinced she wanted to escape Ian's possession. If only she found some way to have both.

"I am willing to stay with him as long as it takes for my father to find the evidence we need to clear his name." Not the complete truth, but not a lie either.

"If that is so, dinna you think you should tell him your real name?"

Marissa gaped at Ian's sister. "How do you... I

mean, you're mistaken."

Fiona gave a sly smile. "Nay, lass, I'm not. I've noticed how it's taken you some time to answer to Marie as if 'twere your given name. 'Tis not."

Marissa lowered her head, staring at her wrists, the leather cuffs Ian had added last night still securely fastened, held in place by tiny locks. Only Ian had the key.

"Very well, you're right." She raised her chin and met Fiona's knowing stare. "I am Marissa Langley, first-born daughter of Royce Langley, the Earl of Montchester."

"Well, Marissa, I will keep your secret for now, but you must tell Ian soon. He should know the woman he... he should know."

"The woman he what, Fiona?" What had the other woman been about to say? She refused to let the hopeful suspicion form.

Fiona sighed. "He cares for you, lass, more than he even realizes, methinks. If you're honest with him, 'twill make it easier for you both."

"You make it sound as if we are a love match, rather than a slave and captor."

"Dinna discount the idea, Marissa. Ian would be lucky to have you, if he had the sense God gave a goat and recognized it."

Marissa giggled, a strange warmth seeping through her. She'd often wished to believe Ian truly cared, but 'twas past time to let that hope die completely. Even so, staying with him as his slave brought a calming sense of acceptance.

She forced her thoughts back to her immediate dilemma. "Fiona, I need to get word to my father." This likely was her only chance to ask her father to help. He hadn't raided the MacCallum clan two years earlier, but he had connections and opportunities to seek the truth. At the same time, 'twould clear his name in Ian's eyes. Then, perhaps, the faraway notion of a real future with Ian might possibly become a reality.

"I'll see if I can find some parchment. How do you plan to send the message?" Fiona asked. Marissa hesitated and Fiona shook her head.

"Nay, lass, I canna. 'Tis too risky."

"Please, Fiona, there must be someone you can ask who won't tell Ian. Someone he won't notice is missing. I know we aren't terribly far from the English border. The journey can be made in two days."

Fiona sighed. "Lass, you're asking for a heap of trouble. Verra well, write your message, I'll see what I can do."

Fiona left the hall, and returned quickly with a sheet of parchment, a quill and some ink. Marissa hurriedly scratched out a note to her father, explaining as best she could with as few words as possible, then rolled the parchment. She had no wax to seal it; instead, she pulled one of the ribbons holding her hair back and tied it around the parchment.

"Thank you, Fiona, I will find a way to repay you for this aid."

"Just hope I can find someone to agree to take the message for you. Now come, we've work to tend to and if I know my brother, he'll be back here to claim you soon."

\* \* \*

After three days of miserable cold rain, the sun finally broke through the clouds. Ian slogged through the muck, heading toward the stables after leaving Marie in his chamber with Fiona, with a strict warning to behave and finish packing. He wanted no more trouble before they left. Though if he were honest, he'd admit he still wished he'd remained abed. Images of Marie laying beneath him this morn still dogged him, and he shook his head to clear it. All he could see was her passion filled face, her lips open and gasping for air as she wrapped around him, pulling him into her welcoming body. His cock stirred, but he did his best to ignore it. More important matters needed his attention, and if his focus remained scattered, he would never get the again-altered plan into place.

He stepped into the cool building and nodded to the stable boy tending his chores. As he made his way to his horse, his clansman's call stopped him. He turned and waited for Jamie.

"What is it?"

"Likely nothing, but I spoke with Edwin Crawford this morn about his trip to York. 'Tis not far from Montchester."

"You think he heads there?"

Jamie shrugged. "Dinna ken, but he seemed nervous. Like he was hiding something."

Alarm soon turned to anger. Could Edwin be traveling to Monchester instead of York? 'Twas but one reason a messenger would go to Marie's home.

"Did he say anything further about his business?"

Jamie shook his head. "Nay. Said he had a private message to deliver, and couldna divulge the sender."

"I know what the message was. I suspect Colin is behind this one as well. What game does the fool play at?" The need to leave with haste grew in urgency.

"Unless the message isna what we think." Jamie rubbed his beard, his face set in thought. "Ian, mayhap it wasna Colin."

"Then who?"

Jamie shrugged. Ian's temper heated, his frustration mounting. "What are you thinking?"

"Nothing. Just wondering why another messenger would be going to Montchester."

Ian turned to look toward the keep, knowing Marie waited inside. Had she sent a messenger? The swift and sharp stab of betrayal left him confused. He shouldna be surprised, of course she wanted her freedom. How could she have arranged it? Who would have helped her? Fiona? The notion his sister had been disloyal to him didn't burn as he expected. Mayhap because the hurt of knowing

Marie still tried to escape him cut so much sharper. He harbored a reckless hope she would choose to stay with him. Not because he forced her, but because she wanted to. Those foolish wishes lay in a broken heap at his feet.

"Has he left yet?" he asked, trying to hear over the blood roaring in his ears. His fingers clenched and unclenched and he tried to re-right his once-again upended world.

"Aye. Do you want to try to catch him?"

Too late. Ian shook his head. "I dinna have the time to chase him down. If he heads for Montchester, we must leave straight away."

"How soon?"

"On the morrow. No later."

Jamie nodded. "As I expected. Will you take Fiona with us as well?"

Ian shook his head. "She's sweet on Edwin and is already missing him. I expect he'll request a handfast when he returns. I willna deny them. I will give Donal my approval for him to bless them."

"I'll admit I'm glad she's staying behind. I have no desire to listen to her constant scolding on the journey."

Ian chuckled. "Nor I. Come, we must make haste."

"Will you take a mount for Marie?"

"Nay, she will ride with one of us. I dinna trust her not to try to flee."

"How's your arm?"

Ian glanced at the spot where Marie's sword had glanced off him a week ago. "Healed."

"Good. Wouldna want it to hinder your ability to travel."

"'Twas naught more than a scratch. You saw for yourself last night it hasna hindered any of my abilities."

Jamie grinned. "'Tis a good thing. I'd hate to have to be the only one to tend to the lass."

"Afraid she'll wear you out?"

A loud laugh echoed in the stable. "She is insatiable."

Ian nodded, unable to resist a broad smile. "Aye, and she danced nicely under the whip last night, didn't she?'

"That she did. I think she liked it, too."

"She certainly did."

Ian recalled how wet and swollen Marie's pussy had been after he'd softly whipped her, her hips jerking into his hand as he'd tested her reactions. When he'd loosened her bonds, she'd attacked him like a wild creature, biting and grabbing, drawing him into her body with a ferocity that even now left his cock tingling. Her passionate screams still sent a shiver along his spine. He found himself eager to whip her again.

"So where are we going?"

"Back to our lands."

Jamie's eyes widened. "But there's nothing there."

"Exactly. None will think to look for us there while we plan the journey to the Highlands."

"Ian, are you giving up your revenge?

Ian hesitated before answering. "Nay, not entirely. But I have given Marie's theory some thought and agree we should investigate further. We will be safe enough on the MacCallum  lands. I suspect no one's ventured there since we abandoned it."

"But 'tis just the three of us. What if we are attacked again? With the possibility of war around us, you canna be sure 'tis safe."

"Donal received word from The Bruce that 'twould appear the English prince does not have the skill of the old king. Most expect the battle to be abandoned."

"How does this help us?"

"The English will retreat, so they pose no more threat. By the time The Panther reaches this village, we will be safely away. Donal has promised to set him on a false trail should he arrive."

"You have something else in mind, don't you?"

Ian shook his head, yet unwilling to share his plans for the coming weeks. The ruins of his home would give him the perfect location to bind Marie to him and his clansman in ways she couldn't imagine. Even if her father did find her, she wouldna want to leave. Ever.

The need to ensure he held her heart in his hands, that she would be devoted only to him, had taken hold of him and colored every decision he made. He couldna bear the thought of her hatred, and this time alone would also provide him with the opportunity to show her the evidence of his clan's destruction. He would heed her theory and examine it thoroughly. If she proved to be correct, he would cease all his plans for her father.

And she would willingly stay with Ian.

\* \* \*

"Royce, find her. Go to the Crawfords, mayhap they want a ransom."

Royce knew if the Scots had wanted a ransom for Marissa, they'd have already asked. "I will go, and I will bring her back. Anyone who tries to stop me will suffer my justice."

He drew Gillian near and vowed again to end the pain his wife endured. The news that Marissa had been taken as a slave by Ian MacCallum left Gillian alternating between fits of rage and deep sorrow. Nothing he'd done eased her agony. Nothing would, except having her daughter back.

He had no choice but to abandon his plans to travel to London. Finding Marissa came before his duties to his country and king. She was being held less than three days ride from Montchester. He could bring her home then still travel to London before summer's end.

He considered a plan to take Rowan and some additional warriors with him while still ensuring enough remained behind to protect Montchester. He looked to the men he'd gathered. Whatever Marissa had endured, these men would know it. Royce would not be able to keep her ruination a secret. He had no illusions his daughter's choices in life had been greatly diminished by her kidnapping. Though he did not want to ruminate on it, he had no doubt what she'd been put through. He prayed to help her recover and mayhap have a chance to be happy again.

"Rider approaching!" The sentry called down, startling Royce.

The gates were already up and no time to lower them, so whoever neared would be able to enter the bailey. He unsheathed his sword, his men doing the same.

Another Scot. Royce scowled at the man who had ridden into Montchester. Something about him seemed familiar. Ah yes, he had been at court last year, seeking aid from the king for his clan. The Crawfords!

Fury now ruling him, he stalked over to the man. "Where is my daughter?"

"I am Edwin Crawford. I bring a message from her."

"From Marissa?" Gillian rushed to Royce's side. "Let me see it."

Royce nodded to the Scot who handed the rolled parchment to Gillian. She broke the seal and opened it.

"It *is* from her, Royce, she's alive." Gillian's brow furrowed. "She says she doesn't want you to find her yet. What have these barbarians done to her?"

Royce stepped closer, but she held up a hand to stop him.

"There's more." Gillian's eyes moved rapidly, reading and re-reading the message. She lifted her violet gaze to him. "A crime has been committed and you need to find the culprits."

"Of course, a crime has been committed. Our daughter has been kidnapped!"

"Nay, not that. Another crime. A raid. Murder. You stand accused of attacking and killing everyone in Ian MacCallum's clan." Her hand shook while she held out the message.

Royce took the parchment from his wife and read it quickly. Marissa's words echoed Gillian's. He met his wife's agonized stare. "I didn't. You know, I didn't. I would never."

She nodded. "I know." Her voice cracked. "But they took our daughter as revenge. Royce, what have they done to her?"

He turned back to the Scot. "This is nonsense!" he roared. "Who ordered her to write this?"

Edwin paled, and backed his horse up a step or two. "Dinna ken. I was given the message and asked to deliver it."

"What is this foolishness about the MacCallums? I have never been anywhere near their village!"

"Ian MacCallum says you and your men attacked his village, and killed almost everyone, burning whatever you could, stealing what you couldna."

"'Tis lies!" Though he knew that, and could and would easily prove it, knowing why Marissa had been taken now seemed so much worse. He didn't want to imagine the horrors she endured, even as he couldn't prevent the images of the possibilities. At least now, he knew what must be done to free her. He hoped this would not re-ignite the war that seemed to be falling apart of late.

He read the message once more. Had his wife noticed this last bit? "Wildcat, look."

Gillian leaned over his arm and read the message again. "Aye. She asks you for help. I pray she is not being tortured to make this request."

Marissa wanted him to uncover the truth and find out who had actually attacked the MacCallums. He turned to his wife.

"We wait. I must investigate these claims." He gave the Crawford messenger a sideways glance. "Rest yourself before you return to your village. I will send a message with you when you go."

"Royce, 'tis not wise to wait! Lord knows what they

are doing to her. The longer she stays there, the worse it could be. You must free her!"

"We will question the messenger. Your daughter has requested I investigate. I will honor her wishes. We will find the truth about the attack on the MacCallums."

Royce held up a hand to silence any further protests. His daughter was as smart and cunning as any of his sons or the knights in his employ. While she might be held against her will, Royce knew his daughter had likely smuggled the message out without her captor's notice. He respected her request, knowing his smart and strong daughter's instincts reflected her honor. She might be a captive, but she was willing to ask a boon in favor of her captor. Her request revealed much about her character and bolstered his pride.

He ran a hand through his hair. With the battle soon to be abandoned, the Scots would disperse across the country. Traveling into the Uplands would be risky, but he had no choice. Anyone he encountered would know he was not on king's business. He would go with the proof his daughter required. Would he be forced to battle his way to her? Didn't matter. He'd do it.

# CHAPTER SEVENTEEN

Ian finished tying his goods to the pack horse and turned to face Jamie and Lachlan. Fiona stood by the keep, her eyes swollen and red. Not only had Edwin still not returned from his journey, Ian and Jamie departed this morn. By her side stood Marie, her face pale and drawn. He frowned. She'd looked fatigued and ashen the last few days and her usual spark had faded. Had she fallen ill? Mayhap he should postpone this trek yet again.

Nay, he couldna. The chance of being found here by her father grew greater every day. Not only that, but there was much she needed to know, and much he still needed to plan. Doing so here would endanger the entire Crawford clan. He wouldna risk his mother's family. He faced very important decisions and wanted to be on his own lands when he sorted through the details. He wondered if any of the dwellings were salvageable. In the days following the raid, he'd been too injured to pay close attention. By the time he'd been well enough to travel, he'd not wanted to look closely at what remained of his lands.

If he'd have thought when he set out over two months ago to make his final preparations for revenge, he would have found himself owning a slip of an English lass with enough fire to light his nights for years to come, he would have thought himself daft. By this point in the summer, he'd planned to have meted out his justice to the murderers and be on his way north. He shook his head. His strategies had crumbled into dust once the lass had upended all his arrangements. Now ... he just wanted to keep her forever, however he could. How had she wormed her way into his heart like this? As much as he wanted her, he still needed to sort out the truth. Was her father the vicious killer he'd sworn to destroy, or was Marie right and the one who slaughtered his clan still unknown? His doubts had grown stronger than his surety and he needed to know.

He strode over to Fiona and pulled her close for a hug. She sobbed loudly, then slapped him away, though her blows were little more than half-hearted shoves.

"Go on with you. I'll be fine. You take care of the lass."

"Fiona, we will miss you. But we will return. Soon."

She nodded and he turned to Marie. "Come lass, 'tis time."

She lifted one hand and placed it in his. The steel cuff around her wrist reminded him of what she still was to him, at least outwardly. The jewels glinting in the morning sun told a more truthful tale. The cuff was a bracelet, akin to fine jewels she had likely worn as the daughter of an earl. He looked to the collar around her neck. Though the most obvious sign of her enslavement, he found he didna want to take it off her. If he had jewels added to the steel to exactly match the cuff, would she be willing to continue wearing it? Somehow, he must find a way to keep her for always.

While Ian he settled her onto the saddle, Jamie said his goodbyes to Fiona. Ian climbed up behind Marie and guided the horse out of the bailey. His clansman fell into place beside him. All felt right; Marie curled in his lap, the last of the MacCallum clan headed toward their former home.

They traveled for several hours and Jamie entertained Marie with tales of their childhood. Ian smiled, recalling those innocent days, when he'd run free with his brothers in the fields, when the most difficult task in his life had been the shearing of the sheep. He'd grown up knowing he would someday lead the clan, not realizing he would never have the chance.

He would rebuild his clan, restore the proud

MacCallum name. As laird, as he had been born to be, he would see his people prosper once more. Soon, one way or another, his plans for vengeance would either see fruition or fall to the wayside, and he could focus on those other goals.

Marie shifted against him and her warm soft body stirred other notions. He smiled against her hair, reaching up to cup her breast. Might as well enjoy the ride. He'd ensure she did as well.

She stiffened and gasped, but the nipple under his thumb hardened. Mayhap this had been a mistake. He wanted her again, now. How easily he got lost in her. The spell she'd woven about him had him forever thinking with his cock instead of his brain. He didn't really fight against his desire, knowing 'twas better for the ride to have such a distraction, rather than his ever present thoughts of violence and revenge to focus on.

"Not fair, Ian."

Jamie's voice cut into the bubble surrounding his logic. Ian turned to find his clansman grinning at him.

"She is mine, Jamie."

"Aye, but to flaunt her like that in front of me ... I'm only made of flesh, and that flesh is protesting being left out."

Ian chuckled at the humorous gleam in Jamie's gaze, though Marie stiffened in his arms.

"I can hear every word you say."

Her words drifted into a moan and she squirmed when he continued to tease her breast through the thin gray dress. He moved to the other, giving it the same lavish treatment and savoring the feel of her heart racing beneath his hand. He suspected she stifled her cries, but he wanted to hear her. With a hard pinch to her nipple, he leaned over and nipped at her neck. She gave a tiny squeak and shuddered wildly. A smile curled his mouth, and he slid his hand down, lifting the kirtle to slip underneath and touch her warm skin.

Her pussy was wet and hot, swollen and pulsing around his teasing fingers. She squirmed again, her arse brushing against his cock. He hardened immediately and longed to feel her wet heat engulfing him. Soon enough.

"But you like it, lass, don't you?" Lifting his head, he turned to Jamie. "I suppose taking a rest wouldna hold us back too much."

Jamie grinned. "And I know the perfect place."

\* \* \*

By the time night fell, Marissa wanted to scream with frustration. With the exception of the one break to tend to their needs, and where she'd been thoroughly wrung out by the two men, Ian had teased her all afternoon. Her body felt like it might combust. She needed release, and she knew he knew it. Did he take delight in torturing her this way?

Yet, his hard cock had pressed against her through his kilt and she knew he was just as affected as she was. When Ian dismounted, he moved stiffly. She held back a smile at his obvious discomfort. Served the cruel bastard right!

He helped her down, and once more, that dreaded chain was affixed to her collar. Yet, she found she rather liked watching the excitement grow in his eyes when he pulled her near. Suddenly the chain seemed so much more than just a means to prevent her flight.

"Stay here, lass."

She sucked in a breath. He would leave her unchained? She managed a nod, holding his gaze. He leaned down, his lips against hers for the briefest caress before he drew away, settling the coiled chain on the ground beside her feet. When he walked away, she looked around. She was somewhere in the wilds of Scotland, she certainly couldn't make an escape now, not with the chain dangling from the collar. The fact he'd left her thus roused a strange tightness in her chest. She sat down under the tree, picking up the end link of the chain and toying absently with it.

Before long, a cheerful fire had been built. She glanced around, seeing only Ian. Where had Jamie gone? A shiver of anticipation crept along her spine. When Ian walked over, the heat in his eyes brought her need to life once more. He hadn't even touched her yet.

She kept her hands clasped before her when he knelt down. He took the end of the chain from her and stood, and she slowly rose with him. Instead of turning and pulling her along behind him, he coiled the chain slowly around his arm, the pull on her neck drawing her closer to him. Her heart thudded and she gave a moment's thought to resisting, but found herself already too aroused to do so. She let him draw her near, until her breasts brushed his chest. The sensation against her hardened nipples was barely a tease, not enough to even bring a full flare of delight.

"Come, lass, we have some time alone before Jamie returns with our meal. Would you like to clean up?"

Her tongue too thick to talk, she nodded and allowed him to lead her to the nearby stream. He unhooked the chain from her collar and allowed her a moment's privacy, before standing patiently beside her while she splashed the cool water on her face and neck. All too soon, he replaced the chain and led her back to the fire. Again, he didn't drag her behind him, he kept her at his side, his hand lightly holding her arm. His fingers moved slightly over her skin, and the touch left her breathing unsteady. She glanced up to find him watching her, a hint of a smile lifting the corners of his mouth. Her throat suddenly dry, she averted her gaze, her cheeks flaming.

He said nothing when he spread her out on his pallet, already in place. She didn't think to protest when his hands moved along her body, squeezing her breasts, pinching her nipples, sliding along her sides, spreading her legs. She reached for him, anxious to soothe the deep burning fire, and bit her lip to stifle a cry when he found his way into her with a furious stroke. She held back her cries as he pumped, his hands at her hips holding her still for his forceful thrusts. His cock seemed to grow ever harder, and the sensation of him filling her stole her breath. Higher and harder, he drove her, the pleasure blinding her, stealing her hearing. Her awareness was only for him, his body satisfying her, his scent surrounding her, his mouth claiming her.

When the explosion burst over her, she did cry out, the sound muffled by his lips on hers, his tongue as deep into her mouth as his cock was into her body. She rocked around him, her pussy clenching hard with soul-searing pleasure. Ian yanked his mouth from her, stiffening above her, his own hoarse cry sounding a moment before his hot seed bathed her sex. She clung to him, their bodies quivering in time with each other, their breathing a perfectly tuned lyre that wove a magical melody.

Several moments passed before Ian drew away, his gaze intent. Marissa wondered why he seemed more somber than usual. An uneasy feeling nibbled at her gut. She forced it aside. 'Twas just hunger.

As if that were a cue, Jamie emerged with a large duck. Marissa hurriedly drew her dress down, but judging from the way his eyes lit with heat, he knew exactly what had just passed between she and Ian. She sighed, eying the fowl, knowing she would be expected to clean the bird. Sure enough, Ian motioned her over, and she rose on shaky legs.

Jamie aided her with the duck, and soon the bird had been spitted and now roasted over the fire. She sat quietly beside the pit, unsure what else was expected of her. She caught Jamie watching her intently. She'd be shared yet again tonight. Her sex clenched in anticipation, and heat warmed her cheeks.

He reached out to turn the duck, his arm sliding against her breast. She inhaled sharply as a slice of desire bolted through her. Jamie leaned back, his gaze on hers. He ran a finger lightly along her lip and she trembled at the touch. Behind her, she heard footsteps as Ian strode over to check on the horses. She pulled away from Jamie. Oddly self-aware, she kept her gaze focused on the bird.

She'd always known Jamie had enjoyed their times together, but for the first time, she'd found herself longing for him to take her alone. God's teeth, she wanted him as much as she wanted Ian. How could she love two men? 'Twas wicked and immoral. Her family would be horrified. She suddenly found she didn't care. The shock and revulsion such thoughts would have stirred a few weeks ago no longer taunted her. A hint of serenity took hold, and she lowered her head to hide her smile.

She didn't care what anyone thought of her. All that mattered was her and Ian and Jamie. Ian's footsteps sounded again as he neared the fire once more. She forced her attention to the duck, noting 'twas almost done.

"Is it ready yet?" Ian asked.

She turned to look at him, surprised to see a hint of annoyance furrowing his brow. Why? Did this have anything to do with the moment she and Jamie had shared?

"Almost," she said.

"Here." He handed her some bread.

"Thank you." She bit into the doughy bread, and thought nothing could taste better. When he handed her the skin with ale, she took a deep swallow to quench her thirst.

When the bird was done, Ian and Jamie ate in silence. Marissa reached to take some meat, and Ian held up a hand to stop her. She gave him a quizzical look.

"You will wait until we are finished." The cold tone of his voice set her skin to gooseflesh. Why did he seek to humiliate her? She suspected she knew the cause of his anger, and that reason helped keep her from lashing out as she wanted to. He ignored her while he continued to eat. She folded her arms and shook her head. Foolish man.

He finally turned and offered her some of the succulent meat. She shook her head, refusing to look at him.

"Lass, you must eat."

She recognized the order in his words, but again shook her head. From the corner of her eye, she saw him stiffen. Yet, she remained still and resisted the urge to fix him with her fiercest glare.

He grabbed her chin and leaned in close. "You will eat, or I'll punish you."

She jerked out of his grip. "I'm not hungry."

"Marie, I am telling you now to eat."

"You'll have to force me then."

"So be it."

"Ian, let the lass be."

It took all of Marissa's will not to turn and stare at Jamie. Her anger over Ian's cruel behavior would burst free if she read understanding in his clansman's expression.

Instead, she finally lifted her head to meet Ian's stormy gaze. The fury in his eyes spurred a sickening feeling in her stomach. He looked over at Jamie. The anger escalated to a rage she didn't understand. When he returned his stare to her, she recognized something else. Possessiveness like she'd never witnessed in him before. Understanding dawned, and with it, her earlier peace returned and diminished a large portion of her anger.

"She will need her strength —" Ian said.

"Let her be," Jamie repeated. "You've done enough to the poor girl. Why must you humiliate her further now? You've taken her from the Crawfords so you can drag her along to face your demons. Have a care, or she'll be the worst enemy you could ever have."

"What do you mean, face my demons? I've no demons to face."

"Aye, you do. You've carried them since your wife and son died. Now they've grown, and you've actually become jealous. Of me."

"I've told you before to mind your own business. You

don't know what you speak of." Ian stood and took a few strides from the fire.

"Don't I?" Jamie followed. "You weren't the only one who lost people. I lost my parents, my brothers that night too, in case you forgot. I miss them every day. But dragging the poor innocent lass all over Scotland is not the way to heal. I've warned you of the dangers this path will bring, and now you've made your own mess. I'll not have you using the lass to appease your misguided resentment. Lest you forget, you were the one who invited me to share. You canna blame me, or the lass, if we feel something for each other. 'Tis your own doing."

Ian spun about and Marissa cringed at the fury on his face. Jamie glanced her way, the reassurance in his gaze easing her worry. A little bit. In silence, she watched Jamie continue to goad Ian until finally, fists clenched, Ian raised his arm.

"Nay!" Marissa couldn't stop the cry. Both men looked at her. She took a deep breath. "He's your clansman. He only wants you to ... to ... "

"To what? Let my family's deaths go unavenged?"

"Nay! Ian, revenge isna what you think. It doesna bring peace, it brings more heartache," said Jamie. "Look what you've done to poor Marie in the name of revenge. Somehow, she came to care for you and for me. She canna help her feelings, any more than I can."

Marissa held her breath waiting for Ian's response. He glared at each one of them then turned and stalked into the forest. She longed to run after him, but even if Jamie hadn't stepped in front of her, she wouldn't have. He needed to sort this all out for himself.

She turned to Jamie. "You are a wise man."

He shrugged and resumed his seat by the fire, grabbing another hunk of the goose. "I doubt Ian thinks so."

"He's angry. And hurt. Jealous."

"He's no reason to be jealous. He brought this whole

mess down on his own head."

"Aye, he has. He's spent a long time nursing his need for vengeance. I imagine 'tis hard for him to let it go."

"You are a wise woman," said Jamie, almost echoing her earlier words. "It's one reason why he isna yet ready to let you go."

The heat in her face drew a soft chuckle from the Scotsman. He leaned over and brushed a brief kiss along her lips. The fire in her core flared to life. She'd never been alone with Jamie, and somehow the thought of doing so now seemed a betrayal to Ian. She shouldn't care, but she pulled away anyway.

Jamie sighed. "You love him, lass, don't you?"

She nodded. "I don't know how or why, but you are right. I do love him."

Jamie said nothing, but the disappointment lining his brow stirred a corresponding ache in her heart.

"I love you too, Jamie. Mayhap not exactly the same, but I do. Tonight, I don't want to hurt Ian anymore."

The grin brightening his face soothed her worry. "You always surprise me, lass."

Certain she'd eased his heartache, she decided to discuss the message she'd sent to her father. Jamie listened patiently while she described her plea for assistance, and her surety her father would do as she asked.

"I am sure he will find the ones responsible."

"I dinna ken, lass. Your father will want vengeance from Ian and me for what we've done."

"I'll ensure he doesn't seek to avenge my honor. He can deny me nothing."

Jamie grinned. "Aye, lass, I suspect he doesna." After a moment, he sobered. "And what will you do if we learn he is the one behind the attacks?"

"I know he didn't. I know my father will find the true raiders."

"But, lass, the pennant. I saw it."

She shook her head. "I believe you're mistaken, and I

understand how that could be. Tell me again what the pennant looked like."

Jamie shook his head. "I've already told you, lass. Was the red banner with the black panther upon it, the gold stripes behind it?"

"Gold stripes?" Here was still more absolute proof. "Jamie, Montchester's coat does not bear gold stripes."

"Are you sure?"

She glared at him. "Of course, I am sure. How can you doubt me on this? Why have you never told me this before?"

"You didna ask about the colors."

She closed her eyes to contain the surge of annoyance. She could have brought an end to this much sooner if only she'd thought to clarify the colors of the flag. 'Twould do no good now. At least she might be able to learn whose coat of arms had gold stripes with its black panther. She opened her eyes and stared at Jamie.

"Whoever did this tried to make it appear my father attacked you. They clearly hadn't expected anyone to survive." She gave a silent prayer of thanks the raiders had not completely succeeded with their murderous plan.

\* \* \*

Ian walked deeper into the forest, needing the distance between him and his clansman. The reality of Jamie's words seemed to mock him, and he growled, wishing for something to hit.

He needed revenge, so Sheila and Duncan could rest in peace. He'd lived the last two years for just that purpose, and now he doubted everything he had believed so strongly. He leaned against the tree, realizing he could no longer clearly remember his wife's face. He missed her, every day, though if he were honest with himself, he'd realize he thought of her far less since he'd taken Marie.

Marie. The dilemma she posed continued to grow. He

cared for her, more than he thought he could ever care for another woman again. He didn't want to ever let her go. He couldna keep her. She was a tool to be used and when his goals were achieved, he had to toss her aside.

But he couldn't do that either. She would always be a part of him, as much as Sheila and Duncan were. He would carry her memory until the end of his days.

Why must she remain a memory? The question taunted him. The idea of always having Marie for his was a dream, one he could never attain. After what he'd done to her, she would never stay with him willingly. He didna blame her if she chose Jamie over him. Much as he wanted to keep her beside him, he found he had no desire to keep her enslaved for the rest of her life.

He would have to let her go. 'Twas no longer any question. He couldna keep her this way. If she chose to be with Jamie, he'd accept it.

"Sheila, what do I do?"

*Do you love her?*

Ian looked around. For the first time in two years, he swore he heard his wife's voice. No one stood in the darkness with him. In the distance, he made out the glow of the fire. He was alone. As he had been for so long.

*You're not alone anymore.*

He shook his head. Madness had finally claimed him. He sank to his knees, tears burning his eyes. Flashes of the night his wife was murdered came at him with blinding speed, until he could no longer breathe.

He choked back a sob. "Sheila, I must avenge you."

*Move on, my love. 'Tis time. Forget revenge and embrace the gift you've been given.*

Great wrenching sobs tore through him and he collapsed on the forest floor. He hadn't shed one tear for his wife and son, and now, he could no longer stop them. When the tumult subsided, he felt weak as a tiny baby bird. Even his anger at Jamie had been cleansed away.

For the first time, he had a clear vision of what to do.

He did love Marie, loved her defiance, her strength and her refusal to break, no matter what he put her through. Her tawny eyes consumed his thoughts, and adoration shone through. Even sharing her with Jamie didna diminish his love. She clearly cared for his clansman in return. Did Ian dare hope she might feel something for him as well?

How could it be possible, after everything he'd done? He didn't know, but he had to find out. There was just one way to do that. He wiped his eyes and stood, feeling stronger than he had in years.

He strode toward the camp.

\* \* \*

Marissa held her breath while she awaited Jamie's response to her admission. Surprisingly, he did not seem angry.

"So The Panther will likely come searching for clues."

"He could." She stared, realization sinking in. "You mean he might go to your lands?"

Jamie nodded. "'Tis a likely place to start the search. If he isn't found by The Bruce and his men first."

Panic stole her breath for a moment. "We travel to your lands too. What if we encounter The Bruce?"

Jamie grinned. "Lass, we'll be safe. 'Tis your father's neck I would worry about."

"My father is capable, and likely travels with his men." Yet, she couldn't help worrying. Even if her father made it through Scotland without incident, what would happen when he reached MacCallum land?

She envisioned a terrible battle, one that ended with her father, Ian or Jamie, or all three, dead. She must prevent that at all costs. Mayhap encountering her father on MacCallum land would be a blessing. 'Twas a place to start in searching for the true murderers. As long as she convinced her father to help. Would Ian agree?

As if her thoughts had brought him back, he appeared at the edge of the trees. She tilted her head, studying him. Something seemed different, but she couldn't decipher what.

"Come, lass, we have to settle some things."

She rose, unable to resist his command. Jamie caught her hand and she smiled at him.

"'Tis all right. If I need you, I'll scream."

He chuckled and released her. She looked at Ian. His dark gaze called to her, and something she'd never seen before beckoned, more fiercely that his hungry passion.

When she reached him, he took her hand and led her into the forest. A moment of alarm crept over her, but she forced it back. After all that had passed between them, she no longer feared he might kill her. She sensed a myriad of odd emotions engulfing him. Her heart raced in response.

He finally stopped and turned to face her, taking her other hand. Several moments passed before he spoke.

"I've treated you terribly, lass. Can you ever forgive me for that?"

"Ian, I don't understand. Aye, you have treated me abominably, but you've also shown me kindness at times. You have not injured or maimed me." She gave a wry smile. "Well, except that I may never make a good marriage."

"I am sorry. You've been ..."

"Ruined. Aye, there is that. But Ian, I know what drove you. Mayhap I can help you find the real monsters who destroyed your clan."

"What do you mean?"

"I've spoken at length with Jamie. What I've learned is proof those men were not my father's."

"Lass, you werena there. I saw it. The pennant."

"Ian, you were injured, it was dark, except for the

fires, and you watched the most horrible thing anyone should ever see. I discovered something else tonight. The pennant you saw bore gold stripes, did it not?"

"Aye."

"Montchester's pennant doesn't have gold stripes. It is solid red."

He stared at her in silence, and despite the sparse light from the moon through the trees, she read the realization in his eyes.

"Just red?"

She nodded.

"The attacker's pennant bore the gold stripes." Her heart raced. She sensed he finally believed her. "'Twas not my father."

He shook his head. "'Twould seem so."

Hope rose swift and pure, obliterating her fears like a cleansing summer rain. "Ian, I can help you find who did this. My father and I, we can both help you."

He slumped, looking oddly defeated. Marissa hated to see him in such a state and longed to draw him near and hold him. She refrained, knowing he would not accept her comfort. Yet.

"Lass, I dinna care anymore who did it. Nothing will bring them back. But I must make repayment to you for what I've done. You're free, lass. I'll return you to your father. On the morrow, we head for Montchester."

She could barely breathe. He was taking her home. Part of her wanted to dance with excitement, the other part of her wanted to curl up and cry.

"Nay, Ian. I don't want to go home."

He stared at her wide-eyed. "What did you say?"

She hesitated, her hands twisting before her. "I... I want to stay with you, Ian, and help you find the raiders."

He shook his head, his mouth gaping. "You want to stay?"

She smiled at his confusion. "Aye. Ian, despite the way you took me, you've become very... important to me."

He stepped closer, placing his hands on her shoulders. "And you, to me. But, lass, the way I took you..."

"You didn't take me. Colin did. You saved me."

Again, he shook his head. "You canna mean that."

She nodded. "I do. I will stay with you for as long as it takes to bring your wife's and son's killers to the justice they deserve."

"Marie, you dinna know what you speak of."

"Marissa."

"Eh?"

The look of confusion on his face almost drew a laugh. "My name is Marissa. Not Marie."

A hint of a smile tugged at the corners of his mouth. "Aye, I suspected you dinna give me your true name. Marissa."

He said it two more times, as if testing the way it sounded in his mouth. Hearing him use her real name inspired intense longing.

"Well, lass, now I know who you truly are. 'Tis glad I am to make your acquaintance."

"I hope I'm more than merely an acquaintance," she said. "And I meant what I said. I will help you find the raiders."

He shook his head. "And if we learn 'tis your father and his men after all... you would go against your own kin?"

"I won't have to. After talking further with Jamie, I am more sure of that than ever. If you'll allow it, I know my father can help."

He hesitated, watching her warily. "After what I've done, I will be lucky if your father doesna slay me on sight."

"'Tis certainly a risk we face. I will not let him."

She moved closer, resting her hand on his chest. He said nothing; emboldened, she stepped still closer, pressing herself against him. The feel of his hard muscled body against hers stirred the now-familiar yearning. 'Twas so wrong to want this, want him, but she did. She loved him, would do everything in her power to help him avoid punishment for his acts against her. If he would allow it, she'd help him find his wife's killers. Above all, she would keep him safe from the noose. If that meant walking away from him once they learned the truth, then she would do it. 'Twould tear her heart out, but she would do it. To keep him safe and alive.

His arms came around her and she sighed with relief. They stood there silently, holding each other, and she had never felt more content.

"Come, let's return to Jamie. If we ride for Montchester in the morn, we need to rest."

He smiled and made no protest when she led him by the hand out of the forest. Jamie had already taken to his pallet, and appeared asleep. Marissa held back a smile. Did he feign slumber, or was he truly sleeping? She didn't care if he heard her and Ian, God's bones, she hoped he would wake and join them.

She'd become such a wanton, but found she rather enjoyed it. She moved toward Ian's pack and settled herself down, lifting her hopeful gaze to his. He grinned and sat beside her, drawing her close once more.

"Jamie seems to be asleep. We might wake him," he whispered.

"Mayhap I want him to," she whispered back.

Ian threw back his head and laughed. For the first time, Marissa saw how handsome he became when carefree and genuinely happy. The giddiness swept over her as well, and when he drew her near for a hungry kiss, she melted against him, anxious to feel his skin against her, his body filling hers. Completing her. This could be the very last chance she would have to lie with him, and she intended to make sure she had memories she would carry with her until the end of her days.

Ian lowered her to the pallet, his hands moving wildly, his kiss stirring her as it never had before. She wrapped herself around him, pressing tightly to his body, conveying her want. A hard muscled chest slid behind her, and she wanted to weep with joy as Jamie curled into her. Ian continued to devour her mouth, his hands and Jamie's moving along her body, removing her clothing, leaving her bare beneath them.

They drew away at the same moment, and she forced her heavy-lidded eyes open to find them watching her with hunger. Her heart raced and her body tightened in response. She reached up for them, and slid an arm around each of their necks. They didn't resist her tug, covering her with their hard bodies.

She felt as if she were already home.

# chapter
# eighteen

The sound of hoofbeats roused Marissa. She could barely move. Ian's arm around her waist held her against him, while Jamie's hand rested on her hip, his legs twined with hers. She didn't want to relinquish their warmth, but they stirred, awakened by the approaching riders.

"Hurry, lass, cover yourself," Ian said, tossing her a dress from his pack. 'Twas not the same drab gray kirtle he'd given her previously. She smiled to find a soft cotton dress in a lovely shade of green. She had no time to admire it longer and quickly slid it over her body.

Both Ian and Jamie stood at alert, searching the horizon. Marissa set about gathering their belongings and packing them. She stepped between them, and took Ian's hand.

"Do you see anyone?" she asked. Her stomach rolled uneasily. Various ideas as to who the riders might be alarmed her.

"There. From the south," Jamie said, pointing.

She and Ian turned. Sure enough, a cloud of dust indicated a group of likely half a dozen men. They traveled across the land at a rapid pace, indicating they were probably not part of a larger train. Marissa flashed back to the day weeks ago when she and Leland had been surrounded by Colin and his men.

"We must go. Now." She tugged on Ian's arm.

He shook his head. "'Tis the Crawford banner."

Marissa couldn't fight the growing sense something wasn't right. She tugged again, then turned to Jamie.

"Make him listen. I have a very bad feeling about

those men."

"Relax, lass. If 'tis the Crawfords, we're not in any danger."

But her senses warned her disaster loomed if they did not flee. She had no weapon, could not help Ian and Jamie if necessary. The taunting voice in her head spoke again.

"Something's not right. It's Colin, and I don't trust him."

Ian looked at her for the first time. "He willna hurt you, lass. I'll kill him first."

"Please, Ian."

He shook his head. "'Tis too late now anyway. They are too close to outrun."

She held back the acid rising in her throat. "Then give me a weapon."

Both men looked at her. Then Ian nodded. "I have another sword in my roll. Jamie, fetch it."

Marissa didn't know whether to trust what she'd heard until Jamie approached and placed the blade in her hand. She looked from the sword to Ian, to Jamie, and back again. Several times. Finally, with a nod, she gripped the hilt and tested the weight. The steel was sturdy and clean, and after a few moves to test her ability, she felt comfortable enough to wield it satisfactorily.

She smiled up at Ian. "Thank you."

"I trust you willna turn it on me." He arched an eyebrow, but the tilt of his mouth gave away his humor. She grinned.

"Never. I'm glad you trust me."

"I've seen some of your skill. If your instincts are as good, we'll need your help."

They all turned to face the incoming men. As they pulled up, Marissa counted seven men. Colin sat to the left of the leader. The man slowly lifted his helm.

Her stomach rolled, her knees threatened to buckle. "Leland?"

\* \* \*

Ian snapped around to stare at Marie ... Marissa. She knew the man in the lead? Ian knew Leland deBurgh as a mercenary hired by many. He was loyal to no one. How did he know Marissa?

"I see you're still alive," the Englishman said. "I'd worried these heathen Scots might have killed you with their foolish antics."

"How can you be ...? I saw you. You were shot with an arrow." Marissa gaped at the man, her face ashen.

"Yes, well, it was blunt-tipped. And I wore protection."

Ian stared as Marissa straightened, her eyes now blazing. The transformation stunned him.

"You set this up? You were in on this?"

She spun about and focused her furious gaze on Ian. He backed up a step. "Nay, lass, I know nothing of him."

She shook her head, and swayed. For a moment, he feared she might collapse. Then she straightened once more.

"I don't know if I can believe you."

Her softly uttered words sliced through him, piercing his heart. He'd just gained her trust and love and now she hated him again.

"Lass, I knew of no plans to kidnap you. Your presence was as much a surprise to me as to you." He spoke steadily and remained still, recalling the sword she now held. Her fingers clenched and unclenched on the hilt. His gaze drifted between hers and the sword.

"I didn't involve the Scot," deBurgh called. "I didn't want *him* to take you. You were supposed to be mine."

She spun back around, and Ian stepped closer to her back, noting Jamie did the same.

"You vile bastard! How could you do this to me?"

The English knight sighed. "You are worth a lot of money. Your father would pay a huge ransom, and there are others who would pay even more to own you. Of course, now that you've been thoroughly used, your value has greatly diminished."

Ian moved at the same moment Marissa issued a loud cry and raised her sword, lunging toward the Englishman. He caught her around the waist, just as Colin Crawford leapt from his horse, sword unsheathed and pointed right at her.

"Been waiting for a chance to take my vengeance on you, lassie," Colin growled, advancing.

Ian stepped in front of her. "You'll have to get through me first." He raised his sword.

An evil smile split Colin's face. "I've been waiting for this chance for two years. Me first mistake was leaving you alive. That wife of yours sure gave me a good ride. Shame she didn't live. She'd have given us all some pleasure."

"'Twas you!" Ian snarled. He struggled to keep the emerging fury at bay, knowing he needed a calm head to take Colin out once and for all.

"Aye, me and Leland there. The English king paid us handsomely to lay waste to those villages," Colin taunted.

"'Tis a pity he passed," the Englishman called out. "He was quite generous and gave us leave to do whatever we wished before we killed the heathen bastards!"

"You're evil!" Marissa cried.

Ian glanced at her. Jamie now restrained her, whispering into her ear. She stopped fighting, but did not lower her blade. The sight of her in her rage, sword aimed at the Englishman, stirred an awe-filled pride. He loved her even more in that moment.

"You will pay, Leland," Marissa vowed. "You murdered those innocent people, simply for the coin."

"Aye, and I'll continue to do so, if the prince chooses

to maintain my employ."

"Never again," Ian swore, drawing the men's attention.

Colin let loose a guffaw. "You think you're gonna stop us? You'll be long buried, as you should've been two years ago. If I'd known you still lived then, I would have taken more time with your lovely wife. She screamed so nicely for me."

A strange calm settled over Ian, the rage now under his control. He stalked closer to Colin, sword ready. He didn't have long to wait before Colin lunged. Ian sidestepped and lifted his blade, averting Crawford's strike with a loud screech when the blades came together. Colin bellowed his anger at missing his target and spun about.

Ian remained calm and simply deflected each of Colin's blows, backing up a step at a time. The clang of the blades against each other echoed in the otherwise still morning air, and the others fell still and quiet, watching the battle. Ian continued his evasive moves, lulling the beefy man into thinking he had the upper hand. Soon enough, Colin began to tire, sweat pouring down the sides of his face. He blinked and wiped his eyes with the back of his hand and lunged again.

Ian eluded the dodge, sending Colin stumbling past. Ian lifted his sword. He brought the hilt down hard on the back of the Crawford's neck, sending him to the ground. He moved to strike, but Colin rolled and lifted his sword. Ian knocked it aside. Before Colin regained any leverage, Ian slammed his blade into the man's chest, piercing his heart.

Colin stared with wide eyes, gasping and coughing. Rivulets of blood spurted from his lips and his sword fell from his limp hand. Ian pulled his blade free, more blood gushing from the wound. Colin grabbed weakly at the gash, a vain attempt to stem the flow.

"You... bastard!" Colin choked and gasped. "She was mine."

With that, he closed his eyes, his life disappearing. Ian spun about. Marissa stared at him with wide eyes set in her very pale face. He bent and wiped the blood from his blade on Colin's shirt before bending to pick up the fallen man's sword.

"Nay!"

Marissa's cry drew his attention and he turned to see the other men dismounting. Leland deBurgh strode toward him, sword raised, his face twisted in a furious scowl.

"You won't escape death today, MacCallum!"

Before Leland could approach, Marissa jumped in front of him, her sword waving in quick strikes that forced the Englishman to retreat as he defended against her furious assault. Ian admired her skill, the way she avoided each of her opponent's blows, while driving him back. Metal screamed when the blades connected and Ian wanted to keep watching how his English lass maintained her advantage over her foe. But another of the knights neared him, ready to attack, and Ian soon found himself in battle.

He used both his and Colin's swords to deflect the other man's strikes, landing a solid blow of his own just under the soldier's helm and catching his neck. The man screamed and fell face forward, but Ian had no time to savor the victory when another charged him. He caught sight of Jamie dispatching another knight and facing a new attacker. Yet one more man came up on Ian's other side. He lifted Colin's steel to deflect him, while driving his own blade into the arm of the first foe. The man howled and dropped his sword, and Ian wasted no time slaying his enemy. He whirled about in time to deflect another thrust, his blade shrieking in protest. Lifting the second sword, he dealt another death blow, nearly decapitating the enemy.

He looked over at Jamie. Only Marissa fought on, and Ian suspected she grew tired. He moved toward the battling pair, his ears assaulted by the metallic wails of the blades coming together. His pride in Marissa's ability quickly gave way to concern when she stumbled and he ran toward her, avoiding the bodies of the fallen men.

He couldn't make himself move fast enough, and from the corner of his eye, saw Jamie also moving toward her.

He watched in horror when her blade was wrested free and deBurgh hauled her against him. She pummeled him with her fists, but the point of his blade at her chin stilled her resistance.

"You're coming with me," deBurgh said. "You two, stay where you are."

"You bastard, you will hang for this!" Marissa cried. She winced as deBurgh pressed the point of his blade into her skin. Ian remained frozen in his place, looking for a chance to free her.

"By the time they find you in some brothel in Edinburgh, I'll be long gone." He ran his fingers along the metal still encircling her neck. "You're nothing more than a slave now, according to this."

Ian wished he'd never placed that blasted collar around her neck. He took another step toward deBurgh.

"Don't move!" the Englishman screamed. "You filthy Scot, you should have died two years ago. She'd have been mine to break."

"You are a sick man, deBurgh, preying on helpless children and women." Flashes of that fateful night intruded on Ian's concentration until he forced them aside, determined to maintain his focus on the man holding Marissa. He dared another step, noting Jamie mirrored his movement.

"Stop right there! I'll kill her now!"

"I thought you wanted the coin she'll bring. I'll buy her." Ian didna dare meet Marissa's gaze, for fear he would lose his concentration. He must remain calm to get the madman to release her.

deBurgh shook his head. "Nay, I'll not miss my chance at sampling what she's learned at your hand." The blade of his sword lowered. "She was to be mine, until I tired of her. Colin Crawford had instructions to bring her to me. You ruined all that! But sullied as she is, she's still a nice piece, one I'll enjoy taking my fill of before I get rid of her."

deBurgh's eyes had taken on a crazed, wild look. Ian's heart raced, his palms sweating while he determined what to do. If the man went mad, he could kill Marissa before Ian could stop him.

"You sick monster!" Marissa screamed, trying once more to break free. deBurgh only tightened his grip around her waist and she gasped, the air forced from her lungs.

Ian's hand clenched on the hilt of his sword, still searching for some weak point in the man's stance. His eyes narrowed to recognize the intense deliberation in Marissa's face. Before he realized what she intended, she'd jerked her head back, catching deBurgh square in the face, the contact echoing with a loud crack. Blood poured from his nose and he howled in pain. The moment he loosened his grip, she broke free, running toward Ian.

deBurgh made one attempt to stop her, but Jamie's blade at his neck halted him. He tried to lift his own blade, but Ian's clansman quickly disarmed him.

Ian caught Marissa when she threw herself at him. He held her tight, relieved she had escaped unharmed. After a few moments, she drew away and turned to Jamie.

"Kill him," she said.

\* \* \*

Marissa turned to Leland. Her disgust and hatred for what he'd done to Ian and what he tried to do to her overrode her logic, replacing it with a powerful hunger for revenge. She wanted his blood. She'd spent weeks worrying and grieving his likely death. To learn he had been the one behind the attacks sickened her further.

"What are you waiting for?" she asked. Why did Ian look so entertained? She found nothing humorous in all this. She wanted Leland's head on a pike. 'Twas all that would satisfy her need for justice.

"Lass, he will taste our vengeance. But I wouldna like to be charged with murdering him."

At his words, the bloodlust ebbed and understanding took hold. No matter Ian's revenge was more than justified. He could be hanged for killing a loyal English subject.

"We will bring him to my father. He will know what to do."

"I expect we won't have to bring him anywhere," Jamie said. He nodded toward the horizon.

In the distance, a cloud of dust indicated another band of riders approached. Marissa bent to pick up her sword where it had landed, ready once again to fight. She glanced up at Ian, but read nothing in his expression. He walked past her and assisted Jamie in securing their prisoner, binding Leland tightly enough so no danger of his escape existed. Yet the foolish man still fought, knocking himself into Jamie's legs, sending the Scot tumbling to the ground. Ian slammed the hilt of his sword to the back of Leland's head. The blackguard fell forward unconscious.

When they finished securing the outlaw, the two Scotsmen came to stand on either side of her. She felt strong and proud to be beside them like this. She savored the feeling a moment before returning her attention to the approaching riders.

Who else could be coming? She glanced at the bodies strewn about. She suspected more would soon be added.

"Who is it?" Jamie asked.

The group neared, and a red banner fluttered in the air. Marissa squinted, her heart racing in excitement. Could it be ... it was! Her father had come!

"Ian, 'tis my father!" She grabbed his arm, unable to

contain her excitement. One glance into his grim face tempered her exuberance. "Don't worry. Once I tell him this is all because of Leland –"

He held up a hand to halt her words. Jamie's hand on her shoulder squeezed gently.

"Lass, he may have set the events in motion, but 'tis I who kept you these past months. Your father will want justice."

She shook her head. "Nay. I will not allow it. I will make him understand."

"Marissa, dinna worry for us. We will face whatever is due us," Jamie said. His vow rang strong, but the crease of his brow betrayed his worry.

She turned to Ian's clansman, laying a hand on his cheek. "I will see you are not blamed for any of this. I won't let anything happen to either one of you."

Jamie gave her a sad smile, his hand capturing hers as he moved closer. She leaned against Ian, savoring the safety of being so close to both of the men she'd come to love.

"I won't lose either of you." She barely had a chance to finish her vow when the riders neared. She recognized her father's helm and happy tears fell freely down her cheeks. She leaned her head on Ian's shoulder, her hand clasped tightly in Jamie's.

Her father halted a few feet from them and removed his helm. The fury in his eyes nearly left her burned to ash. Though she'd expected this reaction, the sight of her father's rage unnerved her.

He unsheathed his sword. "Which of you is Ian MacCallum?"

Ian stepped forward. "'Tis I."

Marissa tried to hold him back, but Jamie kept her close to him and she was forced to relinquish her grip on Ian's hand.

"You are hereby arrested for the crime of kidnapping. The king orders you into my custody. Judgment will be proclaimed at Montchester and you will be sentenced."

"Nay! Papa, don't do this. There is much you don't understand."

"I understand that heathen has you collared like an animal. He will pay for his crimes." Royce Langley dismounted. When he walked over, she broke free of Jamie, running to her father in an attempt to halt him. He grasped her shoulders, holding her still while he visually inspected her then pulled her close for a tight hug. Her tears overflowed once more.

"I am so very glad I've found you," her father said. He turned and nodded to his men, several of whom dismounted and moved toward Ian and Jamie.

Marissa disentangled herself from her father's embrace and ran to Ian's side. "Nay! I must explain first. Don't arrest them."

"Marissa, they kidnapped you, held you as their prisoner."

She looked toward her brother, Rowan, tears burning her eyes once more. She longed to go to him, to hug him as she had her father, but feared if she left Ian and Jamie's side, her father would attack.

She vigorously shook her head. "Rowan, you are a sight for my weary eyes. You must understand, both of you. Mayhap at first Ian held me captive. But 'tis Leland's fault. I stayed because I wanted to. Papa, Ian was going to bring me home."

Royce stared at her blankly, clearly not comprehending her words. "Leland?"

"I thought he was dead," said Rowan.

Marissa shook her head, sneering toward the bound man nearby. "He is right there, and he is the cause of all of this. Of so much worse."

"Explain yourself, Marissa."

She held back a smile to recognize his exasperated tone. She'd succeeded in diffusing his fury, at least a little. She turned to Ian.

"'Twill be all right, you'll see."

Ian shook his head. "Lass, dinna do this. Go home with your family. Jamie and I ... we'll be fine."

"I will not let either of you be arrested. I love you both and I will not lose either of you."

The shock on Ian's face mirrored that on Jamie's. She grinned and placed a kiss on each of their cheeks.

"Trust me."

"Lass, I dinna deserve you," Ian said. "Neither of us do."

"Aye, you should go find someone noble to wed," Jamie added.

She scowled at him. "Both of you hush and allow me to speak with my father. When all is done, we will be together."

"Lass —" Ian began. She placed her fingers over his mouth.

"I am more than capable of holding my own. My father will not hurt me. I will ensure he doesn't hurt either of you."

"Marissa!" Her father's shout startled her. She turned.

"Papa, this is all Leland's doing. He arranged for me to be stolen. He led raids on peaceful villages and killed all the others. Papa, he tried to make it appear the attacks were carried out by you!"

Her father shook his head. "What is this nonsense?" He looked over toward Leland and back to Marissa.

"Are you mad, Marissa? What have those Scots done to you?" Rowan shouted.

"Nay, I am not mad. You will all listen to me!"

She continued to hold Ian's and Jamie's hands, needing the strength she drew from their calloused grip. Marissa called her father and brother closer, not wanting to divulge this before all of the other men.

It took several moments before the men stopped scowling at each other and for her father to silence his insistence that the MacCallums be arrested. When she was certain she had their complete attention, she related all that had happened. She said nothing about the physical relationship that had grown between the three of them, but she made it clear that Ian had saved her from much more brutal treatment at Colin's hands. That he and Jamie had protected her on several occasions.

Her father and Rowan remained silent for several moments, simply staring. Her father's narrowed eyes told her he still didn't believe Ian and Jamie caused her no harm. Rowan, at least, gave her an understanding smile. Her face heated to see his knowing stare and she suspected he guessed the true nature of the relationship between herself and Ian and Jamie.

"They didn't bring you home, or free you, though," Royce said. "That alone is a crime."

She faced him once again. "Nay, 'tis not. Ian has his reasons, and I stand beside him, and Jamie. If not for them, I could very well be dead. Arrest Leland, and make him face justice for the murders he committed."

"Marissa, I realize these last weeks have not been easy for you. Once you are home and -"

"Nay, Papa. I will not change my mind. I want to stay with Ian."

Royce's face reddened with rage. He took another step toward the three of them, but Marissa held her ground, stepping forward and lifting her chin.

"Marissa, go with your brother."

She shook her head. "Nay. Please don't fight me on this."

Her father studied the three of them, his gaze moving slowly over each one of them. His jaw clenched, a muscle in his cheek twitching under the force of his anger.

"Your mother is desperate for word of your safety. You must return to Montchester with me."

"Only if Ian and Jamie accompany us. Not as your prisoners."

"What have they done to you?" Royce asked, his voice

low.

"Nothing I didn't want, Papa." Her stomach knotted with embarrassment, knowing her father would comprehend her meaning. The light in his golden eyes sharpened, and heat flooded her face when he stared knowingly at her.

"You realize...?"

She nodded. "I do."

Silence hovered over them all. A loud groan broke the silence as Leland regained his senses.

He pulled his face out of the dirt. His eyes widened as he saw Royce.

"My lord! You've come! I tried to save your daughter!" he cried out.

"Hold your tongue, you murdering snake!" Marissa yelled.

"She is mad! These heathens have damaged her mind!" Leland argued.

"You lying bastard! I should have let Ian run you through when he had the chance." She clenched her fists, wanting nothing more than to beat the man for his lies and treachery.

"You killed my wife. My son!" Ian bellowed. "This is all because of you!"

Marissa smiled to see Leland cower under the face of Ian's rage. When he caught her eye, his expression softened and he gave her a small, hopeful smile. She returned it.

"He will pay, Ian. For everything he's done," she assured him. He gave her a nod, but remained silent, his gaze flicking to her father. She turned to Royce. "Papa, my mind is as strong and sane as always. Leland is a murderer."

"Do you hear the charges leveled against you?" Royce demanded of his knight.

"'Tis not true!" the mercenary sneered.

"Didn't you say the king paid you well to slaughter all

those innocents?" Marissa asked. She made no attempt to hide the disgust in her voice.

"You little whore! You spread your legs for those heathens!" Leland screamed. He paled when Royce took two steps over to him, sword still at the ready.

"That is my daughter's reputation you disparage! You already stand accused of the murder of many, deBurgh. Don't make me angry enough to kill you now, before you have a chance to be tried for your crimes," Royce said, his voice low and calm.

"But I'm telling you, they lie!" Leland protested. He struggled against his bonds, but Ian and Jamie had tied him securely.

Royce growled and Leland fell still. With a sneer of revulsion, he gave the order to his men to secure Leland for the return to Montchester. Uneasiness stung Marissa when her father deliberately ignored her on his way to mount. Rowan stepped over to her, after ensuring his help was not needed with Leland.

"Are you sure you want to do this, Marissa?" he asked. His green eyes sharpened with concern, then turned cold as he focused on the two men behind her.

"Aye, Rowan. I love them both." She kept her voice low, not wanting her father to hear.

His eyes widened. "What madness is this?"

"Not madness. Love. I will not allow Papa, or anyone, to blame them for what's happened.

Ian saved me, Rowan. What Leland and his men planned..." She shuddered. "I could very well be dead if not for Ian."

Rowan stepped over to Ian. "My sister is determined to protect you, though I don't know why. If I learn you have harmed her in any way -"

"I am willing to face justice for my crimes," Ian vowed.

"Nay! Ian, stop! Jamie, take him away for a moment." She waited until Jamie had led Ian a few feet away before facing her brother. "Rowan, if not for them, who knows what harm would truly have befallen me."

"They kept you captive, Marissa. I can only imagine what they did to you in that time."

"Rowan, I will say it one last time. Ian. Saved. Me. He protected me, as did Jamie."

"But -"

"And I will admit that while he did not always treat me kindly, he had his reasons."

Rowan gaped at her. "What sort of reasons could he have to subject you to God only knows what sort of torture?"

"He thought Papa had killed his family. His wife and son. He acted as I expect you would in his stead."

"But -"

"I will hear no more. My mind is made up. They either come with me, as free men, or I will go with them far away from here."

Rowan seemed to want to say more, but refrained. Instead, he nodded and turned to where his father and the other men waited. Marissa turned to find Ian watching her warily. Jamie seemed uneasy as well. She walked over to them.

"Will you come with me to Montchester?"

Ian looked over at her father. The Panther astride his black destrier could certainly inspire fear, as well as respect. She clasped Ian's hand between hers.

"Please?"

"Doesna seem like a good idea, lass. Your father is likely to want our heads. 'Tis best if we ride north now. Go home to your family."

She shook her head. "Nay. If you will not come with me, I will go with you. Wherever you go. North, east, across the channel."

He said nothing for several moments. Jamie cleared his throat.

"Lass, your family loves you. We are going alone to

the Highlands. 'Tis not a journey for a lady to make."

Marissa rolled her eyes. "You are as much of an arse as he is." She jerked her thumb toward Ian.

"Wait just a minute!" Jamie protested.

"Hush, both of you!" She folded her arms and waited for several moments. "I love you both, despite how we ... started. I can never go back to my old life, not anymore. What's left for me there?"

"Lass, you see? We've ruined your chances for —" Ian said.

Marissa held up her hand. "I am not finished. There's nothing left, because there's nothing there that I want anymore. Yes, I will miss my parents and my brothers and sisters. I'm not the same girl who left to go for a ride with her sweetheart. I am a woman who has very different needs and desires." She lowered her voice with a hint of a smile.

Ian gaped at her, but Jamie threw his head back and laughed. When he quieted, he clapped Ian on the shoulder.

"You should see your face!" He chortled gleefully. "Ian, the lass wants you, even ox-headed as you are. Surely you willna deny her."

"You too, Jamie. I want both of you." She took a large measure of delight in the pleasure in his expression.

Ian ran a hand through his hair. "Are you sure of what you're saying, lass?"

She nodded. "I am. I won't force you to Montchester."

Ian shifted on his feet. "Your father -"

"Will learn to accept it. That he hasn't yet placed you under arrest means he won't."

"Yet."

"If you truly believe that and won't come, then I will leave with you now."

"What about your father?" Jamie asked.

"I will speak with him again. Wait here."

Marissa walked over to her father, tall upon his horse. Aware of the other men's eyes on her, she nodded in acknowledgement then faced her father. He looked every inch the fierce Panther towering over her, eyes sparking with anger, his mouth set in a grim line. She twisted her hands before her, suddenly aware of what these next moments would mean. How she longed to climb up in his arms and let him hold her as he had when she was a child and had suffered some hurt. This time, her pain might be caused by her father. She didn't know if she could bear that. She glanced toward Ian. His dark eyes held hers for a moment, and in them she found the love she knew he felt for her. She looked to Jamie, who gave her a tiny nod. The adoration in both men's gazes strengthened her courage.

She turned back to her father, lifted her chin and took a deep breath. "Papa, I want your word that Ian and Jamie will be treated as my guests while at Montchester. Or I will leave with them now."

He scowled, remaining silent for several moments. His gaze raked over the two men standing several feet away before returning his fiery stare to his daughter. Marissa held her breath as she awaited his answer.

"Very well. If I didn't fear your mother's wrath if I return without you, I'd have their heads." His stern words were tempered by a gleam of humor in his tawny eyes.

She smiled, knowing full well how her mother could make her fierce warrior father suffer under her anger. "I suppose Mama was ready to take up arms and come with you to find me."

Royce nodded. "Aye. Now, hurry. We're a full day's ride from Montchester. As it is, 'twill be long past nightfall ere we arrive."

Marissa nodded, her throat tight with joy. She turned and practically ran back to Ian and Jamie. They caught her between them.

"Please come to Montchester with me. My father will not seek your arrests."

"Are you sure, lass?" Ian asked.

"I am. You'll be safe there, and we can plan where to go."

Ian looked at Jamie. "What about you?"

Jamie hesitated. "I wouldna send you in there alone, Ian. It'll take more than that to get me to leave you and the lass."

Ian said nothing, merely held her tightly before setting her away from him. "Go to your father, lass. We will ride with his men behind you."

"Nay, I ride with you, Ian MacCallum. If you'll have me."

His dark eyes widened once more and she fought the threatening giggle. "Aye, lass, I'll have you for as long as you want to stay."

"Forever. Ian, I love you."

"And I you, lass. And I would show you how much, but mayhap that should wait. Until we dinna have an audience."

She let the laughter free then. "Aye. We'll wait. But not for too long."

He kissed her, and she didn't care if her father watched as she responded with eagerness. When she drew away, the promise in his dark eyes set her sex to clenching in need. Somehow, she would have to find some way to be with him at Montchester, certain her father planned to separate them. If she had her way, she would never be apart from Ian again.

Jamie pulled her near, placing a chaste kiss on the side of her mouth. She wanted more, but knew if she kissed him as passionately as she had Ian, her father, brother and the other men would know she belonged to both Scots, even if 'twas Ian's collar around her neck. While she didn't care what anyone thought of her, her logic and need to ensure her men's safety overrode her desire.

How had she gotten so lucky? A few weeks ago, she'd thought her life was over, with no happy future to look forward to. Now, she had the love of two powerful men who held her heart. Tears blurred her vision. She hugged them both again, unable to believe her good fortune. She had found a new home in the arms of these two men, warriors who'd taught her what it truly meant to be captured.

# The End

Thank you for taking the time to read Warrior's Vengeance. I hope you enjoyed it, and if so, please consider telling your friends or perhaps you wouldn't mind posting a short review. Word of mouth is an author's best friend and more appreciated than you know.

# about the author:

I'm a proud born-and-bred Jersey Girl with Brooklyn roots. And I still live where it all started - I married my very own alpha male many eons ago, and have an amazing college-bound daughter and a 10 year old son who charms and frustrates me at every turn. Free time is always a luxury and I spend the bulk of what time I manage to scrounge up lost in the worlds of my own making. I love to read and write hot, sexy and emotional stories about people both glamorous and not-so-glamorous. Be warned - some of my characters are even downright un-heroic, which is part of what makes them so interestingly sexy, in my opinion!

On the rare occasions I'm not taking advantage of that valuable free time by writing, you can catch me poking around in my other favorite twisted historical worlds of Sleepy Hollow, Reign and the History Channel's Vikings. I'm also a huge fan of Harry Potter, Highlander, Charmed, and

DragonBall Z! Yeah, a strange fandom medley, but each one features some of the sexiest villains ever. Did I mention I love villains? And of course, let's not forget my beloved NY Rangers.

**Find Gianna online:**

**"A Kinky Twist on History!"**
**"Magically Kinky!"**
**Website:** www.giannasimoneeroticromance.com
**Blog:** http://giannasimone.blogspot.com
**Twitter:** @Gianna_Simone
**Facebook:**
www.facebook.com/GiannaSimoneRomanceAuthor
**Goodreads:**
https://www.goodreads.com/author/show/4493720.Gianna_Simone
You can also find me on Pinterest, Google+, LinkedIn!

**I love to hear from readers - don't hesitate to reach out and say hi!**

Gianna Simone

# Coming Soon:

**Warrior's Wrath, Book 3 in the Medieval Warrior's Legends**
**Warrior's Witch, Book 4 in the Medieval Warrior's Legends**

# meɖieɖal
# waŗŗioŗ's leɢeɴɖs

**WARRIOR'S POSSESSION:** Upon her father's death, Lady Gillian Marlowe is ordered by King Edward I to wed Royce Langley, the Earl of Montchester. Worried she is being offered up as little more than a sacrifice in a political game, Gillian is surprised to find herself intrigued by her arrogant and infuriating husband.

Tasked with ridding the border along Wales of rebels who seek to unseat the king, Royce finds subterfuge and secrets everywhere, even with his beautiful wife. Though he only agreed to the marriage because of the king's order, he finds himself both fascinated and incensed by Gillian at every turn. She tries his patience, defies his orders and places herself in danger. To keep her in line, he spanks her, binds her to his bed and uses dominating sexual games to torment her, in an effort to get her to reveal her secrets. But even that is not enough to subdue her stubborn determination to stand beside him and defend her home and people.

Discovering his wife enjoys the same dark pleasures as Royce does only stirs more confusion. He has sworn never to fall for a woman's wiles, but his wife captivates him and stirs a desire deeper than any he has ever known. Trusting her is another matter, as he fears Gillian may bring about his downfall with her continued secrets, which he views as an attempt to undermine his authority.

As the rebel attacks increase and danger lurks everywhere, Gillian falls under suspicion as the traitor, despite her vows of loyalty. Royce must overcome his mistrust and find a way to maintain his possession of Gillian as they battle the enemies both within and without, if there is any hope for them to save each other.

** Featuring A Kinky Twist on History! including male domination, bondage, spanking, anal sex and so much more!

**WARRIOR'S VENGEANCE:** Near the Scottish border during the reign of Edward I, Marissa Langley, daughter of a powerful English earl is captured by a band of marauding Scotsmen. Completely at their mercy, she is desperate to escape. When the leader of the group saves her from certain rape, she believes she will be freed.

But Ian MacCallum is no savior. He takes her for his own, seduces her then makes her a submissive. Her collar and chains are part of his vengeance on her father—the man Ian claims is responsible for the death of his beloved wife and son.

But her immediate death is not Ian's plan. He subjects her to daily suffering and punishments and goes so far as sharing her with another clansman. Yet, her spirit will not be broken. He finds himself drawn to that core of strength within her; finding it most exquisite as it cannot be violated.

When danger from within his clan threatens her, Ian protects her, discovering at the same time that he does not want to lose her, ever.

Marissa makes her own discovery: she comes to crave Ian's torturous touch. When she learns the source of his hatred, she is certain he is wrong. Her father would not commit atrocities. She waits for the moment when she can escape and prove her father's innocence. But that would mean leaving Ian when she is no longer sure she wants to be free.

** Featuring A Kinky Twist on History, including bondage, collars, spanking, multiple partners and so much more!

**WARRIOR'S WRATH:** In 14th century England, a long-kept secret devastates Rowan Langley. Anger sends him on a quest for truth. He trusts no one, keeping others away, except fellow knight Gerard.

Aeron Dawkyns, fleeing Wales and a charge of murder, lives on the street, pickpocketing. She steals Rowan's coin. Later, Rowan catches her attempting to steal his horse. She has a choice – serve them both with her body, or be handed over to be hanged. She chooses Rowan and Gerard.

Serving an angry Rowan has dark pleasures Aeron learns to crave. She feels safe, despite the knights' wicked games. When Rowan drags her back to Wales, she fears that safety will be destroyed.

Rowan learns Aeron's plight and vows to hunt down her enemies, promising to protect and keep her. Yet he worries he's no better than her enemy. Still, he craves his slave's touch, as much as he craves her heart.

Staying with Rowan becomes Aeron's heart's desire – but could mean her death.

** Featuring a Kinky Twist on History! including bondage, spanking, multiple partners and so much more!

# The Norsemen Sagas

**NORSEMAN'S REVENGE:** Being kidnapped by a Viking raider on her wedding night might really be a blessing from the gods.

Geira Sorensdotter awaits her new husband, but she's filled with doubts about the man and the marriage. Those doubts are forgotten when the village is attacked, her husband is struck down and she is tied up and carried off amidst the raid.

Kori Thorfinnson has waited years to take revenge against the man who murdered his wife. But he soon finds the innocent young woman he's taken as his personal slave is not his enemy, despite her marriage to his foe. Her courage in defying him, her caring heart, and the fiery passion she shares stirs feelings Kori hasn't known since his wife died. Afraid to lose Geira, he binds her to him in many ways – not only with rope, but with his body, his collar and his brand.

Geira quickly learns just how despicable her husband was, and despite her difficult circumstances, grows to care deeply for Kori, her captor. Still, dreams of freedom linger. But once she finds herself with child, she must plan her escape, to save herself and her baby. However, Kori has plans of his own.

**NORSEMAN'S DECEPTION:** He saved her life – can the gods save her heart and soul from the mysterious loner's dark desires?

Fearing an arranged marriage, Thora Korisdotter flees her village, vowing never to return home. With her two pet wolves beside her, she is confident in her safety, and protected by the loyal animals. But when outlaws attack, wounding one of her beloved pets, she is thankful for the mysterious stranger who arrives just in time to save her. Now in his debt, she must repay him as he asks – with her body.

Ari Hugisson has wandered for years after being cast out of his clan as an outlaw. The time of his banishment is nearing its end, and Ari has the proof he needs to clear his name and unmask the real murderer – his brother. But when he comes across a beautiful woman under attack, he is compelled to step in and save her. He knows just the way to make her repay her debt, with the passion he senses lurking just under the surface of her fiery nature.

When Thora learns Ari has lied to her and knows well the man she was to wed – his brother – the betrayal cuts deep and she determines to leave him at the first opportunity. But the passion he stirs is unlike anything she has ever known, even if he sometimes insists on treating her as little more than a slave. When he confronts those who would see him killed, will she stand beside him and defend him, even at the risk of losing her family?

The Norsemen Sagas contain explicit love scenes featuring A Kinky Twist on History! including bondage, spanking, multiple partners and more!

Gianna Simone

# The Bayou Magiste Chronicles

**CLAIMED BY THE DEVIL:** Helene Gaudet finds the perfect Dom in an internet chat room. It's as if he can read her mind – and he knows how to make her beg. When they agree to meet in the real world, Helene realizes why her Dom knows her so well – he is none other than Devlin Marchand, the same man who handed her over years ago to a dark sorcerer – to be killed.

She thought she was free from suffering – including a rageful ex-husband who cursed her, leaving her unable to bear children. She wants to forget the past – but her lust for Devlin is so intense after each tormenting, releasing encounter, she doesn't want to leave him.

Devlin wants to repair his past wrongs – but guilt over his past betrayal is multiplied when he learns the curse that has dogged Helene for years comes from the trove of magic created by his very own family. Devlin fears the tentative relationship they've built will be destroyed – and he cannot allow that.

Can they overcome the past to have a future

together?

** Contains lots of explicit Magically Kinky! love scenes of the paranormal kind, including magical sex toys, potions, bondage, spanking and more!

**CLAIMED BY THE MAGE:** Lily Prentiss wishes she could ignore her inborn healing magic so she can live life on her terms, not follow the path her Magiste family chose for her. But when she stumbles across Aidan Marchand in the excruciating throes of evolving into a Mage, her touch is all that stops his pain and she can no longer deny her powers. When the sexy Dom seduces her into willing submission, she finds she doesn't want to resist and actually enjoys giving up control.

Aidan has more to worry about than just his rapidly maturing powers – his business partner is blackmailing him into funding a venture that involves kidnapping young girls both magical and mortal, and selling them as sex slaves. Even as Lily's touch eases Aidan's pain, he knows staying with her puts her in danger from his enemies. But the gift of her sexual submission helps him even more than her healing magic...so how can he let her go?

** Contains lots of explicit Magically Kinky!

love scenes of the paranormal kind, including magical sex toys, potions, bondage, spanking and more!

**CLAIMED BY THE ENCHANTER:** Regine Marchand loves being in control – and the role of domme is the perfect way for her to exert that control. An accomplished equestrian, she has her goals of championship in sight and no one will get in her way. Her life and future are in her hands, she doesn't need to depend on anyone for success and happiness.

Cameron McIntyre is fascinated by the cool façade Regine displays, but he senses the depth of her passion lurking under the surface. Despite her protests to the contrary, he recognizes in her a desire to submit and be dominated. But when he is forced to suspend her from competition due to performance enhancement spells used on her horse, he worries he may drive her away, instead of back into his arms. Believing her innocent of the charges, he vows to help her uncover who set her up while convincing her that submission to him is what she truly wants and needs. Submitting to the tall Irishman brings a new level of pleasure Regine has never known, at the same time making her question everything she knew about herself.

Regine is unaware an enemy from her past has

targeted her for revenge. Together she and Cameron must discover who wants to knock her out of competition for good, possibly killing her in the process.

\** Contains lots of explicit Magically Kinky! love scenes of the paranormal kind, including magical sex toys, potions, bondage, spanking and more!

**CLAIMED BY THE ZYNDEVINE:** In 13th century France, attacked by those carrying out the Papal Inquisition, *Magiste* Enchantress Chantal Belliveau is thankful for rescue from certain torture and death. But she never expected it to be at the hands of Henri Marchand, one of a powerful pureblooded line of ancient *Magiste*, the Zyndevines. Henri holds the key to her survival, but the danger he poses to her heart and soul could turn out to be even more perilous.

Henri is part of *Il Resistasse*, a handful of powerful *Magiste* fighting the atrocities the Catholic Church inflicts on their race. Saving Chantal becomes more than a simple rescue - the innocent young woman with half-trained powers enchants him more than he has ever been before. That she enjoys the dark side of pleasure he inflicts on her makes him question his determination to never give another his heart.

Chantal is horrified when Henri invokes an ancient spell, the *Possede Puissant*. The incantation leaves her little more than his possession. While she finds herself enjoying his dark and wicked sensual delights, she determines to free herself. Still, the security she finds with Henri encourages her to stay by his side, claiming spell or not.

Resentment toward her from Henri's family convinces Chantal she must ultimately break free of Henri's possession. But when the Inquisitioners attack, Henri convinces Chantal to embark on a journey to a new land, a journey that may well mean the survival of the entire *Magiste* race but the loss of her freedom forever.

** Contains lots of explicit Magically Kinky! love scenes of the paranormal kind, including magical sex toys, potions, bondage, spanking and more!